·K·A·N·D·I·D·E·
THE SECRET OF THE MISTS

Kandide and the Secret of the Mists

Diana S. Zimmerman
AR B.L.: 5.0 Alt.: 784
Points: 9.0   MG

·K·A·N·D·I·D·E·
THE SECRET OF THE MISTS

BY
DIANA S. ZIMMERMAN

BOOK ONE OF THE CALABIYAU CHRONICLES

SCHOLASTIC INC.
New York Toronto London Auckland
Sydney Mexico City New Delhi Hong Kong

No part of this publication may be reproduced, stored in a retrieval system, or transmitted in any form or by any means, electronic, mechanical, photocopying, recording, or otherwise, without written permission of the publisher. For information regarding permission, write to Noesis Publishing, a division of Noesis Communications International, Inc., 5777 W. Century Blvd., #200, Los Angeles, CA 90045.

ISBN 978-0-545-29154-5

12 11 10 9 8 7 6 5 4 3 2 1   10 11 12 13 14 15/0

Printed in the U.S.A.   40

First Scholastic printing, September 2010

Cover Design by Stephanie Lostimolo
Book Design by Imaginosis Media Design/Greenleaf Book Group LP

Kandide The Secret of the Mists is dedicated to:

Cynthia Unninayar, who inspired my faery collection; Alice Shultz, who read the first faery story to me; and Stan Shultz, who believed.

As well as those who read, reread, criticized, improved, proofed, and reproofed every page: Dawn Abel, Candice Adams, Sal and Marie Barilla, Tracy Charles, Jeanie Cunningham, Jonathon Debach, Bob Dorian, Paul Elliott, Patricia Fry, Robert Gould, Patrick Grady, Karen Grim, Carol Ivy, Bruce Merrin, Lee and Dan Merrin, Cameron King, Dennis Mullican, Caryn Parker, Brian Sharp, and S. Earl Statler. Also, Ellen Steiber, Ed Massesa, Stephanie Lostimolo and Jake Lebovic for their creativity and support.

With special thanks to my twenty-one junior editors from Sabal Point Elementary School: Alexis, Amanda, Annika, Brianna, Bryanna, Cameron, Christian, Christina, Dakota, Elliot, Ignacio, Jassem, Jacob, J. J., Justin, Kinely, Samantha, Shannon, Taylor, Victoria, Zachary, and their extraordinary teacher, Jeff Smith.

THE KINGDOMS OF CALABIYAU

Within the elemental dimension lies a land not unlike our own—a world that exists in parallel with humankind. Time passes differently, magic is as normal as the sunrise, and four distinctly different kingdoms maintain control.

Calabiyau Proper – The Kingdom of the Fée

Ruled since the beginning of time by Kandide's family, today, Calabiyau Proper is governed equally by its monarch and the representatives from the twelve primary Faery Clans known as the High Council.

Calabiyau West – The Kingdom of the Banshees

When precious gems were discovered in the Year of the Fée 88 BT, (beginning of time) the Banshee Clans split off from the other Fée. Since that time, hundreds of different monarchs have ruled this separatist kingdom. In the Year of the Fée 26,449 BT, King Nastae assumed the throne.

Calabiyau East – The Veil of The Mists

Founded in the Year of the Fée 26,851 BT, the Veil is presided over by Selena and Jake as an independent, democratically governed territory.

Calabiyau North – The Bardic Council

Founded in 20,247 and presided over by High Priestess Viviana, this secretive land is home to wizards and bards.

'Tis not so long ago, nor so far away,
but indeed a time and place quite near, if only we
would see. Some call it the elemental dimension,
others say it is an enchanted realm, and still others
simply call it faery land. Long written about
by scholars, long overlooked by all but those with
innate perception, this world is no less real,
and its reality is of no less consequence.

PROLOGUE

King Toeyad had only enough time to catch a glimpse of the deadly arrow that pointed directly toward him. Although he was standing a good fifty meters away, he did not question that its aim would be precise. Barely hearing the chilling rush of air that signaled the lethal projectile's release, the king fell to the ground. The razor-sharp tip had struck its intended mark. A piercing scream rang out. Crown Princess Kandide, still holding her crossbow, rushed to her father's side.

*"Is nothing here alive?" Kandide whispered,
more to hear a voice than expecting anyone to answer.
"Why would Mother have sent me here?"*

"**W**here am I?" Kandide spoke in little more than a whisper. Her purple-blue eyes darted from tree to tree as she nervously scanned the lifeless forest. Nothing was as it should be.

Dense black fog shrouded the tangled treetops, blocking all but the most persistent rays of sun. "What is this horrible place?" she wondered, trying to take only shallow breaths. Her nostrils stung from the acidic smell of rotting death, and the ground was marshy and slick beneath her open-toed sandals.

Straining to hear any sort of sound, Kandide's ears caught only silence. Not even the chirping of a woodland bird could be heard. *It's as though someone—or something—has scared every living creature away*, she thought, standing frozen in her tracks.

"Is nothing here alive?" she whispered, more to hear a voice than expecting anyone to answer. "Why would Mother have sent me here?"

It was on that very morning that Kandide was to be

crowned Queen of Calabiyau Proper, the kingdom of the Fée. Her otherwise perfect brow furrowed with confusion as her mind flashed on the image of her all-white marble castle. Only a short time before, she had been standing on its grand balcony with its glistening brass rails, speaking to her subjects. "Mother gestured and now I'm here in this awful land. How could she have done this to me—her own daughter?"

Careful not to slip on the slimy ground, Kandide cautiously took a few steps, first looking in one direction, and then the other, trying to establish some sort of bearing—*a landmark, something that can tell me where I am,* she thought.

But she saw no landmarks, only thick, tangled vines hanging from gnarled branches that reached out and clawed at her like so many bony fingers as she tried to make her way through—to where, she did not know. *At least Mother could have let me change clothes,* she thought, tugging her skirt free from a reluctant bush full of thorns.

Still wearing her pearlescent cape and the formal attire of the court, Kandide could not have been more inappropriately dressed. Glancing down at the hem of her long flowing gown, she saw that it was already caked with black mud. The delicate fabric seemed to snag on the dense underbrush with every step she took. And yet, even in her distress, the Fée princess had the proud look of nobility. She was poised and beautiful beyond compare, with high cheekbones and skin that was silvery-white like freshly fallen snow. Her nearly waist-length hair shimmered gold one minute and platinum the next.

Forcing herself to keep walking, Kandide's head suddenly jerked backward, leaving her throat bare and exposed. She dared not move or even breathe. *Stay calm,* she tried to tell herself, fearing that her pounding heart could be heard by whomever— or whatever—had grabbed onto her.

Kandide's eyes slowly focused upward. Only then did she catch her breath. There was nothing to see—nothing except the twisted branch that had become entangled in her hair. Reaching up, she hastily snapped it in two, freeing herself from its thorny grasp.

As she stood there pulling one splintered piece of wood after another from her long golden braid, anger began to set in—anger at her mother, then at her sister. *I can't believe Tara didn't help me,* she thought. *And the court healers, they just stood there staring at me like so many cowering deer. They could have done something.*

Each time she moved her left arm, a sharp pain shot through her shoulder and wing. It was a constant reminder of the terrible accident. "They didn't even try to heal me," she mumbled, tossing the last sliver of bark to the ground. "They're jealous. They're all jealous of my beauty, that's why. But they're not going to get away with it. I won't let them. I'll find my way out of here. I will."

With each step she took, Kandide's annoyance increased, as did her sense of helplessness. She was disoriented, exhausted, and completely alone. Panic began to replace common sense. Her anger quickly gave way to all of the other emotions that she had kept pent up for so very long. The pain. The fear. The guilt. The shame. The sadness—the terrible sadness over losing her father—all of her emotions streamed forth at once.

Mother sent me away. Why does she hate me so? Tears began

to well up in her eyes. *Mother blames me for what happened to Father, that's why. Now she hates me—they all hate me because I'm . . . I'm an Imperfect now!*

"No!" she shrieked, desperately trying to maintain some semblance of control. "I'm not an Imperfect. My wing will be healed." Kandide glanced back at what was once a beautiful iridescent wing that now fell limp, crumpled, and broken.

"I will be perfect again. I'm too beautiful not to be. I mustn't think about my wing, or Mother, or Tara, or the healers—only about what to do right now. If I just had my crossbow, at least then . . ." She paused for a moment to listen. It was so quiet, so very quiet. The few remaining leaves that clung to the mostly barren trees dared not even rustle, lest they awaken the voiceless land.

Her father's words resonated in her head. "Strength and courage are what matter most when times are not as we wish, my daughter," the great king had told her as he lay dying. "Strength and courage—that's it. Strength and courage." Under her breath, Kandide repeated it with each step she took. She was determined to transform her panic into purpose. "I will find a way out of this horrible place."

Gazing around at a forest of dead trees, she watched the heavy fog settle closer to the ground, making it difficult to see more than a few meters ahead. Kandide began picking her way, albeit slowly, through the spiny underbrush. With each step, oily black mud oozed through her shoes. *Watch where you walk,* she scolded herself as the thick black muck nearly swallowed her right sandal. Yanking it free, she scraped the smelly stuff off on a nearby rock, and then forced herself to keep pressing onward.

"There has to be a path or something—and I shall find it. I always do. Like when I was a little girl and father and I got lost in the woods. I was the one who led us home. I did it then and I'll do it now."

For several hours, she walked, searching for any type of identifiable landmark. But with the sun almost completely obscured by the dense fog, maintaining any sort of direction was nearly impossible. The small strips of cloth that she tore from her numerous under-slips and tied to every third tree, kept her from walking in circles. But as she soon realized, they did nothing to stop her from going deeper and deeper into the shadow-laden woods.

Pausing for a moment to rest, Kandide spotted what appeared to be a small cave just a few meters ahead. It didn't look like much—just an opening between two boulders—but with night approaching, it might at least be some shelter.

She made her way over to the crude refuge and cautiously peered inside. "Seems empty enough," she whispered, "and dry." Kandide pulled her cape tightly around her shoulders, trying to ward off the shivering wave of cold she suddenly felt. Although winter had not yet set in, the fog-laden air was damp and chilly. "Yes, I shall stay here until morning." She ducked her head to go in.

It was a far cry from her own luxuriously appointed bedchamber with its cozy plush blue comforter and soft satin sheets, but at least for this night, it would have to do. Kandide sat down on a flat rock that protruded from the ground near the cave's back wall. Her shoulder and wing throbbed with pain, and her stomach rumbled. She couldn't even remember the last time she'd eaten a meal.

Not that there would be anything even remotely edible in a place like this, she thought. *At least the floor isn't wet. I wonder where all the sand came from?* She scooped up a handful and let it flow through her fingers. *Maybe someone else is living here.* She peered outside, but saw only shadowy blackness. Night was quickly approaching.

Although exhausted and trembling, both from cold and fear, Kandide was determined not to let her emotions regain control. She thought of her family and the events that led up to her being sent away. *If only Tara hadn't said she'd go to the Meadows that day. If only Teren hadn't created that silly spell. If only Father hadn't ... if ... if ...*

A bittersweet smile crossed her face, as she, once again, remembered her father's counsel. *"If* could put a thousand hectares in a bottle," King Toeyad would say when she tried to use "if" as an excuse to justify her actions. *"If* is a master you must not serve, my child," he would patiently tell her, "for it will only hinder your ambition, not enable your task."

"And my task right now is to make some light." She sat up with a renewed sense of determination. Rubbing her hands together in a slow circular motion, a bluish glow appeared between her fingertips. "From flame to light, now grow, be bright. I command you this moment to enable my sight." The tiny blue orb grew larger and larger until it was bright enough to completely illuminate her small shelter.

"There, that should do it." Placing the softly flickering light in a crevice in the large granite rock that made up the cave's back wall, she mused, "Well, at least my little brother is of some use. Guess I'll have to thank him for teaching me that bit of magic . . . if I ever see him again."

Cold, hungry, and truly alone for the first time in her life, Kandide could not help but think about all that had happened. Her thoughts drifted back to the days before, when everything began to change . . .

*It was as though all in Calahiyau were
holding their breath, awaiting word—all but
Princess Kandide, that is. She had simply vanished.*

TWO

"It isn't that Kandide means to be unkind, my love," King Toeyad whispered to his wife, Queen Tiyana. "She has simply been raised to be queen."

"She has been raised to think that the world, including you, should indulge her every whim." Tiyana frowned as she placed her hand on her husband's cheek. "Oh why, my darling, why did you have to play that deadly archery game with Kandide? Why now?"

"It was to be my final lesson to her," he softly replied. "One she needed to learn." It took a great deal of effort for him to do so, but he forced himself to lift his head up.

King Toeyad and Queen Tiyana ruled over Calabiyau Proper. It was Toeyad's long-ago ancestors for whom this land was named. The Biyau family, of the Water Clan, had been the sovereign monarchs since the Year of the Fée, 08 BT (beginning of time). When the family assumed control, the word *cala*, meaning "land" in the language of the ancients, was added to their own name—hence Cala-biyau, land of Biyau.

Toeyad had been king of this enchanted realm for nearly four hundred years. And while it is not uncommon for Fée to live a half a millennium or more, no one but the eldest of the elders could remember a time when he did not rule.

From his richly carved canopied bed with its deep purple satin sheets and overstuffed pillows, the dying king looked up at Tiyana with a reassuring smile. "Kandide will have many battles to face when she inherits the throne. She must truly know, not just in her head, but deep within her heart, that lives are dependent upon her skill and expertise."

"Just as your life was during that silly game," Tiyana replied.

"Just as my life would have been had her skill with a cross-bow not been so great," he corrected her. "For as you well know, it was not Kandide's arrow that caused my collapse. This old heart is simply not as strong as it once was."

"That is my point, exactly." Frustrated with her daughter's behavior, Tiyana shook her head. "Knowing that your health has been failing, she should not have kept you out there for so long."

"Oh, Tiyana, if only you could have seen her." King Toeyad's eyes lit up. He seemed invigorated as he talked about their archery game in the lush green forest that surrounded the castle. "Kandide played with the skill of an absolute master. Her arrows struck my gaming shield twenty-six times—each a perfect center hit. That kind of score simply does not happen."

"Exceptional talent does not justify exceptional selfishness." Tiyana placed a second purple satin pillow under King Toeyad's head. "And it certainly does not excuse Kandide's behavior now, disappearing like this."

"As usual, my love, you are right on both counts."

"And as usual, my darling, you chose not to deny your daughter—on twenty-six counts!"

Looking at Tiyana with a flirtatious grin, Toeyad softly kissed her hand. "Just as I could never deny you, my beloved, on any account."

Although her husband was greatly weakened, Tiyana still found his smile irresistible. "I wouldn't mind your indulging her so, if Kandide actually learned some of the lessons you attempt to teach her. Even now, with all that is happening, she continues to think only of herself."

"All of her life she has been told how very special she is. How very beautiful. How very perfect."

"How very spoiled!" On this Tiyana would not relent.

"Kandide is young and has not yet realized that her authority must be tempered with respect. But worry not, my love, it will come. Age does find wisdom, you know."

"We can only hope."

"Please send her to me as soon as she is found. I fear I have very little time left. The fates will not be denied much longer. I must transfer the Gift to Kandide before my strength completely fails. As you well know, all life depends upon it."

"I have everyone looking for her." Standing up, Tiyana walked over to a nearby table and poured him a cup of steaming ginger tea. "Now, I want you to drink this, my love. It will be good for you." She held the cup up for him.

"You do make a wonderful nurse," he teased. "A bit pushy, but wonderful, nonetheless." He took a sip of the tea. The lingering effect of the hot ginger felt good on his throat as he rested his head back on the pillow and closed his eyes.

Reports of King Toeyad's imminent passing had spread throughout the land. Greatly saddened by the news, the Fée, out of deep respect, had all but stopped their daily activities. Bread ovens began to cool from fires not stoked, pumpkins and crooked-neck yellow squash lay unharvested in the fields, and shops of every kind stood empty as most villagers waited in the central square for some sort of message about their beloved king. It was as though all in Calabiyau were holding their breath, awaiting word—all but Princess Kandide, that is.

She had simply vanished.

"Hey, remember the time I put a spell on Kandide so that she sneezed every time she looked in a mirror?"

THREE

"Well, she's not in the Meadows!" Prince Teren swooped into the king's chamber. "She's not in the library, either. I was just up there."

Having just reached his fourteenth birthday, Teren was the youngest of their three children and their only son. Although he looked exactly like Toeyad had when he was young, with the same roguish smile, high forehead, yellow-brown eyes, and tousled sandy blond hair, that was where the similarity ended.

Known more for his mischievous pranks than his princely manner, Teren's primary goal in life was to become a great and mighty mage—a worker of wonders who could conjure wizardly enchantments. His talent already far exceeded his age.

"I'll keep looking for her if you want me to, Mother," he offered. "Maybe she went to that little chocolate shop down in the village that she likes so much. You know, the one where she always goes when she feels sorry for herself. I could look there, or maybe—"

"No, Teren," Tiyana replied, "you stay here with your father. I shall go search for her myself. Perhaps I will have better luck." Her eyes suddenly narrowed. She looked at her son suspiciously. "You didn't put one of your spells on Kandide, did you? That's not why she's missing, is it?"

"Mother! Would I do that?"

"It has been known to happen. In any case, I want you spend this time with your father." Attempting a smile, Tiyana's face revealed only anguish at the thought of leaving her husband's side, even for a few minutes. But her eldest daughter must be found, and soon.

"Worry not, my love," King Toeyad reassured her with the same confident look that made Tiyana fall in love with him so many years ago. "As you can see, I am actually feeling a bit stronger just now. Find Kandide. The Gift must be transferred to her while I am still able. I shall not pass before you return."

"You had better not." Turning to depart, she briefly paused to look back at him, and then straight at Teren. "And you had better make sure of it!"

"I will, Mother! I'll make sure."

King Toeyad's bedchamber was dimly lit, reflecting the somber mood that prevailed throughout the castle. The subtle fragrance of violet oil filled the air, and the softly glowing embers inside his ancient flagstone fireplace were barely burning. Throughout the castle, forlorn faces replaced the gaiety of happier times. Only Toeyad didn't seem to be sorrowful. He had a smile and positive words for everyone who entered his room.

"I'm happy you're here, Teren," the king whispered. "I've not been able to spend enough hours with you these recent weeks, and for that I apologize."

"It's okay, Father. I understand. Really I do." Biting his lower lip, he stared at the floor. "It's just that—"

"It's just what, my son?"

"It's just . . . I want you to be well—that's all." Teren quickly turned away so his father would not see the tears in his eyes. *I'm fourteen and a prince,* he reminded himself. *I'm not supposed to cry.*

"I also want to be well, Teren. And I am feeling a bit better. So, why don't you open those curtains and let the sunlight come in?" Toeyad motioned toward the floor-to-ceiling purple and gold brocade drapes across from his bed. "I don't know why everyone insists upon closing them."

Teren started to walk over to do so, then hesitated and looked back at his father. "Are you sure it's okay?"

"I assure you, it is 'okay.' I am still King, you know."

"Are you really feeling better, Father?" A glimmer of hope crossed Teren's face.

"A little. Now, open the curtains, then come over here. I have a question for you—and I want you to be truthful with me. You didn't turn Kandide into a frog or anything, did you?"

"Of course not!" Teren hastily pulled back the curtains. Rays of sunlight streamed in, instantly giving the room a much cheerier feel. "Besides, I haven't gotten that spell to work yet."

"You're quite sure?"

"I'm sure." He walked over and sat down on the purple and gold chair next to his father's massive bed. "Hey, remember the time I put a spell on Kandide so that she sneezed every time she looked in a mirror?"

"I remember that she sneezed almost constantly for three weeks, until your little spell finally wore off."

"Yeah, it took me forever to figure out how to unweave that one." Teren chuckled at the memory. "Kandide never could walk by a mirror without admiring herself."

Toeyad also started to chuckle at the memory of his son's prank. "You're probably right, but I don't think she thought it was funny. And you didn't do much laughing, either, when you found out that you would be spending the next two weeks confined to your bedchamber."

"Now, that's the part that wasn't funny." Teren stopped laughing. "Anyway, I've been spending a lot of time in the Royal Library studying the really old books on magic. I think I've finally figured out how to undo my spells." He glanced up to see a serving Fée enter the room. Her arms were wrapped around a huge bouquet of orange and yellow tiger lilies, which she artfully arranged in a large purple vase. Looking at her, Teren flashed a mischievous smile. Leaning close to his father, he cupped his hand to one side of his mouth and whispered, "Want me to show you how it works?"

"Absolutely not!" Toeyad acknowledged the Fée with a regal nod and a smile of thanks. She graciously curtsied to the king, and then promptly exited, knowing all too well what that look on Teren's face meant. "I am, however, pleased to hear that you are making progress with your lessons." He reached over and patted his son's hand. "Would you like me to tell you a secret?"

"A secret?"

"Yes, a secret. I was known to weave a few good-natured

spells myself when I was your age."

"You, Father? Did you really? Tell me about one. Please."

"Only if you promise not to try it yourself—at least, not until you've practiced," he added, seeing the eager look on his son's face.

"I promise."

"Then help me to sit up and I will tell you about it." Although it was difficult, Toeyad leaned forward, holding on to his son's arm while Teren placed several more large purple pillows behind his back.

Realizing how frail his father had become, Teren's excited expression changed to one of concern. "Are you sure you're all right, Father?"

"I'm fine. Now, listen closely. There was an old wizard named Melini. Max, we used to call him. He was the most amazing wizard I have ever known. Rumor had it he was related to Merlin."

"Really?" Teren had several paintings of Merlin in his bedchamber, for he was, indeed, the young prince's idol. "To Merlin himself?"

"So they say. Max never denied nor acknowledged it, but he did teach me a spell that I think you may find quite handy . . ."

*"May the earthly spirits help us
when that girl is crowned!"*

FOUR

"Where could your sister possibly be?" Queen Tiyana was speaking to her youngest daughter, Princess Tara, as the two of them walked down the long circular hallway that spiraled back to King Toeyad's chamber.

Except for having green eyes, Tara looked like her mother, with orange-auburn hair and pale green skin. A bit more elfin in nature, she preferred to wear britches and boots, and, unlike Tiyana or Kandide, was almost never seen in the more formal attire of the court.

"I fear your father is not as strong as he would have us believe," Tiyana continued.

Tara looked up at her mother. Her almond-shaped eyes were red from crying. "I wish there was something more I could do. What good are my healing skills, if I can't even help my own father?"

Tiyana stopped walking and put her arm around Tara, giving her a gentle hug. "You must never feel that way. You may be the most powerful healer in all of Calabiyau, but even you cannot remedy time's passage. All we can do now is be with him. I only hope we find Kandide—and soon."

"She'll be along, Mother. You know how Kandi is." Princess Tara was the only one permitted to call her sister "Kandi." It was an endearment that the crown princess had allowed Tara from the time she first started speaking and couldn't quite pronounce Kandide. "She just does everything on her own time."

"And in her own way." Tiyana sighed.

"Your Majesty!" Mylea, Kandide's lady-in-waiting, came rushing up to them. "We have finally located Princess Kandide!"

Tiyana and Tara turned to acknowledge the anxious Fée. "Thank the earthly spirits. Where is she?" Tiyana asked.

Mylea curtseyed to the queen. "Her Royal Highness has just now returned to her chamber from the gaming fields."

"The gaming fields!" Tiyana threw up her hands. "Of course, I should have thought to look there. Her father is close to the passing, and Kandide is out practicing games of skill. Why does that not surprise me? Please, Mylea, send her to Toeyad's chamber, immediately."

Mylea wrung her hands, looking awkwardly at the floor. "I have tried, Your Majesty, but she says she must finish braiding her hair and will yet be a while."

"May the earthly spirits help us when that girl is crowned!"

"Now, Mother, you know how Kandi is about looking perfect." True to her nature, Tara tried to minimize her sister's unfathomable behavior. It was something she seemed to be doing more and more since their father had become ill. "Let me go and see if I can hasten her. Come Mylea, perhaps the two of us will stand a better chance."

As Tiyana watched them rush off, she couldn't help but wonder: *How could we have raised two daughters who are so completely different? One spends all her time in the forest healing injured animals, and the other does everything but what her courtly duties require.*

Walking into Toeyad's antechamber, Tiyana hesitated, deciding to wait for Kandide before going into his bedroom. *I must speak to her before she sees her father,* she thought, sitting down on the lavender loveseat where she and her husband had shared so many quiet conversations. *How Toeyad loves purple.* She gazed around the room. *He probably would have painted the entire castle that color if I had let him. Maybe the entire village!* The thought of thousands of purple thatched roofs almost made her smile.

On this day, Tiyana was wearing Toeyad's favorite gown. It, too, was purple. Delicate lavender lace framed her face, and folds of deep royal purple velvet, tightly gathered around her waist, accentuated her still-perfect figure. Long, graceful sleeves almost covered her hands. She was also wearing her favorite piece of jewelry, the amethyst, diamond, and imperial topaz collar necklace that Toeyad designed for her upon their engagement.

A sad smile crossed Tiyana's face as she fought back her overwhelming sorrow. Her entire body ached from the thought of living without him. She and Toeyad had ruled together for well over a century. To her, it seemed like only yesterday that they first met. "Where has the time gone?" she whispered to herself while looking at her long auburn curls in the gilded mirror that adorned the east wall of the King's antechamber. "And where did all of these silver streaks come from?" Piled atop her head, curls randomly spilled over her diamond and amethyst-encrusted tiara, the one Toeyad had presented to her on the day he made her his queen.

"Time only enhances your beauty," he would say when she fretted about the fact that even the Fée must age, albeit far more slowly than humankind.

Tiyana's thoughts drifted back to the day they first met. It was in her tiny forest village with its pointy green roofs. She was barely twenty-five years of age in human years. Running out of her cottage to find out what all the excitement was about, Tiyana looked up to see Calabiyau's king sitting atop his all-black steed. His smile took her breath away. Little did she know when he was introduced to her that, in just three months, she would be queen of this great land. "I have searched for three centuries to find you," he told her as they strolled through the woods near her home. "But in less than an instant, you've stolen my heart."

For a few fleeting moments, she also remembered the seldom and oh-so-precious carefree times that they shared when, together, they would fly off into the woods, or tumble to the ground laughing as they gathered sunbeams in the Meadows. On one of those days, Toeyad wove the brightest ones into a crown that he fashioned out of freshly gathered red and pink fuchsias. Placing it on Tiyana's head, he stood back and looked at her. Then, with a frown, he shook his head, saying, "No, no matter how hard I try, nothing can outshine your beauty, my love."

Tiyana tried to blink back the tears that kept welling up in her purple-blue eyes. Before she could wipe them away, the antechamber doors burst open.

"Mother, what do you mean sending Tara to hasten me?" an irate Princess Kandide demanded as she stormed into the chamber.

Jolted back to reality, Tiyana quickly stood up. "Kandide, I asked you to stay near. You know your father no longer has the strength to deploy the Gift. It must be transferred to you immediately."

"Can't it wait just a few minutes longer, Mother? I haven't yet finished my braid." Kandide held up a section of her long silver-gold hair and began weaving it together. Turning to look in the mirror, she continued, "You know I must look perfect for Father—especially now."

Perfection was important to all Fée. To Kandide, however, it was an obsession. And while it was true that each clan measured perfection differently—some clans were tall, others short, some were green, and others were dark or light skinned— all had unwavering standards of beauty and physical perfection that were used to judge an individual's worth and status. Dressed in an off-white iridescent cape that seemed to change color with each gesture, Kandide was, indeed, the personification of perfection, in spite of her still unfinished braid.

"You look great, Kandi. Really you do." Tara had followed her sister into the room.

"Well, of course I do, Tara. But I'm told that Father is feeling stronger. So, I'm sure he won't mind if I—"

"No, Kandide." Tiyana's expression made it clear that her

eldest daughter was to say no more. "Your father's renewed strength is merely a sign that his time draws near. Now stop thinking only of yourself. You may be Calabiyau's next queen, but you are Toeyad's daughter first, and that means showing respect."

With the defiant poise of a captive snow leopard, Kandide grudgingly acquiesced. "Yes, Mother." Nodding her head in the slightest of bows, she followed Tiyana and Tara into her father's bedchamber.

Kandide was dripping wet,
but no longer in pain.

FIVE

Kandide seldom showed emotion. "Leaders simply don't do as such," she would say. As she swept past her brother and sister, and approached her father's bedside, her stoic posturing suddenly seemed meaningless. Seeing her father so very pale was more than even she could bear. *I must be strong*, she thought, fighting back her emotions. *I am King Toeyad's daughter, heir to the throne, and the very essence of his being.* Struggling to compose herself, she sat down in the gold and purple chair at his bedside.

King Toeyad reached up to wipe away a tear glistening on her lower lashes—softly whispering, "You must remember your destiny, my child. Strength and courage are what matter most when times are not as we wish."

"But, Father, I do not wish you to pass." Kandide spoke as though her very words could alter his fate.

"All seasons must change. To live is also to die, for only then can the cycle start anew. I have raised you to take my place—

29

to be a great leader, and that you must now be."

"And so I shall, Father."

Kandide could do no wrong in Toeyad's eyes. The only thing that he and Tiyana ever argued about was how to raise her. "Self-confidence is good," he would say when Kandide was being particularly arrogant. "After all, she will have many challenges to face as queen." It was King Toeyad who pampered and spoiled Kandide so. He simply could not say no to his eldest daughter.

"Rule with strength and courage, my child," he told her. "And always with a kind and accepting heart. The power of the throne, as well as the Gift, will soon be yours. They give you the ability to change the world—for better or for worse."

A deep pout crossed Kandide's otherwise exquisite face. "Yes, Father. But I still don't want you to—"

"Hush now, my daughter. I have something to give you before I transfer the Gift." Toeyad handed Kandide a large white feather with a thin silver band spiraled around its quill.

"A feather?" She turned it over and looked at it quizzically.

"Is it not the simple feather that allows eagles to soar, that protects waterfowl from freezing, or that, with a stroke of its quill, has altered destiny? Always look beneath the surface, my child. Truth is rare at first glance."

"But I—"

Toeyad closed her fingers around its quill. "Keep this simple reminder near. It will serve you well."

"As you wish, Father." Having no idea what he meant, Kandide placed the white feather in the pocket of her cape.

"And now, my daughter, you must ready yourself to accept the Gift."

"I'm ready, Father." She sat up straight with the confidence of a born aristocrat.

"Then let us begin." Looking up at her, Toeyad spoke the words his father had said to him so long ago: "Since the beginning of time, each generation of our family has guarded the Gift of the Frost. Now, as rightful heir to the throne, it is your turn, and you, Kandide Biyau, are to be its sole keeper. Do you willingly accept the Gift, my daughter?"

Kandide nodded. "Yes, Father." *It's what I have been trained for,* she thought, holding her head up proudly.

"Do you understand its true power and importance to all the creatures of our great land?"

"Yes, Father." Speaking in strict ceremonial fashion, Kandide recited the oath Toeyad had taught her: "The Gift of the Frost is that most precious and crucial of all Gifts. Without its deploy, the leaves cannot fall, winter cannot settle in, and spring cannot bring forth a new beginning. All life would soon perish. Just as you have, and your father, grandfather, and their fathers and mothers before them—since the beginning of time—I shall faithfully deploy the Frost each year."

"Do you willingly agree to be the guardian of the Gift, placing its care even above your own life?"

"Yes, Father, I do—even above my own life."

"Good. Are you ready then for the transfer, my daughter?"

"I am, Father." *I just wish it didn't have to be so soon.* Kandide looked down at the floor, then back to her father. She fought to hold back her tears, for she knew all too well, what the consequences of the transfer would be. Sliding her chair closer to the king, she held up her hands.

In a precise rhythm, Kandide and her father's index fingers touched, then their middle, ring, and little fingers. King Toeyad closed his eyes and chanted a magical incantation, slowly bringing his thumbs to meet hers. Instantly, a powerful electrical current began wildly arcing from the king to Kandide.

Momentarily stunned, her hands began to quiver; a sudden freezing sensation shot through her entire body. Every fiber of her being vibrated with a series of intense sensations that ranged from euphoria to excruciating pain. As the force of the current steadily increased, each new jolt became more powerful and more unbearable than the last. *Father told me it would be painful*, she thought, *but . . .* Kandide gasped as she struggled to maintain control. Had her hands not been fused to Toeyad's she would have surely fallen over.

Wide-eyed, Teren watched his sister. With every jolt of her body, he also flinched. "Is she going to be okay?" he whispered to his mother.

Holding her son's hand, Tiyana's voice was hushed. "Toeyad warned us it would be difficult. I just didn't think . . ."

"Perhaps I—" Tara started toward her sister.

"No, Tara." Tiyana held out her other hand to stop her. "Kandide must do this alone." *I only wish we could do something*, she thought, feeling completely helpless.

As the transfer continued, Kandide began shaking so violently that she almost passed out. The endless jolts from such a tremendous infusion of enchantment were far worse than she could have ever imagined. Her muscles screamed from what felt like hundreds of needle-like jabs penetrating each cell. Every nerve was on fire, and yet still it continued.

I can do this, she told herself. *I will do this.* It was all she could do to keep her body from going into spastic shock. *I must remain conscious. I must.* She wanted to scream, but nothing came out. Beads of perspiration streamed down her face. Her breathing became more and more erratic. She gasped for air.

The force of the Gift had become so strong that her entire body was engulfed in a glistening iridescent halo of pure electrical current. Her hands, her legs, her face, every inch of her skin burned as though it was being seared on a white-hot griddle. Magic infused her very being.

Then, as suddenly as they started, the agonizing jolts abruptly stopped. The intense heat simply melted away. Kandide was dripping wet, but no longer in pain. Numb, her muscles slowly began to relax as the dreadful spasms subsided.

Virtually drained of the Gift, Toeyad was, at last, able to separate his hands from hers. Falling back onto the pillows, the King spoke in short, strained phrases. "You must now . . . finish . . . my work . . ." He inhaled deeply several times before attempting to speak again.

With the enormous power of her newly acquired gift, Kandide's breathing quickly returned to normal. *I'm no longer exhausted,* she thought, feeling more alive than ever before. Barely hearing her father's words, she stood up and gazed into his large gilded chamber mirror. Blotting the last few drops of perspiration from her forehead, Kandide couldn't help but think, *I look even more amazing than normal.* Her entire body radiated with a magnificent silvery glow.

Struggling to speak, Toeyad watched his daughter. "Use the Gift and the throne wisely, my child. You must become the leader of *all* Fée. Only then will you have earned your right to be the true queen."

"Yes, Father," Kandide half-heartedly answered. Her attention was fixed on her own glorious reflection. *Why did no one ever tell me her how astonishingly gorgeous I would look once I had the Gift?* she thought. *Is this not as important as the Gift, itself?*

"Kandide," Tiyana spoke up. She would have no more of her daughter's selfishness. "Your father . . ."

Kandide glanced back at him. The color was completely drained from Toeyad's face. "Father!" she cried, rushing back to his side. "Oh, Father, I love you." Tenderly kissing him on both cheeks, she whispered, "I'm so sorry. I never meant to keep you out in the woods that long. I love you so very much."

"And I love you, Kandide." He looked into her watery eyes. "I chose my destiny, not you, my daughter. Your actions did not alter the fates. Of my time for passing, even you have no control. Remember my words—*all* of them. And keep the feather close."

"I will, Father." She felt it safely in her cape pocket. *Although I have no idea why.*

"Good. Now I must speak to your brother and sister." With one last reassuring nod, Toeyad smiled at his eldest daughter. Reluctantly, she left his side. Walking over to her mother, Kandide fought to keep from sobbing. *I will not cry. I am Toeyad's daughter, heir to the throne*, she repeated to herself. *I am strong.*

With Tara and Teren kneeling by his side, Toeyad whispered, "Take care of Kandide, my children, for the two of you are also written in the fates. She may be older, but you, Tara, are wiser, with far greater perspective. Kandide needs your compassion and gentle spirit. And you, Teren, she needs your humor, optimism, and that remarkably clever and magical mind. Both of you will ultimately help her along her path of serving *all* Fée. Only then will each of you be free to pursue your individual destinies."

"Us, Father?" Tara had no idea what he meant.

"Help Kandide?" Teren echoed. "Kandide never accepts help from anyone, especially me."

"Teren's right." Tara looked at him with a bewildered expression. "How can we help her?"

"I confess, my children, I do not know. I'm only certain that Kandide will need you both. Guide her well."

As confusing as their father's request was, Tara nodded. "Of course, we will do as you say, Father."

"We promise," Teren vowed.

"Thank you. Now, know that I have lived a good and long life, and that the two of you have been so very much a part of my joy. Carry with you at all times the undying love of your father. This is my parting gift to you both."

"No greater gift could we want," Tara answered, wiping away her tears.

"We love you, Father." Teren hugged his dad.

"Your words mean everything to me," the great king replied. "Now it's time for me to speak to your mother." Toeyad reached out to take Tiyana's hand as she approached. "My beloved Queen, no one has ever had a better partner. You, and you alone, provided me with unyielding strength when my own resolve would falter. My accomplishments are equally your accomplishments. Will you do me the great honor of accepting my last kiss?"

Tiyana's heart sank as her thoughts adjusted to the inevitability of the moment—for that kiss would be his last. "I have always loved you," she whispered. "That will always be."

Kneeling beside him, their lips met, and she, too, became surrounded by a glowing radiance. Toeyad's final kiss was offered so that a small portion of his essence would remain within her. Among the Fée, this was the ultimate gift of caring—the Gift of Everlasting Love.

It was also King Toeyad's final gift. Only the fading glow of his body now remained where once lay Tiyana's most mighty love and the greatest ruler the Fée had ever known. His passing was complete. He was forever gone from her side.

Tears streamed down her face as she watched his essence vanish into nothingness. Tiyana placed a small bouquet of purple violets on his empty bed. They were his favorite flowers. "Your father has returned to the eternal river from which all life flows, and to which all life must return," she told her children. "Now we must return to our lives and honor his legacy."

Tiyana and the three siblings slowly left Toeyad's chamber. Momentarily turning back, she paused, then softly whispered, "Good-bye, my beloved. Journey well, until we meet again along the shores of time."

Word of King Toeyad's passing quickly spread throughout the clans. Not a crop was picked nor a shop left open as all paused to bid farewell. Even Mother Nature grieved as the sky brought forth a warm gentle rain. From mountains to sea, all the land mourned the loss of a true and mighty friend.

Fée from every corner of Calabiyau came to the castle to

pay homage, leaving thousands of flowers of every color and type along the courtyard walkways. Their rich fragrances filled the air with exotic scents. Deer, squirrels, skunks, bears, birds, and raccoons also paused to say good-bye as Fée and creatures joined together for one last tribute to their beloved king.

It was the beginning of a new cycle, and with it, a new leader. Like the changing of the seasons, one had relinquished its claim, and another was about to take its place. King Toeyad was gone and Kandide, now possessed with the Gift, was to be crowned.

The High Council, Calabiyau's governing body, had been ordered by Toeyad to perform Kandide's official crowning on the fourth sunrise after his death. Normally, the Fée set aside seven days in reverence for a king's passing, and then another week before the crowning. But her father, as his last official mandate to the Council, had forbidden it. He made the twelve Council members promise to have no reverence at all and to crown Kandide on the fourth day after she received the Gift.

Toeyad argued that four days was plenty of time to make the necessary preparations. "Crown my daughter quickly, rejoice in your new queen, and let the cycle begin anew. I fear there are dangers yet untold, and Calabiyau must not appear vulnerable to Fée or Banshee. Their King Nastae must not think we are without a strong leader. The Banshee raids on our border villages are already far too prevalent and vicious. Do as I request, and I shall rest as I have lived, in peace and harmony."

The Council members had no choice but to abide. It was, after all, the law that the passing king had the final say in these matters.

And while, like most of the High Council members, many of Kandide's subjects did not like her arrogant ways, it was also true that few of them had actually met the crown princess. Rumors, however, abounded of her selfish, spoiled nature.

"Surely, Kandide has inherited a few of her father's better traits and is not as intolerable as they say," some of her subjects would optimistically propose. "After all, she is of her father's essence."

Others would vehemently disagree, stating that they personally knew someone who had felt the wrath of her self-centered whims.

Nevertheless, Kandide was to be their queen. Arrogant or not, it was her destiny. That was the law of the land.

*Tara's heart nearly stopped.
Over the piercing clap of thunder,
she heard Kandide's terrified scream.*

SIX

In the days that followed her father's death, Kandide became even more radiant, with the Gift of the Frost glowing strongly within her. *Even my wings look as though they've captured a rainbow,* she thought as she readied herself to go outdoors. Never had she been more beautiful—or more cold and dispassionate to those around her.

She had always had her father for support. Now that support was gone. And, if the truth be known, the crown princess was terrified of not having him to guide and protect her. That truth, however, must never be known. Kandide would not even admit to herself how much she missed him. *After all,* she rationalized, *was it not Father who taught me that I must be strong and never reveal my emotions? Was it not he who insisted that I be crowned in just four days? I can't just sit around and mope until then.*

"Father would be so very proud of how beautiful I look today," she told Teren as they ventured out to the gaming fields. "I do so wish he were here . . . to see how beautiful I am, I mean.

Don't you just love the way my wings glow?"

Teren stared at his sister in disbelief. He was, as usual, completely unimpressed with her carrying on, and found it especially objectionable so close to their father's passing. "I'm sure Father would be proud of the way you are gloat . . . uh, I mean the way your wings are glowing. Now, come on, let's go."

On this bright sunny day, Kandide and her brother were headed off for an early morning game of aerial cane fighting, or aercaen, as the Fée called it. Requiring far more strategy and speed than physical strength, aercaen was one of the more challenging of the faery battle games. It was also one of Kandide's absolute favorites. She had won many a match because of her considerable skill and wit in out-maneuvering her opponents.

She was dressed entirely in white. And while her attire was perfectly designed for playing aercaen, typical of the future queen, it was far more ornate than necessary. Teren, on the other hand, was dressed in the traditional dark blue practice uniform.

"It's such a shame that I have to deploy the Gift to change the seasons." Kandide twirled her fighting stick between her fingers. "I just hate the fact that when I do, my wonderful radiance will fade."

Teren rolled his eyes. "Your 'wonderful radiance' will build back up before you have to deploy the Gift again next year. Let's just get this game over with, so I can go back to the Royal Library."

Kandide stopped twirling her stick. "You can't keep hiding out between the shelves of those old books, Teren. I know you're upset over Father's passing, but it's not good to stay up there and feel sorry for yourself."

"I'm not feeling sorry for myself," he fired back. "I just want more time to be alone. Not everybody is like you, you know."

"That's it!" Kandide exclaimed.

"What's it?"

"More time. I'll bring about the Frost *after* my crowning parties. And I shall order the festivities to continue for days. That way, all of my subjects will have more time to see how incredibly beautiful I look with the radiance of the Gift."

"They already know how beautiful you look."

"Well, of course they do, Teren, but now—"

"But now, big sister, I think they'd rather see how beautiful the Frost looks. It's already late for the seasons to change— way past Samhain."

"Yes, but look at all the lovely weather I am allowing." Kandide gestured with open arms toward the bright blue sky.

The air was fresh, and the morning sky was indeed clear, with only a few wispy clouds. The temperature was ideal for being on the gaming field.

"That's it. I've made up my mind," Kandide declared, while flitting about and practicing maneuvers with her cane. "Deploying the Frost will have to wait until my crowning parties are over. After all, delaying winter for a few more days will also give me—I mean, my subjects—more time to spend in the Meadows."

"I'm sure they'll be thrilled," Teren muttered. There was no sense trying to talk Kandide out of anything. She always did exactly what she wanted, anyway. *I can't believe I even agreed to come out here,* he thought. *I wouldn't have, except for her non-stop badgering. And the fact that I've yet to beat her in a single match.*

But that's about to change. Teren had a brand new spell up his sleeve, one that his father had made him promise not to use until he had practiced. *However,* he told himself, *Father didn't say anything about whom I should practice it on.* Watching his sister flit about, Teren called, "Are you ready to play?"

"Of course." Kandide flew over to him and called the signal to start the match. "Cotell!"

They both lowered their protective face guards and the game began. Soaring above the field, their hard, wooden sticks began clashing as they tumbled and whirled through the air. Kandide was, as always, the epitome of poise. Even in battle games, her graceful carriage never seemed to falter. And while Teren was much clumsier, she couldn't help but notice how much he had improved since last they competed. *He's actually getting better,* she thought, as she twisted out of the way to avoid being hit. *It's nice to see he's taking an interest in something other than his books on magic.*

Ducking and dodging, the two siblings swung and hit at each other, each trying to win the game by causing the other to drop his or her stick. With a carefully executed flip, Kandide was just about to smash the cane from her brother's hand when she instantly froze in midair.

"It works!" Teren hollered. "It works!" Seizing the advantage, he easily knocked the cane from a very stiff Kandide's hands. "It really works!" he repeated, astonished by the results of his new spell. "Father said it would!"

Suddenly waking up, Kandide shook her head. "What . . . was that? What happened?"

"I beat you," Teren gloated as he floated to the ground.

"No, you cheated, that's what you did!" Still a bit dazed, Kandide nonetheless managed a graceful landing. "You put a spell on me, and that, little brother, is not allowed!"

"Where does it say so in the rules?"

"Well, it certainly isn't proper gaming etiquette." Seeing Tiyana and Tara standing to one side of the field, Kandide called, "Is it, Mother?"

"I'm not quite sure." Attempting to keep a straight face, Tiyana flew over to her daughter. "I don't think it's ever been an issue before."

"Well, it's an issue now! And I am quite sure that I will not play with you again, little brother, if you must resort to using your silly spells to win!" Shoving her facemask at him, Kandide abruptly turned to leave.

"You're just jealous because you can't cast that spell," Teren called after her.

"All right, Teren, that is enough." Tiyana reprimanded her son.

"Oh, now it's my fault. It's always my fault!" With his arms crossed and his feet firmly planted on the ground, he glared at his older sister.

Unable to resist, Kandide spun around to face her brother. "It usually is."

"That is not what I meant, Kandide, and you know it." Tiyana spoke to her daughter in the same firm tone that she had used to scold Teren. "Now, you're needed back at the castle. There's a great deal to be done for your crowning ceremony tomorrow, not to mention the parties that follow."

"Better run along, Kandide!" Teren chided, quickly turning

his attention to Tara. "Hey, Tara, want to see how my new spell works?"

"Sure, I'd—"

"She can't!" Kandide cut her sister off. "We're going to the Meadows, aren't we, Tara?"

"Right now? Well, I . . ."

Ignoring Tara's hesitation, Kandide was insistent. "That's what we shall do. In honor of Father, we shall go to the Meadows and bring back some pomegranates for my crowning parties."

"Absolutely not!" Tiyana exclaimed. "You have much too much to do to ready yourself for the ceremonies. Besides, the Air Clan has warned of a storm coming in."

"Oh, Mother, you never like it when I go to the Meadows," Kandide protested. "I want one last bit of freedom before I become a captive to my crown! You know I love it there—even more than playing aercaen."

"Kandide—"

"Mother, don't you remember when I was little? Father would break away from his courtly duties and take me there to pick pomegranates." Images of the two of them breaking open the ripest fruits and eating the jewel-like ruby seeds as they relaxed under a shady tree flashed through Kandide's mind. "That's it. I'm going to go in honor of Father," she insisted.

"Kandide, please don't go there today," her mother implored. "You know what happened to Selena."

"But I want to go. Besides, if you tell me one more time about Aunt Selena being injured in the Meadows, I think I shall explode." Kandide turned to her sister. "Are you coming?"

"I, uh . . . ?" Tara looked at her mother to see what she

should do.

"Go ahead, Tara. If Kandide must go, then maybe you can ensure that she doesn't stay too long." *This is one battle I probably won't win,* Tiyana thought, shaking her head. *And even if I do, Kandide will spend the rest of the day pouting.* "There is much to be done."

"I'll be glad to help you, Mother," Teren offered, seeing the exasperated look on Tiyana's face.

"Thank you, Teren. There are, however, still some decisions that only Kandide can make."

"Then I shall make them when I return." Kandide flicked her long golden braid back over her shoulder. "Let's be off, little sister."

Tara started to gesture so that the two of them might magically transport to the Meadows. Kandide, however, had already decided that they would take advantage of the warm weather by flying all the way there, just as she and their father had done so many times before. She grabbed her sister's hand, insisting, "No, I want to fly." Pulling Tara off the ground, Kandide led the way as they sailed above the treetops.

"Teren, don't you dare!" Tiyana ordered, seeing that her son was about to "practice" his new spell again.

"Aw, you never let me have any fun."

"Come along. There are a few things you can help me with, and that is not one of them." With a magical phrase and a wave of her hands, Tiyana gestured to transport the two of them back to the castle. Instantly, they vanished, dissolving into a shimmering spray of silvery faery dust.

Across the castle grounds, over three tiny villages, and out into the open spaces the two sisters flew. Below, they could see thousands of Fée bringing flowers for their father—*and my crowning, of course,* Kandide thought. "Tonight I will deal with all of the arrangements," she told Tara, "but right now I'm free. I have the entire day to enjoy the Meadows."

Together, they flew between hills, across streams, and down into the valley. It was a beautiful day—perfect for catching sunbeams. The sisters laughed and giggled, playing with butterflies and songbirds along the way. Before long, they reached the Meadows, which were very beautiful, very peaceful, and so very full of wild pomegranate trees. The vibrant green grass stretched out like a vast emerald carpet, and since the first frost had not yet fallen, hundreds of late-blooming flowers still dotted the terrain. Pink and yellow, red and gold, the blossoms glistened in the sun with the last drops of morning dew. Their fragrances made the air smell fresh and sweet.

Fluttering up to the top of a tree, Kandide plucked a luscious pomegranate. Laughing, she tossed it to Tara, and a game of aerial catch ensued. The sisters darted from tree to tree, selecting the largest of the fruit for their own and tossing the smaller ones to the animals waiting below. Foxes, raccoons, deer, and white-striped skunks all joined in the feasting.

The hours flew. "I haven't had so much fun since Father and I used to come here," Kandide told her sister. "We really need to do this more often."

"We do, but right now we need to think about heading back." Tara looked up at the sky. She felt a prickle of alarm. The air felt heavy, and thunderclouds were rolling in. She knew all too well that the Meadows were no place to be in a storm.

With a sudden wind whirling around her, and large drops of rain starting to fall, even the animals were rushing to take shelter. "We'd better go," Tara called to her sister.

"In a minute. I just want to gather a few more pomegranates." Kandide flew back up to the top of a particularly tall tree. She tossed her sister a large red fruit. "See how perfect these are."

But before Tara could catch the pomegranate, a blinding flash of lightning streaked down from the sky. Her heart nearly stopped. Over the piercing clap of thunder, she heard Kandide's terrified scream.

"No!" Tara gasped. "It can't be!"

But it was.

Branches came crashing down, and, with them, Kandide plummeted to the ground.

*Tiyana watched yet another
fiery bolt of lightning strike.
Thunder reverberated throughout the castle.*

SEVEN

"Kandi!" Tara screamed, rushing to her sister's side. "Wake up! Please, Kandi, wake *up*. Tara felt her sister's pulse. Kandide's heart was still beating, but the silver radiance that surrounded her body was starting to turn dull and gray.

The rain began to pound. It went straight through Tara's thin cotton shirt like piercing needles. She started to shake from the cold and bone-deep panic. Her brain seemed stuck in a circle of questions: *What if Kandi doesn't wake up? What if I can't get her back to the castle? What if she . . . ?* Forcing back her fears, Tara whispered, "I won't let you die, Kandi. I promise."

She took a deep breath, then drew upon the cool white light of her healing talent, and chanted a magical phrase: "Light of body, mind, and soul, enter my sister and reclaim this toll." As Tara passed her hands over Kandide's body, silver beads of light began to flow from her fingertips. Over and over again, she repeated the incantation. But her sister didn't respond, not even with the tiniest movement. *I just don't have enough power of my own,* she thought. *I have to get help from the other healers.*

Tara knew that she had only minutes to get Kandide back to the castle. But first, she would have to transfer more energy into her sister. Transferring too much would mean that she would be left without the strength to get them both home; not enough and Kandide's essence would continue to fade.

With thunder crashing overhead, and the rain pouring down, Tara mustered all of her strength. She placed her hands on Kandide's temples, and forced her own precious life into her sister. "Light of body, mind, and soul, use my strength to reclaim this toll." This time, she could feel her sister respond, but only slightly. Kandide's life source was almost completely drained by the lightning strike. Had it not been for the extra power she inherited with the Gift, she surely would not have survived even this long. Tara knew that getting her home quickly, where many healers could link their energies together, was the only chance to save her.

But how? We can't fly home, she thought. *If lightning strikes while we're in the sky, it will kill us both.* Using magic to transport her sister back to the castle was almost as dangerous, but with Kandide so weak, it might be her only hope. Timing was everything. *If I choose the wrong moment to transport, our essence will be sucked into the electrical surge caused by the lightning.*

Tara looked up at the sky. Lightning flashed against the dark clouds, forking in crazed, jagged patterns. "We have to transport during a break between the flashes," she whispered to her sister. Listening to the thunder, she counted the seconds between each lightning strike. It seemed as though they were coming in fifteen to twenty second intervals.

Terrified, shaking, and soaked from the pounding rain, Tara gently lifted Kandide up and then pulled her sister tightly against her own body. As soon as she saw a streak of lightning flash across the sky, she instantly gestured to transport home, hoping beyond hope that another strike would not occur anywhere near them. *May the earthly spirits be with us,* she thought, as she felt her body dissolve from its solid state into shimmering light particles.

Even in their transported state, Tara was aware of thunder booming all around them. Brilliant flashes began erupting in the distance, one right after another. She could only trust that luck would be on their side and that they were far enough away from the deadly strikes. Hopefully, she had guessed right on the timing.

Inside the castle, the sounds of crashing thunder sent Tiyana rushing toward a large window that looked out in the direction of the Meadows. Memories of her twin sister, Selena, lost from just such a storm, made her heart contract with fear. She gazed out at the dark sky and torrential rain. "I do hope they get back soon, Teren."

"I could go look for them." He walked over and stood next to his mother, staring up at the darkened sky.

"No, you know it's far too dangerous." Tiyana watched yet another fiery bolt of lightning strike. Thunder reverberated throughout the castle. The Fée have few natural enemies worse than lightening. "Even the Fire Clan wouldn't dare go out in this kind of a storm," she told him, clutching the white satin drape that framed the window.

"Mother!" Tara screamed for help. Materializing on the landing atop the grand stairway, she clung to Kandide's wet lifeless body.

"May the spirits help us!" Tiyana cried as she looked up to see her two daughters. "Teren, gather as many of the healers as you can find, and send them upstairs, immediately!"

Tiyana helped Tara take Kandide to her bedchamber, where they removed her soaked clothing and gently placed her into her bed. With virtually all of her essence drained, Kandide was unconscious and growing ever more translucent. Racing against time, both Tiyana and Tara knew they had to act quickly—she wouldn't last much longer.

Servants, then the healers began flooding the chamber. Upon seeing the crown princess, each displayed the same expression—fear then panic. "If Kandide dies," one whispered, "the Gift of the Frost will be lost forever."

"Then we'll all die," another gasped as she stared, wide-eyed, at their soon-to-be crowned queen.

"She hasn't got very long, has she?" a panicked young serving Fée asked. "What will we do?"

"Silence!" Tiyana shouted above the commotion. "Talk like that helps no one. I want everyone except the healers, Tara, and Teren to leave this room now. And I want no one told of what you've seen. Is that understood?" They sheepishly nodded their heads, and then quickly left. The horrified look on several of their faces told Tiyana that their promises might be difficult to keep.

Tara instantly began issuing orders to the court healers.

"Gather around me and join hands. Call on the whitest of the healing lights, and the brightest red of the heart's renewal. I need as much of your talent as possible."

All five of them immediately created a linked circle so that their power could be braided together. Tara began chanting, "Light of body, mind, and soul, join our talents to reclaim this toll." Once again, silvery light streamed from her fingertips into Kandide's body. This time the pulses were much stronger, and yet still nothing happened. Even after several minutes, Kandide showed no sign of responding.

"I need more," Tara ordered. She was beginning to turn pale from already having used up so much of her own strength.

"You need to rest," Lars, one of the senior healers insisted. He, like the others, was also starting to lose color from expending so much energy.

"Not until my sister is better." Tara, who was barely able to stand, sat down on the side of the bed next to her sister and placed her fingertips on Kandide's temples. "Instead of linking with me, place your hands directly on each energy point of her body," she told the others.

"But, Your Highness," Lars objected, "that many different healing patterns pouring into her at once isn't safe."

"Just do it, please. It's the only idea I have left, and I won't let my sister die." Tara looked at her mother for reassurance. Tiyana nodded for Lars to try.

Although the other healers also disagreed with Tara's request, they did as she asked. Each of them placed his or her hands on the various points where Kandide's energy flows intersected—her chest, wrists, abdomen, forehead, legs, and feet.

"What about her wing?" Lars asked. "It looks pretty bad."

"We'll deal with that later. Now, all of you, start on my cue." Following Tara's lead, they began to chant the incantation again. "Light of body, mind, and soul, use my strength to reclaim this toll."

As their healing light flowed into Kandide's body, Tara could feel her sister's pulse grow ever so slightly stronger. She also noticed that the dull gray color of her skin began to lighten, but there still was no sign her wakening. "Again," Tara ordered, barely able to speak. But as they started, two of the healers, also drained of their strength, collapsed on the floor.

"That's enough for now." Tiyana took her daughter's hand to stop her from continuing.

"But, Mother—"

"Tara, you can't save your sister by killing yourself—or the others. You need rest. All of you." She helped her daughter to a side chair, while Lars and Teren attended to the two healers who had fainted.

"Needless to say, each of you are sworn to secrecy regarding Kandide's condition," Tiyana insisted, once they were revived enough to listen.

"Of course, Your Highness," Lars replied. "What about Lord Salitar and the High Council? What should we say to them?"

"I shall attend to them, myself." Tiyana poured six glasses of fresh mulberry juice. She handed one to Tara and each of healers, and then poured herself and Teren a glass. "I want all of your focus to be on getting my daughter well. As soon as your strength returns, we must try again." She sat down next to Kandide and stroked her daughter's forehead. But there was no response, nothing at all.

For the next two days, Kandide lay motionless, barely clinging to life. Tara, Teren, Tiyana, and the healers all kept watch. Their future queen was never left alone, even for an instant. Mylea made sure food was aplenty, although most barely ate. Each time Tara felt a little of her own strength return, she and several of the healers immediately channeled more energy into Kandide.

In spite of their efforts, there was still no sign from Kandide that she would survive. Their only hope was that she was becoming less translucent.

"The important question is," Lady Batony continued,
"what do we do if Kandide does not recover?"

EIGHT

Inside the mahogany-paneled chamber of the High Council, every conversation revolved around Kandide. The Council of Twelve, as the members were called, represented the twelve primary Fée clans—Earth, Water, Fire, Air, Plant, Animal, Science, History, Creativity, Wisdom, Healing Arts, and the Heart. Collectively, the Council members were quite powerful and often extremely vocal when it came to deciding matters of state, especially as they related to their new queen.

"If only Kandide hadn't gone to the Meadows," Lady Alicia said with a sigh. She represented the Animal Clan and, more specifically, was a guardian of the reptiles. Tall, with short black hair and olive skin, she had been a member of the High Council since its inception, nearly one hundred years earlier.

"Unfortunately, Lady Alicia," Lord Socrat of the Wisdom Clan replied, "*if* might be Kandide's favorite conjunction, but it cannot help her, or us, right now."

His wife, Lady Socrat, who was one of the forest guardians,

and represented the Plant Clan, nodded in agreement. "Her life—and ours—remain at the whim of the fates."

"You're absolutely right, Lady Socrat." Lady Corale nodded in agreement. Her clan was of the Water, and she was a guardian of the oceans and seas. "Kandide has placed us all in a most dangerous situation. She hasn't even taken the crown yet, and already we're suffering the results of her selfish behavior."

Lady Karena, of the Heart Clan, was always the most tolerant of Kandide. Her golden hair shimmered under the flickering light of the wall torches. "You mustn't be so critical, Lady Corale. Surely she will recover, and all will be—"

An intensely bright scarlet flash of light interrupted her words. Lady Aron, of the Fire Clan, materialized in all her blazing splendor. "Perhaps, Lady Karena, we will all be blessed and Kandide will not . . . die." As always, Lady Aron was dressed in vibrant reds, scarlets, yellows, and ambers, with hair and wings that shimmered as though they were forged of flames. "I don't mean to imply that this untimely accident was poetic justice, but we all know that Kandide has never shown respect to the Council or to anyone except her father. Had she attended to her duties instead of going to the Meadows, none of this would have happened. I'm quite sure we can all agree that this time her actions set a new standard for reproach."

"Speaking of reproach, must you always enter like that?" Lady Batony glared at her. She was from the Creativity Clan and a guardian of music. "It's most annoying, Firenza. Besides, it's the Gift of the Frost that we must be concerned with now."

"Surprisingly enough, Lady Batony, I agree with you— about the Gift, that is." Lady Aron nonchalantly walked over to assume her place at one end of the large crescent-shaped Council table and took the seat next to her husband, Lord Aron.

"The important question is," Lady Batony continued, "what do we do if Kandide does not recover? What of the Gift?"

"We must at least consider that possibility," Lord Revên, from the Science Clan, answered. His voice was as deep as his concern. "This is a very serious situation."

"That it is," Lord Aron concurred, nodding his head. "And from what I have been told, there is a possibility that she may indeed not recover." Soft-spoken, he was from the Earth Clan and a most handsome Fée. With milk chocolate colored skin, and dark-brown hair and eyes, Lord Aron was the complete opposite of his fiery wife. "We all know that the Gift must be—"

"Preserved at any cost," Lady Aron interrupted, something she did quite frequently.

Lady Batony straightened in her seat. "Are you suggesting that—"

"I'm not suggesting anything. I simply—"

"All right, all right," Lord Rössi cut her off. "You two . . . please." His clan members were the Historians and the keepers of the records for all time. As the Council chair, Lord Rössi had his hands full keeping peace between the various members. "Must you bicker even at a time like this? You're certainly not helping the situation—either of you!"

Both Lady Aron and Lady Batony glared at him; nonetheless, they stopped their banter.

"I am told by my healers that Kandide has some color returning," Lord Salitar hastily stated. His clan members were the guardians of the Healing Arts.

"We can only hope they are right," Lord Standish, of the Air Clan, added with a deeply concerned frown. At nearly four hundred fifty years old, he was the eldest member of the Council.

"While many of you are quick to express concerns, and rightly so," Lord Rössi stood up as he spoke, "none of you have any idea what to do about the injured crown princess, and more importantly, the Gift. Perhaps we can focus on coming up with a plan, instead of just berating our new queen." He glanced at Lady Aron.

"Hopefully, our new queen," Lady Batony corrected him.

Completely ignoring Lord Rössi's request, Lady Aron, again, spoke up. "I, for one, simply don't see why you're all so eager for Kandide to take the throne. She's been a problem since she was born. Even as a small child, she would make her opinions on important matters of state well known."

"That's true, Lady Aron, but it was King Toeyad who encouraged her to do so." Lady Karena defended Kandide's actions. "He felt it was good training."

"So he did." Lady Aron's amber eyes with their piercing blue pupils flashed in unbridled annoyance. "Unfortunately, most of what she said then wasn't any more intelligent than what she says now. If it weren't for the Gift, we would certainly be much better off without her. In any case, if what you say is true, Lord Salitar, and Kandide is gaining at least some strength, then as soon as she shows any sign of consciousness, she must be ordered to transfer the Gift to someone who can immediately deploy it."

"Someone like you, Lady Aron?" Lady Batony crossed her

arms and glowered at the fiery Fée.

"That I would never agree to," Lady Karena protested. "Besides, transferring the Gift could kill Kandide in her weakened state."

"And so it might." Lady Aron leaned back in her chair. "But again, I ask, do any of you have a better solution?"

Silence filled the chamber. All looked around for an answer, but none of the Council members could suggest a single workable idea.

Taking the floor again, Lady Aron ultimately convinced them to agree that, "Above all else, the Gift must be preserved, regardless of the cost—even if it means Kandide's life."

"Why won't you answer me?" she shrieked.

NINE

On the third day following the accident, Teren thought he noticed his sister stir. The movement was so slight that he couldn't even be certain he had seen it. "Mother! Tara, come here."

Tiyana, who had fallen asleep in a chair near her daughter's bedside, woke up with a start. "What is it, Teren?"

He pointed to his sister. "I think she moved her head. Maybe she's waking up."

"Her face does look like it's got some color back." Tara placed her hand on Kandide's forehead. "She feels much warmer."

"That's a good sign." Tiyana knelt down beside her daughter. "Kandide . . . Kandide, can you hear me?"

Slowly, Kandide's eyes fluttered open. Although still groggy, she managed to whisper, "Mo . . . Mother . . . ? What . . . what hap—?" As she struggled to sit up, the other healers quickly gathered around her bed.

"Hush now, my child." Tiyana gently stroked her daughter's

forehead, brushing a golden wisp of hair away from her eyes. "Be still. You're still very weak. You were struck by lightning. Tara brought you home."

Kandide's eyes began to focus, and a faint smile crossed her lips. "Tara, I . . ."

"You're going to be all right now, Kandi. You're going to be all right." The elated young princess reached down to hold her sister's hand. The moment Tara touched her, a sudden surge of power flowed through Kandide's body, penetrating every muscle. The radiant glow of the Gift began to reappear, once again surrounding her with an iridescent halo.

Instantly, Kandide could feel her strength returning. "Mother, look!" She held out her hands, turning them from back to front for all to see the glow. "The Gift is back. I'm going to be fine. Teren, look!"

Kandide was alive, but all was not fine. As she leaned forward, her left wing did not unfold. Teren's expression changed from joy to shock. Not daring to speak, he simply stood there, staring at his sister.

"What's wrong? Teren? Mother? What's . . .?" Looking back at her wing, Kandide shrieked. "No! My wing! My beautiful wing! It's . . . it's . . . bent!"

Kandide's left wing was no longer full and beautiful. Instead of silver and gossamer, it looked like crumpled parchment— dull, twisted, and grotesquely deformed. She tried to move it, and an intense pain shot through her back and shoulders. She tried again, but the pain only got worse. She felt as if red-hot wires had been strung beneath her skin. As the realization of her plight began to sink in, Kandide became frantic. She turned to Tara and the other healers, her eyes wild with fear. "You must fix it!" she ordered. "I command all of you to fix my wing. Now!"

One by one, the healers lowered their heads, unwilling to meet Kandide's eyes.

"Why won't you answer me?" she shrieked. "How could you have let this happen? You must fix it! I can't be . . . a crumplewing. Not me! I won't be a . . . I won't be an Imperfect! Not even for a minute!"

"Kandide, please, calm down." Tiyana attempted to take her daughter's hand, but she quickly jerked it away. "Healing your wing will take time, and you need rest."

King Toeyad's words of strength and courage reverberated in Kandide's head. Taking a breath, she managed to speak with the cool regal tone she had been trained to use. Her back was straight and her head was high. "You will heal my wing, right now. As your queen, I command it." *Who do they think they are, leaving me like this?* she thought. Fear pulsed though her body.

"Of course, they will try," Tiyana gently responded, hoping to lessen her daughter's anguish.

"I don't want them to try, Mother. I want them to fix it. Now!" Kandide looked at her sister. "Tell me you can do it, Tara. Tell me you can fix my wing."

"Of course we'll do our best, Kandi." From experience, however, Tara knew that, unless Kandide's wing had been repaired immediately after it was damaged, there was little hope of it ever being perfect again. "You were so weak when I got you home that it has taken all of us just to keep you alive."

"Well, I am alive now, so fix it!"

Lars, who also had a great deal of experience with injured

wings, spoke up. "Your wing is severely damaged, Your Majesty. Even if Tara were at her full strength, I don't think it is within our combined powers, at least not immediately, to repair it. Perhaps over time . . ." The others nodded in agreement.

His words only served to enrage Kandide. With nowhere else to vent, she screamed at her sister, "This is your fault! You've always been jealous of me!"

"But, Kandi, I—" Tara desperately tried to make her sister understand. "We've done everythi—"

"You've done nothing. You're jealous because I'm going to become queen—that's what it is!" Breathing heavily, Kandide continued her shrill tirade. "Now go! All of you go!" Turning away, she sank back into her bed and pulled the thick blue satin comforter over her head.

"You may go," Tiyana told the others. "Let me talk to Kandide alone." Seeing Tara and Teren's hesitation, Tiyana motioned for them to also leave. Sitting on the edge of the bed, Tiyana placed her hand on her daughter's huddled form. "Kandide, listen to me. I know you're frightened and your wing—it must hurt you terribly, but none of this is your sister's fault. She's barely had any rest, just trying to save your life. Healing your wing will require patience and belief in her—"

"Go away!" Kandide's hysterical shriek was barely muffled by the covers. "Leave me!"

"But, Kandide—"

"Go!" Kandide pulled the covers even tighter over her head. *If father were alive,* she thought, *he'd make them do it.* "I said, GO!" she screamed, only slightly lowering the comforter so she could look her mother in the eye. "You're my mother and you can't even help me!"

Kandide's words cut through Tiyana like a knife. Her daughter was right. There was nothing she could do. Perhaps nothing anyone can do. Her beautiful and oh-so-perfect daughter, the soon-to-be queen, was now a crumplewing— an Imperfect.

To the Fée, and more importantly, to Kandide, it was a fate of unimaginable horror. Since the beginning of time, Imperfects, as the Fée called those who were not physically perfect, were considered a disgrace, and Tiyana knew this all too well. They were not accepted. They must be sent away.

Before leaving Kandide's room, Tiyana pulled a long velvet rope to summon Mylea. "Please stay near," she ordered Kandide's lady-in-waiting. "I shall return as soon as I have spoken to the Council."

"Yes, Your Majesty." Mylea curtsied.

The two siblings were waiting for their mother in Kandide's antechamber. Teren was nervously making a crystal ball float from hand to hand. "Guess it must be broken," he told Tara, holding it up and looking into it. "The only thing I can see in it is my own reflection."

"You know those things never work." Tara stopped her pacing long enough to comment. "No one can tell how the future will unfold, not even you." She looked up to see Tiyana walking in the room. "I'm so sorry, Mother," she exclaimed, rushing over to her. "I don't want to be queen—really I don't. I hate politics."

"I know, Tara, I know." She gave her youngest daughter a reassuring hug. "You saved Kandide's life, child. No one could have done more to help her than you. No one. She's just terrified and angry right now."

"Maybe I could create a Glamour spell," Teren eagerly suggested. "I'd have to find just the right incantation that would make her wing look perfect. But it might work—at least until Tara can heal it."

"If I can heal it, Teren." Tara sat down on the pink settee close to where her brother stood. "I honestly don't know if I can, not even if I had the help of every healer in the entire kingdom."

Tiyana sat next to her daughter. "And I'm afraid it would take an extraordinary amount of magic and glamour to conceal that much damage. Even then, the spell probably couldn't be sustained for very long—not even with your talents, my son."

"So what are we going to do, Mother?" Teren placed the crystal ball back on Kandide's desk.

"I'm not sure. But in any case, I must inform the High Council."

"You can't!" Teren's voice rose in alarm. "You know how Lady Aron feels about Imperfects." He began to recite one of her more frequent speeches: "'Physical perfection is imperative to the survival of the Fée. Imperfects are weak and an embarrassment to our race. They are a threat to our strength and all we have stood for since the beginning of time.'"

"Teren's right, Mother." Tara nodded. "Lady Aron's always saying how 'Imperfects must never be allowed to remain in our land—or before you know it, they'll expect to have full rights.'"

"We've all heard her say it a hundred times," Teren added, continuing his impersonation of Lady Aron: "'Our governing Articles have never accepted Imperfects. That is the way it has always been, and that is the way it will remain—as long as I serve on the Council.'" He walked over to his mother. "She'll insist on banishing Kandide."

"I know." Tiyana's voice was barely audible. "Your father did his best to amend the Articles, but since the vote of the Council must be unanimous, Toeyad had little choice but to concede to her demands."

"Yeah, and even after nearly a hundred years of trying," Teren added, "you know the most Father could get was an agreement to let Fée with minor imperfections conceal their flaws—and even then, they're stuck in lowly jobs."

"With her wing that badly damaged, the Council will never let Kandi be queen," Tara insisted. "Even the idea would be—"

"Unfathomable." Tiyana had to agree. "You're right."

"I think we shouldn't tell them what's wrong." Teren picked up the crystal ball again, looked at it, then set it back down. "At least not right this minute. That way Tara can have some time to at least try and fix it."

"What do you think, Tara?" Tiyana looked at her daughter.

"I'm just not sure, Mother. Even after Aunt Selena transferred the gift of Healing to me when she was so badly injured, I couldn't heal her. You know I will do everything I can. But it could take months—and even so, it might only be a partial healing. I can't guarantee . . ."

"Then, I guess it's settled." Tiyana stood up. Pain and inevitability were etched across her face. "We don't have months, and the Council must be told the truth. Better I tell them now, than they hear it from someone else—and they surely will."

"But the healers are sworn to silence," Tara objected.

71

"They are," Tiyana replied. "I think, however, that some of the serving staff may have said some things. Rumors are already flying."

"Yeah, and we don't know who Lady Aron has bribed— or what they've told her," Teren added. "It could be anything."

"You're right, my son. Mylea does her best to hire good help, but loyalty seems to be a rare commodity where Imperfects are concerned. No, we shall simply have to deal with the consequences of Kandide's injuries when she is stronger. Right now, I must go speak to the Council."

Teren pointed to one of the crystal torch lamps that lit the chamber. Instantly a ball of flames erupted.

TEN

Each of the twelve members of the High Council stood, bowing to Tiyana as she, Teren, and Tara entered the room. The somber look of the dark wood paneling in the Council Chamber seemed appropriate at that moment.

"Welcome, Tiyana." Lord Socrat was the first to speak. He and Lady Socrat were Tiyana's closest friends. "Kandide, is she . . . ?"

"My daughter lives." Tiyana forced a smile. Sighs of relief spread throughout the chamber, but a gesture of her hand indicated that there was more to tell. "She lives, however . . ."

"However?" demanded Lady Aron. Her words, like her beauty, contained no semblance of softness. She was the most belligerent and argumentative Fée Tiyana had ever known, and perhaps the only Council member she did not like or trust.

"Kandide is injured," Tiyana explained.

"Injured?" Lord Rössi's tone revealed only concern. "In what way, Tiyana?"

"She . . . she has an injured—" Before Tiyana could finish her sentence, the Council Chamber doors flew open.

Kandide stood in the doorway. The radiance of the Gift glowed around her. *There's no need for them to know the truth,* she thought, looking from Council member to Council member. *At least not until after my wing has been healed.* Her gaze rested upon Tiyana. "What Mother was about to say is that my wing has been injured." Kandide's cloak was tightly wrapped around her shoulders to conceal the awful truth of just how badly her wing was bent and broken.

"How injured is it?" Lady Aron pressed.

"I assure you it is only a temporary condition." Kandide tried not to flinch as a fierce pain shot through her shoulder.

"Surely Tara will be able to heal it." Lady Karena nodded encouragingly to Kandide.

"Well, Tara," Lady Aron stared straight at the young princess, "can you heal Kandide's wing?"

"I—"

"Of course she can." Kandide cut her sister off. *At least say you can, Tara,* she fumed. *At least do that much for me.* She walked over to her crystal throne and sat down, facing the Council's crescent-shaped table.

Lady Aron eyed the crown princess. "Perhaps you should show us just how badly your wing is damaged." She started toward to Kandide.

Catching his wife's arm, Lord Aron stopped her. "I don't think that will be necessary, my dear."

"I agree," Lady Batony spoke up. "Please, Kandide, do spare showing it to us."

Jerking her arm free from her husband's grasp, Lady Aron was not about to relent. "I'm sorry that you're so squeamish, Lady Batony, but as Council members, we have the right to know just how badly our future queen is damaged. I, for one, demand that you show us, Kandide."

"How dare you demand anything of me," Kandide retorted. "Let me remind you, Lady Aron, that I am the rightful heir to the throne, and you have no authority to insist that I do anything."

"And let me remind you, Your Highness, the majority vote of the Council is equal to yours. I'm quite sure that I am not alone in my desire to know if we are about to crown an Imperfect—something I assure you will never happen." The fiery Fée turned to one of the other Council members. "Do you agree, Lord Standish?"

"Well, we certainly can't crown an Imperfect." He carefully avoided Kandide's stare.

Lady Aron turned to the guardian of the seas, whose long, flowing black hair was adorned with tiny seashells. "And you, Lady Corale? As the representative of the Water clans, what is your opinion?"

"It definitely would not be in compliance with our Articles of Law," she stated.

"And you, Lord Revên? You are the guardian of the Sacred Arts and represent the Science Clans. How do you feel?" Lady Aron looked directly at the red-haired Council member.

"Philosophically, I do not agree. But practically, I'm afraid I must concur with Lady Corale." He, too, avoided Kandide's gaze. "We simply cannot have an Imperfect as our queen.

The Articles are most definitive on that matter."

"But we don't even know how badly Kandide is injured," Lady Karena objected. Her blue eyes were full of compassion. "I say we give her wing time to heal."

Of course, you would say that, Lady Karena, Lady Aron chuckled to herself. *Well, in spite of your pitiful bout of sympathy, Kandide will be out of here in no time.* She could barely contain her glee. "Lord Rössi, as Council Chair, I think you should call for a vote to force Kandide to show us her wing."

"And I think the matter requires much more serious consideration," he shrewdly answered. "Perhaps, Kandide, we should discuss your prognosis with Lars and Tara in private so that we may determine how long you might possibly be infirmed."

Kandide's purple-blue eyes blazed in defiance. "Perhaps, Lord Rössi, I will speak to my subjects first. I'm told that several thousand of them have gathered in the courtyard and are waiting to see me." Standing, Kandide walked over to the door, turning back only to say, "Are you coming Mother?"

Lady Aron spoke before Tiyana could answer. "Your subjects have no vote, Kandide."

"Not in this matter, but certainly for your re-election to the Council. May I remind everyone of the warnings my father issued? Even before my accident, the Banshee raids on the villages near the border of our two lands were becoming more frequent—and vicious. Our subjects will not be happy if you delay crowning a queen."

Lady Aron could barely keep a straight face. This was simply too good to be true. "Well, then, Kandide, as I see it, the solution is in your very own words. You must be sent away—at least until your wing is healed—if it can be—and your sister will immediately be crowned."

"Me?" Tara gasped. Her thoughts began to whirl with panic. *I don't know the first thing about running a kingdom. I belong in the forest healing animals, not trying to deal with an out-of-control Council.* "No, no, no! I can't be queen."

"Well, we certainly can't crown your brother," Lady Aron insisted. "He's, well, far too . . . young."

Standing just to the left of Tiyana, Teren was becoming more and more upset. "I don't ever want to be king. Kandide is the rightful heir. She's our queen. Besides, I'm a wizard." He pointed to one of the crystal torch lamps that lit the chamber. Instantly a ball of flames erupted. Dancing through the air, it disintegrated over the heads of the Council into a burst of golden sparks.

"And stunts like that are exactly why we don't want you as king," Lady Batony flicked a fallen spark from her shoulder. "Using your talents so frivolously at a time like this—it's unacceptable, it is."

Lady Alicia also brushed a few sparks from her own shoulder before speaking. "Teren's antics are not the point—as annoying as they are. May I remind all of you that the Gift of the Frost must be our priority?"

"Yes, the Gift," Lady Aron agreed. "And since it appears that Kandide will be leaving us, I insist that she immediately transfer it to someone else."

The entire Council erupted in argument. "Lady Aron's right." "Perhaps and perhaps not." "I say, it must be transferred."

"But what if Kandide isn't strong enough?" "We mustn't wait." "I agree, it must happen now!" "Who will it go to?"

"Silence!" Lord Rössi banged his wooden gavel on the table. "Can we please discuss this in an orderly fashion?"

"Thank you Lord Rössi." Tiyana scanned the faces of the twelve Council members. "As a mother and your former queen, I am appalled by the Council's behavior. My daughter is barely well enough to stand before you, and yet here she is—and all you can think of is the Gift!"

"All, Tiyana? The Gift is *all* that is important. Your daughter is an Imperfect—a crumplewing!" Lady Aron's voice became even more biting as she turned from Tiyana to address Kandide. "Respectfully, Your Majesty, you no longer belong among us. You not only injured your wing due to your own self-centered actions, but now you disgrace and humiliate your entire family by coming in here and demanding to rule. Your behavior is a grave dishonor to your father and to the crown. I insist that you transfer the Gift of the Frost—and that you do it immediately!"

Kandide responded with the icy cold of a winter storm. "Once again, Lady Aron, your demands mean nothing to me. I shall speak to my subjects, and then we shall see about the crown, the Gift, and my future."

"Well, I do hope that you will show your dear father some respect and leave Calabiyau—at least until your wing can be healed." Lady Aron's golden eyes were blazing. *Which my sources now tell me can never happen,* she added silently. *It's amazing what insights a few baubles can buy.* "May I also remind you that winter is severely past due? At least have the decency to immediately deploy the Frost."

With each word Lady Aron spoke, Kandide grew more defiant. "When and how I deploy the Frost is my decision. I am Calabiyau's rightful queen, and that means no one—least of all you—has the authority to order me to do anything." She pulled her cape tightly around her shoulders and swept out of the Council chamber.

"We'll see who orders whom," Lady Aron muttered under her breath. "Go speak to your subjects. You may be surprised at what they say."

For a split second, Kandide was unaware of what was happening. Then she panicked.

ELEVEN

"**A**re you sure you're up to doing this, Kandide?" Tiyana rushed to catch up with her daughter as she headed toward the speaking balcony. Teren and Tara were only a few paces behind.

"Perhaps you should wait a bit, Kandi," Tara suggested. "Until—"

Kandide whirled around to face her sister. "Until what, Tara? Until the entire kingdom knows about my wing? Lady Aron has eyes and ears everywhere. It wouldn't surprise me if she's already blackmailed one of the healers into revealing what they've seen. No, I must deal with my subjects now, while I can, on my terms. They are not so silly as the Council, nor as vindictive as Lady Aron. Once I stand before them, they'll see how beautiful I look, and that the Gift radiates within me. I am their queen and I must lead with strength and courage; that's what matters. Father has said so."

"Then lead you shall, my daughter." As the four of them

stepped onto the grand speaking balcony, Tiyana could only hope Kandide was right. Thousands of Fée from every clan were gathered in the courtyard below. The afternoon was bright and sunny, and all were awaiting word of their new queen.

With every bit of the nobility she was born with, Kandide stepped to the front of the wide marble platform. She was standing exactly where her father had, when he spoke to his subjects so many times before. An image of him holding her hand as they stood there on her sixth birthday, flashed through her mind.

They loved me then, and they'll love me now, she thought, listening to the sound of the long-horned trumpets that heralded her arrival. Kandide placed her right hand on the curved brass railing that surrounded the balcony. Her long silver-gold hair glistened in the sunlight. For all to see, the crown princess looked to be the personification of perfection. She raised her left hand to greet her subjects with a regal wave.

The anxious crowd began wildly cheering. Cries of "She lives!" and "Long live Queen Kandide!" broke out, followed by applause and even louder cheering.

"See, Mother, how much they love me," she whispered, raising her hand, once again. This time, it was to silence the crowd. "Yes, I live." She told them, and more cheers poured forth. Feeling confident and assured, Kandide continued: "You are my loyal subjects, and I am soon to be crowned your queen. It is my destiny to serve in the footsteps of my father, our greatest and most beloved King Toeyad."

Again, cheers erupted, and again she silenced them with a gesture of her hand. *What I'm about to say next will determine my destiny*, she thought. Feeling her pulse quicken, Kandide chose her words carefully. "Hear me now." Her voice was clear and strong. "I must take leave for a brief while so that I may fully regain my strength. I will remain here, at the castle, in seclusion. As soon as I am strong again, I shall return to this balcony and stand before you as your rightful monarch."

"Why?" "What's wrong?" "How long?" She could hear uncertainty spread throughout the assemblage.

"Do not fear," Kandide hastily reassured them. "I shall return to my duties in a very short time. It was with strength and courage that King Toeyad led you, and it was only through my own strength and courage that I survived the lightning strike. And survive I did. It is my destiny to be your greatest and most beloved ruler, and that I shall be."

The crowd went quiet again. This time the silence was different. Kandide felt a prickle of unease. *They must think I'm leaving them without someone to rule,* she thought, completely unaware of the arrogance of her own words. An idea popped into her head. "Worry not. My sister, Princess Tara, will reign in my brief absence."

Almost too shocked to speak, Tara stammered, "Kandi, I—"

But Kandide silenced her. "I ask that you embrace Her Royal Highness Princess Tara, as your temporary queen." With a deep, formal bow, Kandide curtsied to her sister. As she rose, however, one of the trumpeters who had turned to assist her stepped on the hem of her cape.

Gasps erupted from the crowd. For a split second, Kandide was unaware of what was happening. Then she panicked. "My cape! No, it . . ." She grabbed for the pearlescent fabric as it slid off her shoulders, but she was too late. There, for all to see, was her terrible secret—a bent and broken wing.

Frantically wrapping her cape back around her shoulders, Kandide tried to speak over the jeers and laughter that were erupting as awareness of her imperfection spread through the crowd. "My wing will be healed. I assure you, it will."

Ignoring her words, someone hollered, "She's a crumplewing!" Another called out, "She's an Imperfect!" More taunting cries resonated across the courtyard. "Kandide's a crumplewing!" "You're not our queen!"

"I am your queen," she shouted back. "I'm not an Imperfect. It's only a temporary injury. Listen to me."

The more she tried to speak, the louder the crowd became, until suddenly a pomegranate pelted her in the shoulder with the force of large rock. Knocking her backward, it instantly created a dark purple bruise on her creamy white skin. *I must make them understand,* she frantically thought, ignoring the pain and forcing herself to remain regal. *I will be perfect again.* Before she could say another word, a second tangerine-sized pomegranate grazed her wrist, and another narrowly missed her head.

"Kandi!" Tara rushed to her sister's side, as did the trumpeter who had stepped on the hem of her cape. Together, they attempted to form a shield in to protect her.

"Stop it! I said stop it! All of you!" Teren shouted from the edge of the balcony. His pleas, however, were met only with more jeers. The castle grounds were immediately teeming with guards, but even they had little effect on the growing fury of the crowd.

"Send her away," someone shouted. "Yeah, send her away!" This time, a small rock was hurled onto the balcony.

Fearing not just for her daughter's life, but for the safety of everyone involved, Tiyana frantically gestured. With a wave of her hand, Kandide disappeared in a shimmer of silver sparks. The jeers stopped. The crowd became silent as they watched their future queen vanish into nothingness.

"My daughter has been sent away," Tiyana called out, hoping to ease the hostility. All eyes were glued to her. She scanned the massive assembly. They were her subjects—the very same Fée who had loved Toeyad and her for all these years. She knew they were waiting for her to say something more—to provide reassurance. She stepped forward to speak. "Her Royal Highness Princess Tara shall be crowned queen. Now go to your homes and tell your clans. I must meet with the Council. Long Live Calabiyau!"

The crowd echoed her words, "Long Live Calabiyau!"

Saying nothing further, Tiyana, along with Tara and Teren left the balcony. "May the earthly spirits protect you, Kandide," she whispered, as they started down the hall that led to the Council chamber. *I must now protect Tara.*

"Mother, wait!" Tara caught Tiyana's arm. "You can't tell the Council that I'll be queen. You know me; I'm not trained in politics. I can't rule over Calabiyau."

"You can and you will, my child. Forgive my tone, but this is not a time to be fearful."

"But—" Tara protested.

"You must trust me on this," Tiyana said softly. "Now, say no more. Teren, take your sister to her chamber and stay there until after I speak to the Council. Tara, you will not meet with them until tomorrow, when it can be from a position of strength." The look on their mother's face told the two siblings not to argue.

Tiyana continued to the Council chamber alone. She took a deep breath, then walked inside, and stood directly in the center of the Council's crescent table. Only silence could be heard as all waited for her to speak. "Kandide has been sent away," she repeated, in the same firm manner she had used to tell her subjects. "She has abdicated the throne to Tara."

"What about the Gift?" Lady Aron demanded.

"The Gift, Lady Aron?" Tiyana's expression revealed only contempt. "The present is the gift we have now, dealing with it will determine how we unwrap our future. I suggest the Council consider its actions here today most wisely, and crown my youngest daughter at first light."

Halting a sudden eruption of heated controversy, Lord Rössi smashed his gavel down on the table. "Silence!" he ordered. "I said silence." Backs stiffened as hushed murmurs permeated the chamber. "May I please speak?" One member after another finally stopped talking. "Good. Each of you knows that it is the law of the land to uphold an abdicated monarch's wishes. Tara will be queen."

All knew he was correct, and none, not even Lady Aron, had the power to challenge Fée law on this matter.

"And I, as Council Chair, agree with Tiyana," he continued. "She must be crowned at first light. We have been long enough without a ruler. There are far too many sightings of Banshee troops along the border. They must not be allowed to learn of any disruption of power." With that, he banged his gavel again and dismissed the Council.

Tiyana had always admired how forceful Lord Rössi could be. It was the reason Toeyad had appointed him as the Council's Chairman. *Tara will need his strength,* she thought, before saying to him, "I shall be in my chamber if you need me."

Feeling only emptiness, Tiyana's body was trembling by the time she got to her room. *First Toeyad and now Kandide, this is surely a time that will require a great deal of strength and courage—perhaps more than I have left.*

She looked up at the full-length portrait of her husband. He seemed so life-like, as though he could simply step off the canvas. "I know what you would say, my darling, Tara and Teren need me now. It's their future that I must safeguard. But first I need a few minutes to get my own emotions under control. Then I shall be able attend to Tara. Oh, Toeyad, how could things have gone so very wrong?"

Tiyana settled into a nearby chair. Her chamber was decorated in the lush greens of the forest. It reminded her of the woods where she and Selena grew up. *I thought losing my sister was the worst thing in my life. Now I have two more pieces of my heart that can never be replaced—my beloved husband and my eldest daughter.*

Sitting there alone, she thought of all she and Toeyad had achieved during their rule. As little as a hundred years ago, things were very different for the Fée. Calabiyau was in constant turmoil. Although King Toeyad's family had ruled almost since the beginning of time, jealousy, arrogance, and struggles for power dominated faery politics for as long as anyone could remember. *Not much has changed*, she thought. *Each clan still considers itself to be more important than the other.*

Tiyana knew full well that had Toeyad's ancestors not possessed the Gift of the Frost, they surely would have been dethroned millennia ago—and that worried her as well. *Tara doesn't have the Gift to protect her title, nor the experience to control the Council. And yet, like you, my husband, diplomacy is a skill she fortunately does possess—that will surely help.*

Toeyad's skill as a diplomat was what ultimately united the clans, and for the greater part of the past century, they had all lived in harmony. *All, that is, except the Banshees.* Tiyana's worries shifted to how Tara would be able to deal with them. As powerful and strong a leader as Toeyad was, even he had been unable to bring them into the High Council. Their volatile and fierce, warlike nature simply would not allow it. The best he could do was to negotiate a truce with their leader, King Nastae, to not wage all-out war.

"We've come such a long way, my love," she told her husband, looking back up at his portrait. "I so wish that Kandide would have been able to finish your work and create a true peace with the Banshees. I was so proud of her on the balcony, today—the way she took charge. She certainly has your spirit. But being queen is not her destiny, and now I must go speak to Tara."

Tiyana stood up and straightened the mint green lace collar that framed her face. It was the first day since Toeyad's death that she had not worn purple in his honor. She was about to leave her chamber when she heard her daughter's voice.

"Are you okay, Mother?" Tara rushed into the room.

Teren was right behind her. "What did the Council say?"

"They had no choice but to agree. Tara, you will be crowned."

"Are you sure I can do this, Mother?"

"I'm sure you must do this," Tiyana told her. "I know it's not what you want, but unless you abdicate to Teren—"

"Oh, no you don't!" He started to back out of the room. "There's no way I'm going to let you do that. Sorry, Tara, you're the one who's next in line."

"But do either of you really think that there's any way the Council will ever listen to me? They know my talent is in healing. I'm just not prepared to be queen—everyone knows that."

"Sometimes, my daughter, preparation isn't part of the plan." Tiyana tried to reassure her daughter. "There will be many challenges, but I have every confidence that you will grow to be a wonderful ruler. And remember, you will not be alone. I'll be there to help you, as will Lord and Lady Socrat—and Lord Rössi, and Lady Karena."

"And me," Teren added. "I'll help you, Tara."

"Thank you, Teren. I know you will." Deep down, Tara knew she had no choice but to agree. "If my being Queen is what you really think best, Mother, then I shall do as you ask."

"Good." Tiyana knew how hard this was for her daughter. "It will be fine, Tara. I promise. Now, there is much to do."

"Like maybe finding Kandide," Teren said. "Then Tara can try to heal her wing and she can come back."

"Where is Kandi, Mother?" Tara asked. "Where did you send her?"

Ignoring her question, Tiyana reached over to turn up the flame in the oil lamp on her desk. "It's a bit dark in here, don't you think?"

"I think you should at least tell us why you won't say where Kandide is," Teren persisted.

"What's done is done, Teren. We must focus on Tara now."

"But, Mother, what about the Gift?" Tara's anxiety only deepened. "Even if I am crowned, I can't bring about winter. Only Kandi can do that."

"Perhaps." Tiyana looked out her arched window at the rising full moon. Its harvest-orange reflection shimmered on the pond below. "Now, I want both of you to try and get some rest tonight. Our future has taken an unexpected turn, but Calabiyau's destiny is yet to be written. And I must have this night to think."

The only sound was the occasional twig cracking underfoot. Not even the wind rippled through the trees. There was only silence—deathly silence.

TWELVE

K andide hadn't intended to fall asleep, only to rest until daybreak. Emerging from the last remnants of slumber, it took a few minutes for her to remember what had happened—that her mother had sent her away, and that she had taken refuge in this small rock cave just before nightfall.

Maybe I'm dreaming, she thought, stretching her arms. The severe pain in her shoulder and the bruise on her wrist told her otherwise. Staring up at the jagged ceiling of her tiny shelter, Kandide attempted to make sense of it all when she became aware of something cold and wet nudging her arm. Slowly turning to look, she saw a huge silver-grey wolf looming over her. It was the biggest wolf she'd ever seen.

"H-hello," she managed to stammer. Knowing better than to move quickly or show fear, Kandide held out her hand for him to sniff. But the wolf merely glared at her, his amber eyes glowing in the dim light of the cave. "N-nice boy. I . . . I won't hurt you. Really, I won't."

For what seemed like an eternity, the wolf stood there, watching her. Then, with a deep-throated growl, he turned and ambled out of the cave. Pausing for a brief moment to look back at her, he then disappeared into the shadows.

I need to get out of here, and fast, Kandide thought, hastily standing up. She straightened her dress, pulled her cape around her shoulders, and cautiously stepped outside. Her crumpled wing was throbbing, but that was something she would just have to endure for the time being. Kandide stood for a moment, looking around. *Which way should I go?* she wondered.

Although the sun had risen, the forest was still engulfed in the same strange dark fog. The early morning rays of light that did shine through cast ominous shadows, making the gnarled, dead forest appear even more menacing than when she had first arrived. Taking a few steps in one direction, Kandide spotted the wolf standing only a dozen meters away. Partially hidden behind a massive old fallen oak, his glowing eyes watched her every move. Again, he growled.

Maybe not that way, she thought, quickly turning in the opposite direction. Being extra careful not to slip, Kandide slowly began making her way through the tangled tree branches and marshy underbrush. Reaching out to snap a twisted branch that blocked her way, she had a sudden thought. *Maybe these are the Mists? Maybe this is where Imperfects are sent. Maybe that's the reason no one ever sees them again.* She remembered back to the time when she believed that sending Imperfects to a place like this was merely a legend—a ruse to make young Fée behave. A wave of terror swept over her. *Maybe it's all true. If so, then*

I'll never see Calabiyau or my family again . . .

"No!" she said aloud. "I can't think about that. I must keep focused." Repeating her father's words—"Strength and courage. Strength and courage. Strength and courage"—Kandide forced herself to keep walking, although still very slowly.

She headed away from the wolf. Curiously, whenever she glanced back, she saw that he was following her, but always at a distance. *What's he doing all by himself in a place like this, anyway?* she wondered. *Wolves normally live in packs.* A chill crept up her spine. *Does that mean there are more of them? Maybe he's waiting for his friends to show up and then he'll attack. No. He could have easily killed me back there in the cave.* She winced at the thought. "Just keep walking, Kandide," she mumbled, "and pay attention to where you're going."

Except for an occasional glimpse of the wolf, she could neither see nor hear another living creature. The only sound was the occasional twig cracking underfoot. Not even the wind rippled through the trees. There was only silence—deathly silence.

Maybe I should just transport out of here—to wherever I end up. But without knowing where she was, how could she even begin to set the coordinates? Transporting only worked when the Fée knew where they were starting from, as well as where they were going. She could end up anywhere—or nowhere. *No, I have to find some sort of identifiable landmark first. Then I can transport. If only I had my gaming boots,* she thought, as a glob of slimy black mud oozed between her toes. *At least then I could walk faster. I'll never wear sandals again!*

As Kandide continued making her way through the dense

maze of forest, other thoughts began to consume her—thoughts of her future, of the way she was treated by the Council, how much she disliked Lady Aron, and how much she missed her father. *I will be healed. I will be perfect again. I will get out of here. I won't let Lady Aron win. I won't let any of them win! It's my destiny to be queen. Father said so.* Like so many vivid pictures, each image that flashed through her mind made her more and more determined to find the way out of this horrible place.

Her empty stomach rumbled, but she pushed back any thought of food, and instead tried to focus on remembering what Teren had told her about the Mists. "What did he say about them?" She knew no one would answer, but it made her feel better to hear a voice, even if it was her own. "Where are they supposed to be located? Think, Kandide, think! You're brilliant—Father has said so many times. You can figure this out. You always do."

"If only I could fly, I could see above the trees. I could find a landmark." Looking up at the tangled canopy of branches above her head, she began to chuckle at how silly she sounded. "If I could fly, I'd be gone already."

"Okay, no more *ifs*, Kandide. Father was right. *If* won't solve the problem, and it certainly won't stop my wing from aching." Snapping off another branch and tossing it out of her way, Kandide flinched. The constant throbbing in her wing was bad enough, but every time she twisted a certain way, sharp pains shot up her back.

"I could do without that," she muttered. Rubbing her shoulder, Kandide pressed on a nerve near her neck. It seemed to help lessen the pain, at least for a while. "I could also do without this disgusting smell!" The putrid, acidic stench was getting stronger, and it was starting to make her feel nauseous. At least the revolting odor kept her from wanting anything to eat. "Not that there would be anything even remotely edible in these woods—except maybe me!" She shuddered at what might be out there, and began walking faster.

"Oh, yuck!" Kandide looked down just in time to stop herself from stepping in a gaseous pool of black slime. "What's in there?" Tufts of brown fur floated on the pool's oily surface. She could only imagine what lay rotting underneath. In truth, she did not want to know.

While trying to figure out the best way to go around the slime, she noticed what appeared to be a clearing no more than fifty meters ahead. Kandide stood there staring at it. *Am I imagining this?*

Shafts of sunlight illuminated some sort of an opening. Could she actually have found the edge of these dreadful woods? Her heart began to pound. "I knew I could do it. I knew I could find my way! I always do!"

Careful not to fall or step into anything else that looked overly slimy, Kandide made her way toward the clearing. The rays of sun got brighter and brighter, until, to her absolute amazement, she saw an immense golden gate. Its ornate filigree glistened in the midday sun. The gate was set in the center of the highest, longest stone wall that she had ever seen. It seemed to stretch toward infinity in both directions. Through the gate, she could see a magnificent castle with two identical towers.

"I don't know where I am," she happily admitted, "but at least I'm somewhere!" As Kandide drew closer, the massive gate swung open. It was as though her arrival had been expected. *Could this be where the Banshees live?*

Uncertain about entering, she hesitated, glancing back at the dark, fog-laden woods behind her. The wolf stood just a short distance away; its golden eyes were watching her.

Kandide made her choice.

*"What is this place?
Where am I?"*

THIRTEEN

In complete contrast to the dark, putrid forest that she had just come through, Kandide found herself standing in an exquisitely landscaped garden. Fuchsias, hydrangeas, pansies, cockleshells, bluebells, orchids, jasmine—flowers of every kind and color filled the air with their rich fragrances. She inhaled deeply to take in their splendid aroma, hoping to clear her lungs of the acidic stench of the Mists. Everywhere she looked, exotic botanicals formed wondrous pathways that led to the golden château. Its towering spires reached upward toward the clear blue sky. Vividly colored stained glass windows sparkled in the sunlight.

Kandide could only stand there, staring in wonder and awe. *What is this place? Where am I?*

The flawlessly manicured grounds were bustling with activity. Fée from virtually every clan were busy trimming shrubs, planting flowers, and going about their duties as if this were any ordinary castle. But this was no ordinary castle. It was different somehow, truly strange in its absolute perfection, and even more extraordinary than her own palace. *I've never heard of a kingdom like this,* Kandide thought, bewildered by what she saw. *Neither Father nor the Council has ever spoken of it.*

She managed a "hello" to one young couple who returned her greeting and then, giggling, flitted off before she could inquire as to where she was.

At least they aren't Banshees, she happily thought, making sure her cape was pulled tightly around her shoulders to conceal her damaged wing. Kandide started to ask another Fée, but he also extended a polite greeting and then quickly flew off. Looking around, she became aware of a woman approaching. As the lady drew closer, Kandide was completely taken aback. She pressed her nails into her palms to make sure she wasn't dreaming.

"Mother?" She stared at the woman in disbelief.

"Kandide? Is it really you?" the lady replied, even more astonished than Kandide.

"Yes, but—"

"I'm Selena, your mother's twin sister."

"Selena?" Kandide's jaw dropped open. "Aunt Selena? But how? I-I don't understand? You . . . you died when I was young." She slowly looked around. Everything was so beautiful, so perfect. It all seemed real enough—and yet . . . Any number of thoughts raced through her mind. *Is this where Fée go when they die? Could it be that I actually didn't survive the lightning strike? Perhaps Father is here.* Staring at Selena, she finally asked, "If I'm here, does that mean that I, too, have . . . have died?"

"Goodness no, child." Selena couldn't help but chuckle. "I assure you that you are very much alive, and so am I."

"That's a relief—I think."

"My, how you've grown, and so very beautiful. Tell, me, how is Tiyana? How is your sister? And little Teren—how is he?"

"They're all well, but—"

"And your father? How is King Toeyad? I trust he is well?"

"Then you haven't heard?"

"Heard? I'm afraid we don't get much news out here."

"Father has recently passed."

"Oh, Kandide, I am so very sorry. A greater leader the Fée could not have known, nor a kinder one. And now . . . why, that means you must be queen." Selena curtsied with a deep bow. "Your Majesty!"

"Well, I . . . I'm . . ."

Kandide started to explain, but Selena continued, "Let me be the first to welcome you to the Veil of the Mists. We're so very honored. Oh dear, how rude of me. I'm just so excited to see you. Do come inside, Your Majesty."

"Thank you. But please, Aunt Selena, call me Kandide."

"Then Kandide it is."

They walked through an elegant golden archway that led into the château's Great Hall.

"We simply had no idea you were coming," Selena remarked apologetically as they entered the large room, "or we would have sent a welcoming party to meet you." Looking at Kandide's torn gown and mud-stained shoes, she knew something was wrong. But decided, as she had done with so many new arrivals, to delay questioning her niece, and instead wait for Kandide to explain her sudden appearance. "I shall have fresh clothes prepared for you immediately."

"That would be most appreciated. My trip was . . . uh . . . hastily arranged," Kandide replied, looking around at the marvelous décor.

The inside of the château was even more resplendent than its exterior. Intricately woven tapestries, majestic sculptures, and colorful paintings graced the walls. The furnishings were exquisite in every detail, masterfully carved with upholstery that was obviously the work of superior artisans. Spectacular jewels—rubies, emeralds, sapphires, and diamonds—adorned a massive, yet splendidly carved marble fireplace. Each faceted stone sparkled as it captured the light of the flickering flames. They, too, were unlike anything she had ever seen in size and color.

"Please, do be seated." Selena gestured toward a richly embroidered blue and gold chair. "I can't believe that you are actually here in the Veil, and that you know about us. Tell me, dare I hope that the Council has finally amended the Articles to allow those with injuries to live there? Can I finally visit my sister? It has been so very long. Oh dear, I am going on. With so many things I long to know, I'm afraid I'm just full of questions."

"I have a few, myself," Kandide murmured, still gazing around the magnificently appointed hall.

"How long will you stay?" Selena sat down in a chair across from her niece. *Perhaps that will get her to loosen up*, she thought.

"My plans are, well . . . flexible."

"Good. Then I do hope you'll stay a while. There's so much to show you and to talk about."

"That would be lovely." Assuming that Selena knew nothing about her crumpled wing, Kandide decided that there was no point in telling her, at least not yet. "I'm afraid I'm a bit confused, however," she continued. "I thought the Mists were only a legend—an imaginary place created to frighten young Fée into behaving."

"I assure you the Mists are quite real, and, as you undoubtedly saw when you were outside the Veil, quite dangerous."

"The Veil?"

"Perhaps I should start at the beginning," Selena answered. The way Kandide had arrived, all alone and so disheveled, she wasn't surprised by her niece's lack of knowledge about their land.

"Yes, please." Kandide sat up straight, trying to sound regal and not too uninformed about where she was.

"It all seems so long ago now. Your mother and I used to love to visit the Meadows—"

"The Meadows? Mother? But, Aunt Selena, mother abhors the Meadows."

"She does now, but it wasn't always so. We would often go there to gather wild berries, or to just sit under a pomegranate tree and talk—sometimes for hours. Then we'd catch moonbeams to light our way home."

"That sounds like Tara and me." Kandide suddenly thought of how much fun she and her sister used to have. They, too, would fill their pockets with moonbeams, and then use them to find their way home. "So, what happened?"

"One day, we were caught in a terrible lightning storm." Selena let her cape slide off her shoulder. "That's when my—"

Before she could finish her sentence, Kandide gasped, "Your wing, it's bent!"

"Why, yes. I thought you knew."

"You're a crumplewing? You were sent away?"

"I didn't mean to startle you. Oh dear." Selena was beside herself at the thought of upsetting her niece.

"No, I'm . . . fine. I just—I'm just surprised, that's all." *The same thing happened to Selena that happened to me,* she thought. *If only Mother had told me, maybe I wouldn't have gone out that day.* She stared at Selena's wing and simply shook her head. "We were told you had passed—but you didn't. And now . . ."

"That's what your father wanted everyone to believe."

"But why? How? All this?" Kandide gestured at the château's beautiful furnishings.

"When the accident happened and we realized that my wing could not be healed, your father couldn't bear to send me away. He knew that to do so would break Tiyana's heart. Toeyad pleaded with the High Council to change the law so those of us with permanent injuries could remain in Calabiyau. While some were willing, Lady Aron led a powerful fight to oppose it."

"Lady Aron. Of course." Kandide shrugged. *She's still doing it.*

"In the end, she won by convincing enough members of the Council so that a vote was never even taken. That's when your father created this sanctuary surrounded by the Mists—a secret place, where I could live in safety."

"Father created the Veil?"

"Why, yes." Selena was now convinced that Kandide's lack of knowledge meant she had probably not arrived of her own accord. Nevertheless, she continued her story: "Although most Fée probably don't realize it, King Toeyad was quite accomplished in the wizardly arts. I'm surprised he didn't tell you about the Veil's formation."

"Well, not everything," Kandide hastily replied. "He . . . his passing was rather sudden. That's why."

"I see." Selena regarded her niece curiously. She had a few questions of her own. But they would have to wait until Kandide felt more comfortable speaking about why she was really there. "Well, as you stated, even though many think the Mists are merely legend, in truth, they have existed since the beginning of time. No one knows how they were formed. Your father wanted a safe place for me to live, so he cast a spell in the heart of this dead land—where he knew no one would venture. Not only did he create a paradise for me to live in, but he also placed a protective shield—a Veil—over this entire area, making it impossible for anyone to transport directly in—or out, for that matter."

"I had no idea." Kandide's voice was soft with amazement. "I mean, I had no idea that Father created so vast an area. And that he built this château for you, as well."

"The château he did not build. You see, at first there was just me, a small cottage, and the griffins, of course."

"Griffins?" Kandide's eyes lit up. As a child, she used to dream of seeing a griffin.

Selena smiled at her niece's sudden enthusiasm. "You're fond of griffins?"

"I've never actually seen one," Kandide admitted. "But Father used to say I reminded him of them."

"And he was right. Even as a small child, you had a proud, fiercely independent nature. Griffins are just the same."

"That's exactly what Father used to say." A blush of

genuine excitement crossed Kandide's face. "How many griffins are here?"

"Less than a dozen, I'm afraid. Toeyad brought all that he could find to the Veil so they'd be safe and we could try to restore their numbers."

"That's truly wonderful. I didn't think there were any still alive. I'd love to see them."

"Perhaps you will. They live up in the mountains and come down every few days for food."

"I hope I am still here when they do. But tell me, how . . . where did everyone else—"

"Come from? Please, have some hot tea and shortbread." As Selena was speaking, a dark-haired young Fée entered with refreshments. She poured Kandide a cup of hot tea. "We make it with fresh pomegranates," her aunt explained. "They're grown right here."

Almost choking at the thought of more pomegranates, Kandide managed a polite "Thank you. It sounds lovely." Ignoring the tea, she reached instead for a piece of shortbread. "Do continue with your story, Aunt Selena."

"Of course, and then, Kandide, perhaps you can tell me what prompted your sudden visit to the Veil."

"He's exactly what I have been looking for," Lady Aron thought. *"And I have a feeling he knows a great deal more than he's saying."*

FOURTEEN

"Y ou asked to see me, Lady Aron?"

"Yes, do come in." She motioned for the tall, lanky uniformed soldier to enter the antechamber of her living quarters in the castle.

The room's décor perfectly reflected Lady Aron's fiery personality. Nothing was understated in design or color. With vivid red and orange furnishings scattered throughout, the room also contained a large area rug that looked as though it was woven from actual flames.

"How may I be of service, My Lady?" the soldier inquired as he stood at the edge of the carpet. He was almost afraid to step on it, lest it scorch his boots.

Lady Aron wasted no time getting to the point. "I wish to know why a trumpeter of the Royal Guard was so clumsy as to step on the cape of the crown princess."

"It was an unfortunate accident," he replied, nervously fumbling with his cap. "I have apologized most profusely to Her

Royal Highness Tiyana."

"So I hear. And yes, it was an unfortunate accident, wasn't it?" With a flick of her wrist, the cap flew out of his hands and landed on a nearby table. "No need to be nervous, I don't bite. Please, have a seat." Gesturing toward a chair, she continued, "I just might have use for someone such as you. Tell me your name again."

"I am called Asgart, My Lady," he answered, still standing. "Begging your pardon, but I believe it is the same name you were given when you asked my commander about me."

"Don't be impertinent," she snapped, then quickly softened her tone. "Please, do be seated, Asgart. I really don't bite unless, of course, I'm given reason to."

"No, My Lady, I mean . . . I don't have much time." Asgart was fully aware of her bite. He had seen it from afar many times. It was not at all uncommon for her to lash out at members of her own staff for no other reason than they said "Good morning" in too cheery a tone. He glanced toward the door. "Duty calls, you know."

"No, I don't know. I also don't know why you intentionally stepped on Kandide's cloak. And, unless you would like me to submit a report to the Council that contains—well, let's just say, some evidence that I have recently uncovered regarding your 'malicious intent' in the cape incident, I suggest you be a little more agreeable. Now, sit."

"Yes, Ma'am." Asgart walked over to the chair she had motioned to and sat down.

"That's better. Now, won't you join me in a cup of tea?" Without waiting for his answer, she snapped her fingers. The tea, in the two cups that had been sitting on the table in front of him, instantly burst into flames.

He jerked backward, not daring to touch them.

"Don't worry, I'm just making sure it's nice and hot for you." She picked up one of the cups, blew out the flames, and then took a sip. "Things tend to get cold rather quickly around here. Perhaps you'd like some sugar?"

"Uh, no. Just the tea is fine, thank you." Asgart watched as the flames died down in his cup. Still afraid to touch it, he picked up his cap instead.

"So, now that we're friends," Lady Aron sat her cup down, "why don't you tell me what really happened with Kandide's cape—and why."

"As I said, it was an accident, nothing more." Lady Aron might serve on the High Council, but he was not easily intimidated, even by her. Tiyana had issued an order of forgiveness and, in his mind, that's all that mattered.

"I know what must have happened." Lady Aron's large fire-opal ring flashed with color as she placed her hand on his. "You merely wanted to see if the rumors about Kandide being an Imperfect were true. Is that why you did it, my dear?"

Asgart quickly slid his hand away. "On my life," he insisted, "I would never do anything to harm Princess Kandide."

"Well, there certainly is no harm in wanting to know the truth about her condition, now is there? After all, you do have the right to know if your future queen is an Imperfect."

"I—"

"You don't happen to think that an Imperfect should be queen, now do you?"

"Of course I don't, but . . . please, I can say no more, My Lady."

"Oh, I think you can. Tell me, are you pleased with Tara's crowning?"

"Indeed," he answered with a firm nod. "Princess Tara is young and inexperienced, but I have no doubt that she will be a fair and devoted leader. She is, after all, most gracious and kind."

"And Kandide is not?"

"That's not what I meant." Asgart wasn't at all sure how to answer such a question.

"I understand that you have had firsthand experience with Kandide's . . . shall we say, lack of graciousness?"

"Respectfully, My Lady, I'm sure that is something you need not be concerned with. Besides, it was a very long time ago."

Lady Aron put her hand on his knee. "My dear, dear Asgart, when it comes to you, everything is now my concern. We're friends, remember—and we are going to become even closer."

"Begging your pardon, My Lady, I'm married, and my wife . . . she'll be serving dinner soon, and I have yet to finish my duties. I really must be going." Asgart stood up to leave.

"Yes, your wife. I was hoping we could discuss her." Lady Aron favored him with a smile. "I understand that your wife is also employed here in the castle. It would be such a shame if she lost her position at the same time you lost yours. Why, what would your two lovely children do? You wouldn't want that to happen, now would you?"

Asgart could only glare, knowing she would not be denied.

"You do understand what I'm saying, don't you, trumpeter?"

"Yes, My Lady."

"Good. Then sit back down." She pointed to the chair. Grudgingly, he obeyed.

"Now, tell me about what happened 'a long time ago.'"

"I . . . I was a most respected soldier. It was my privilege to guard King Toeyad—that was until Kandide decided that I should become her aercaen partner. Even though she was young and inexperienced, she severely injured my leg in one of our games of combat."

"I'm sure it was just an unfortunate accident," Lady Aron mimicked his words, "though undoubtedly embarrassing."

"Well, I could have dealt with that. Even the best competitors occasionally lose to lesser players. But the princess, she . . . she humiliated me even further by publicly apologizing and then ordering her healers to fix my leg, right there in front of my peers. At least she could have let me leave the gaming field on my own. I had strength enough for that, yet she made me look like a weakling."

"Why do you think she did it?" Lady Aron pressed, curious to know how he felt about the crown princess.

"It was Her Highness' first big win, and she wanted to make sure everyone knew it. After that, I suppose she no longer considered me worthy of being her aercaen partner, so the next day, I was assigned to be a court trumpeter. The guys in my legion had a lot of fun with that. 'Job too tough?' they would say. 'Gone soft, have we?' I haven't been able to advance in the ranks since."

"How very unfortunate for you." *He's exactly what I have been looking for,* she thought. *And I have a feeling he knows a great deal more than he's saying.* "So, Asgart, tell me, do you have any idea where Kandide . . . I mean, where Imperfects are sent? I've heard that, in certain cases, King Toeyad personally took charge of that duty."

Asgart rubbed his chin. "Well, there are rumors among the guards."

"Rumors?" Lady Aron was most anxious to hear about these rumors.

"It's probably nothing." He shook his head.

"I'll be the judge of that, my dear Asgart. Incidentally, now that we have become such good friends, I may be able to help you finally get a promotion—especially since you did act so very bravely in trying to shield Kandide from all of those pomegranates that were being hurled at her."

"I never meant for her to get hurt. I only—"

"Of course you didn't." Lady Aron couldn't have been more pleased with her latest conquest. Asgart, it seemed, was a real find. He was not terribly bright, but he was resolute in his feelings. And he had absolutely no loyalty to Kandide. "Please, do tell me," she prodded. "I just love rumors."

Wondering if he had already said too much, Asgart hesitated. Still, a promotion was more than he had dared hope for in a very long time. *And I did stop one or two pomegranates from hitting Kandide*, he reasoned. *Besides, I deserve a promotion after all I've been put through.*

"Well?" Lady Aron urged him.

"Well . . . there are rumors that King Toeyad created a secret place in an area called the Mists."

"A secret place in the Mists?" *So, it truly does exist*, she thought. *Now you just need to find it for me.* "So, where in the

Mists do you think this secret place is?"

"I'm not sure. You might ask your husband."

"Lord Aron? Why would my husband know about it?" In all their years of marriage, Lady Aron had never heard her husband mention the Mists, let alone a secret place.

Asgart shifted uncomfortably in his seat. "A number of years ago, I overheard King Toeyad talking with Lord Aron about a place of safety for Imperfects. That's when he mentioned the Mists."

"Go on." She took a sip of tea.

"I think King Toeyad said that he had created a valley— or did he call it a veil—in the Mists? I'm not sure. Anyway, I remember thinking how odd it sounded, because I always thought the Mists were just a legend. And why would Lord Aron care about what happens to Imperfects?"

"Yes, why would he? Tell me, do you think you can find out where this secret place is?"

"I really wouldn't know where to look. The rumors say that the Mists cover quite a large area, and that they're extremely dangerous."

"Dangerous—yes, I suppose they could be dangerous." Lady Aron passed her hand over her cup and again, it burst into flames. "I just hate cold tea." She waited a few seconds then blew out the flames. "You've done well, Asgart. Just one more thing. What do you know about garglans?"

"Garglans?" He looked at her alarmed. "You mean those awful creatures that the Banshees use to guard their jewel caves?"

"Exactly."

"Why do you want to know about garglans?"

"An excellent question," she mused. "Why would anyone inquire about garglans?" Lady Aron stood up and motioned toward the door. "Because you, dear Asgart, are about to go and get some for me."

"In a way? You suppose?"
Jake's voice was hot with disbelief.

FIFTEEN

Noticing that Kandide had instantly devoured the first biscuit, Selena offered her niece another piece from the tray next to her on the table. "Please, do have more shortbread."

As they sat in the large Receiving Hall in the château, Kandide eagerly ate one piece, then another, and another, until she had almost finished the entire plateful. Never could she remember anything tasting so good. She even could feel her strength beginning to return. "They are quite delicious," she said, half apologizing as she eyed the last biscuit on the plate. "I must get the recipe for our pastry chef."

"I'm glad you like them," Selena replied. "Margay will be pleased."

"Margay?"

"She oversees the kitchen. Her pastries are truly incredible. Now, let's see, you were about to tell me about your arrival here?"

Kandide stammered a bit before answering. "Oh, uh, you

mean why I look such a fright?" She glanced down at her torn, mud-stained skirt. "Well, uh, you see, when I set the transport coordinates to come here, I must have miscalculated and got lost . . . and, uh, I turned the wrong way. That's all. I just took a wrong turn. I'm sure it happens to everybody. In any case, you were telling me about how the château came to be." She quickly grabbed the last biscuit and took a bite from it.

"Of course. That explains it." Knowing that her niece was not yet comfortable enough to reveal the real reason for being there, Selena felt it best to continue with her own story. "Shortly after arriving here, I was searching in the woods for wild mushrooms, and I met Jake."

"Did I hear my name?" A tall, extremely handsome Fée bounded into the room. With tousled black hair and vibrant green eyes, he had a boyish smile that Kandide instantly found irresistible. "Well, hello." Jake's eyes seemed even brighter as he smiled at her.

I can't believe he actually winked at me, Kandide thought, having never heard the word "hello" sound so flirtatious. *He is sort of cute—in an odd kind of way.*

"Jake," Selena motioned for him to join them, "I'd like you to meet my niece, Her Majesty Queen Kandide. Kandide, this is Jake."

"Q–Queen Kandide?" Jake's jaw dropped almost as low as his very formal bow. He managed to stammer out an embarrassed, but certainly more appropriate, greeting. "Your Majesty, begging your pardon. I-I didn't realize. I mean, your attire . . ."

"I got lost coming here. And there's no need to apologize." Kandide addressed him in her most royal tone. Offering Jake her hand, she added with an amused smile, "It is my pleasure, I'm sure. Do join us."

As though he had been hit by a block of marble, Jake dropped into the nearest chair. Looking from him to Kandide, Selena hid an approving smile. "Well, now that we have the formalities out of the way, may I continue with my story?"

"Please do," Kandide murmured, having trouble looking away from Jake. Never had she seen such beautiful eyes—*except my own, of course,* she thought. Her heart began to flutter. *There's something about him . . .*

"As I was saying," Selena continued, barely able to get their attention, "I was walking in the woods one afternoon when Jake came bounding out."

"He seems to do a lot of that," Kandide responded with a slight laugh. She dared not let her eyes meet his again.

"I do not!" Jake protested. "Do I?"

"It does seem to be a trait of yours." Selena looked over at him and smiled. "Jake also had to leave his clan."

"Why? You're so . . . so perfect." Realizing what she had just said, Kandide suddenly blushed. "I mean . . ."

"Jake was a victim of the after-wars," Selena explained.

"The after-wars?" Kandide had heard about them, but only in passing.

"Before your father was able to convince the twelve clans to sign the Unification Treaty, Selena continued, "there were many battles. And while we were quick to brag about how few Fée were killed during these skirmishes, many hundreds of others were badly injured—even after the Treaty was signed. Pockets of fighting went on for years. They were known as the after-wars. Jake was attempting to stop a rumble that had turned particularly violent when a burning timber fell on his legs."

Kandide eyed Jake's seemly perfect physique, searching for some sort of imperfection. *He looks okay to me,* she thought, commenting, "At least you're all right, now."

"Sort of." Jake suddenly flew straight up. His boots, however, remained on the floor.

Kandide could only stare at him, stunned with disbelief. She felt her stomach start to churn; for a few seconds she wasn't sure she could keep down the shortbread.

"I lost my feet." Jake sounded almost proud of his misfortune.

"But when you came into the room," Kandide stammered, "you . . . you walked perfectly."

"Thank you. It took years to develop feet that work like real ones. Now we've figured out how to do arms, and legs, and—"

"You mean to say that you can make limbs that work like real ones?" Kandide wasn't sure she believed him.

Jake's green eyes studied her. "Yes, Your Majesty, that's one of the things we've been working on here."

"Can you make wings?" she asked, far too eagerly, almost forgetting about his lack of feet.

"Not perfectly yet, but we do have a prototypal set. I'll show them to you if you'd like." Sitting down, he pulled his boots back on.

Watching him, the reality of his imperfection returned. It took all of Kandide's composure not to reveal the repulsion that she again felt. Nevertheless, she managed a polite reply. "That would be nice. If I'm still here. I do have a kingdom to run, you know." Quickly turning to her aunt, she whispered,

"Father sent the rest here as well?"

"No, not in the beginning. Jake told me that there were others who were also injured and living in the Mists. And while they should have been able to return home from the fighting with honor and glory, they were instead 'discreetly' sent away. Many of them did eventually join us. Unfortunately, many others were never found. Still more were too far gone for anyone to help, and simply would not leave the woods. We don't know what happened to them, but we fear the worst."

Kandide wasn't sure how she felt about what she was hearing. "They're Imperfects, and yet the reason they're Imperfects is because they were injured when they joined with Father to help unite the clans and end the fighting. In a way, I suppose they are heroes, but . . ."

"In a way? You suppose?" Jake's voice was hot with disbelief. "There's no question, Your Majesty, they are heroes." He crossed his arms and leaned back in his chair.

Kandide stiffened. *How dare he contradict his queen?* she thought. *But then, he is after all, an Imperfect. I suppose I can overlook his rudeness this one time.* "Well, Jake," she said, in what she felt was a very reasonable way, "I'm not sure that sending them away was the right thing to do. But what else could be done with them? They are, after all, Imperfects. They could hardly live among the rest of us. It just wouldn't be right."

"No," he retorted, "I suppose 'it just wouldn't be right,' Your Majesty!"

I really shouldn't have to justify anything I say, she thought, *but I am a guest, so I suppose that I should at least try and make him understand how the real world works.* "The laws pertaining to Imperfects are in our Articles, Jake, and they're very specific. Even Father wasn't able to get the High Council to change them. Not even for Selena."

"And that is exactly why King Toeyad granted the Veil its independence," he blurted out. "So that we govern ourselves and aren't subject to the Articles of Calabiyau—or its rulers!"

Taken aback by the idea that her rule might not extend to this area, Kandide, nonetheless, pushed her annoyance aside. Why, she did not know. "Yes, and that was . . . well, it was very wise of Father to create a safe place for Imperfects to live." *Why are you even bothering with him?* she asked herself, quickly turning her attention back to her aunt. "So, then what happened?"

"What happened?" Selena gave her niece a curious look. "Oh, at the Veil, you mean. Well, we began building this château and the surrounding villages."

"Imperfects built this?" Kandide exclaimed. *How could Imperfects build something so beautiful?*

"And why not, Your Majesty?" Jake stood up. "We may be missing feet or have crumpled wings—some of us have even lost legs or arms while fighting so that you and your kind can live in a land that's safe—but we certainly aren't helpless. Or useless." With a curt bow, he walked toward the door, turning back only to say, "By your leave, Your Majesty. My duties require me elsewhere."

Kandide wasn't sure if it was Jake's audacity or what he was saying that disturbed her more. *I should know better than to get into conversations with Fée like him,* she thought. *And I won't ever do it again.* But as he left the room, her eyes followed. She found herself unable to look away.

Watching her niece, Selena commented, "Jake is very proud of all we have accomplished, and with good reason. He is the one who persuaded most of the Fée who were living in the Mists to come here. He convinced them that they are worthwhile and could live full and productive lives."

"But he seems to be so happy. I don't understand. I mean . . . he . . . he doesn't have any . . . well, you know, feet," she whispered.

Selena arched one eyebrow. "Jake may not be perfect, but then, who is?"

Kandide started to answer. "I cert—" Thinking better of it, she sank back down into her chair. "It's all so confusing, so very confusing."

"I'm sure it must be." Selena knew she still had more to explain. "To one clan, perfection is being tall, to another it is being short, and to yet another, it is being fair or dark. Some clans are wiser than others; some are more clever or creative. Your mother and I are greens, while you are pale, like your father. We're all different. But all Fée, whether they are born with physical challenges or become permanently injured, have something to offer, Kandide, if only they are given a chance to develop and utilize their individual talent and skills."

Kandide stared out the large window at several Fée who were doing gardening chores. "Are you saying that every one living here is . . . is an Imperfect?"

"Well, we don't use that term, but yes, I suppose we are."

"Then what are they called?"

"Oh, well, let's see. That's Salara over there with Ilene and

Robbi." Selena pointed in the direction of three Fée who were polishing a large marble outdoor fountain. And there's Jessita and Margrite—the two young girls in blue who are trimming the hedge."

"Of course." A slightly embarrassed Kandide pulled her cloak even tighter around her shoulders. *They seem normal enough,* she thought. *But then, so did Jake.* "So, how do you live? Where do you get food?"

"We grow all our own food and only eat food that is grown. We respect all life."

"Father would like that. He too respected all life."

"Yes, he did—*all* life. I was hoping that you had come to learn about us, and to help convince the Council that we are valuable. But I'm sensing that is not the case."

"Uh, well, of course it is, Selena—that's exactly why I'm here—to learn about the Veil."

"Good." Selena stood up. "Then, why don't I take you on a quick tour before dinner?"

"That would be lovely." Kandide also stood up, trying not to flinch from the pain that kept shooting through her shoulder. Nonetheless, she was determined not to let her aunt know about her wing. *I mustn't let anyone know,* she thought. *Especially Jake, he must never know. I'm not like them. I'm just here to learn about the Veil—a royal visit—that's all.*

"Are you sure you feel up to it?" Selena noticed that her niece suddenly seemed very pale. "You must be exhausted from all your travels. Would you prefer to rest this evening? We can take the tour tomorrow."

"I assure you, I'm fine. Just a little stiff from sitting so long."

She twisted her back to try and stop the pains. "And if we can avoid seeing Jake, I'm sure the tour will be most enjoyable."

Tara could contain herself no longer.
"A small sacrifice, Lady Aron?
You call giving up her life a small sacrifice?"

SIXTEEN

Inside their chamber, the entire High Council was in an uproar. Having crowned Tara as the new queen at first light, they turned their attention to what to do about the Frost.

Sitting uncomfortably on the crystal throne, the young queen spoke not a word—instead letting the Council members have their say. On the rare occasion that she had visited the Council when her father was alive, she had watched the great king use silence as a ploy to gain control. *Perhaps it will work for me,* she thought, wishing she were in the forest with her beloved animals.

Lady Aron was, as usual, the most vocal. "Tiyana, you simply must tell us where Kandide is. The seasons must change. We are running out of time."

"I have told you, I sent her away." Tiyana's voice was cool and firm. "There is nothing that can be done right now."

"There is always something that can be done," the Fire Fée retorted. Her stoic expression seemed to hold a hidden secret.

"Toeyad gave you his last kiss and, with it, at least some of the Gift. If you cannot find Kandide, then the solution is simple: You must use what you have been given to trigger the Frost."

"While I hate to agree with Lady Aron," Lady Batony spoke with a sigh of resignation, "I am afraid, Tiyana, that you may be our only hope."

Lord Socrat's eyes widened in astonishment. "Lady Batony, are we to understand that you actually concur with Lady Aron in this matter? Do you not realize that deploying the Gift could be fatal to Tiyana?"

"I—" Lady Batony started to defend her comments, but Lady Aron cut her off.

"Lord Socrat, would you prefer that all of Calabiyau suffer for Kandide's reckless behavior? Is it not better for Tiyana, her own mother, to make a small sacrifice? That seems a perfectly just solution to me."

Tara could contain herself no longer. "A small sacrifice, Lady Aron? You call giving up her life a small sacrifice?" She stood up; her pulse was racing. *I'm not about to lose Mother to Lady Aron's manipulations,* she thought. "How can you even suggest such a thing, especially you, Lady Batony?"

Looking rather sheepish, Lady Batony stammered, "Well, I . . . I simply meant, Tiyana might be our only solution. Oh, dear, if only Kandide had not gone to the Meadows. I remember when I was a little girl—"

"But you're not a little girl," Tara sharply cut her off, "and Kandide did go to the Meadows." Whether from frustration or anger, her voice suddenly became strong and clear. "As Father would say: 'It is today that we must deal with, nothing else.'

I suggest we all heed his advice."

"You're quite right, Tara." Lady Aron surprised everyone by agreeing. "And, as you well know, the consequences of not dealing with the Frost, today, will most assuredly be fatal."

"So could Mother's attempt to deploy it!" Tara exploded in anger.

Lady Aron responded with a tone that was as cold as her words. "We all realize the price Tiyana might pay, Tara, but each of us must pass at one time or another. And since it appears that we won't be seeing your sister again, it is the greater good that we must all think of now."

"Well, I've had just about enough of your greater good, Lady Aron." Tara slammed her hand down on the Council table. "You may be of the Fire Clan, Firenza, but it is ice that runs through your heart. The High Council is dismissed—until I call you back!"

"How dare you speak to me that way?" an incensed Lady Aron fired back.

"How dare I? Well, as your queen, I . . . I . . . command you to leave!" Tara was shaking inside, but managed to speak with the authority her new title demanded. "I said you're dismissed. All of you."

"Bravo, Tara!" All eyes instantly shifted to Teren, who had been sitting quietly in the visitor section of the chamber. *Oops!* he thought, quickly melting into a far corner of the room. "I mean, Your Majesty."

"Why, thank you, Teren." She turned her attention back to the Council members. "Well?"

Grumbling, they filed out of the chamber. Only Tara, Teren,

and their mother remained.

"That should keep them quiet for a while." Teren walked over to his sister. "You were great, Tara. I knew you could do it."

"Thanks." Her heart was still pounding. "I hope I wasn't too mean. I really hate being like that."

"Nor should you ever have to be," Tiyana told her daughter. "You did well, Tara. But we may need to seriously consider what the Council says. The seasons must change. And I'm sure that I have enough of your father's essence to trigger the Frost—at least this year."

"I can't believe you're saying that, Mother?" Teren would hear none of it. "You're not going to sacrifice your life. I won't let you!"

"*We* won't let you." Tara was just as adamant. "You may be able to change the seasons this year, but if you die, what happens after that? Your triggering the Frost is not the answer. Finding Kandide is. Please, Mother, you must tell us where you sent her."

"Tara's right." Teren sat down on the edge of the Council table. "We have to find her."

Tiyana regarded her children with a mixture of pride and exasperation. "I cannot let you go in search of her—either one of you. It's far too dangerous. Tara, you are queen, and the Council needs your compassion and common sense more than ever right now."

"Then I'll go alone," Teren insisted.

"May the earthly spirits help us if something should happen to you, my son. Lady Aron would be next in line for the throne."

"What?" Tara's almond-shaped eyes widened to the size of harvest moons. "What do you mean Lady Aron is next in line?"

Teren pushed himself to his feet. "That's impossible. How could that scheming—"

"Sit back down and I'll tell you the story." Tiyana motioned for them both to do so. "It was a long time ago, when the clans were still at war. Part of the preliminary treaty negotiations included Lady Aron marrying your father."

Tara nearly fell off the throne chair. "Father and Lady Aron? He'd sooner have married a scorpion."

Biting back a smile, Tiyana continued: "At the time, the leaders felt that if the Fire and Water Clans were united, all of the other clans would join rank. Everyone knew that there would never be any real peace until those two clans stopped fighting. There was just one problem—Toeyad refused to marry her."

"Well, no wonder," Tara exclaimed, "he was in love with you."

"Actually, at that point, we hadn't yet met. Your father refused because he didn't want to marry, as you so aptly put it, a scorpion. Fortunately, as king, Toeyad had the authority to override the clan leaders in this matter."

"I still don't understand." Teren picked up Lord Rössi's gavel and began twirling it in his fingertips.

"Well, within a week of his refusing to marry her, we met. So, naturally, from Lady Aron's perspective, not agreeing to marry her was my fault."

"That's why she's so nasty to you," Tara said. "It all makes sense now."

"According to your father, Lady Aron has always been extremely malevolent—even as a child—and has never changed."

Teren placed the gavel back on the table. "Father knew her

when she was a young girl?"

"Yes," Tiyana replied. "As a child, Firenza, used to come with her parents to the clan conclaves that were held here in the castle. In spite of the constant fighting, the meetings went on for decades before the treaty negotiations started and the High Council was formed. Toeyad said she was quite the bully, even back then, always picking on the other children and causing them to get in trouble. Of course, if she got caught, she would just lie and place the blame on one of her playmates."

"She's no different today." Tara motioned toward Lady Aron's chair.

"Not really. It was even rumored that Firenza betrayed her own brother to a Banshee raiding party, simply because she felt that their father paid too much attention to him."

"I didn't know she even had a brother." Teren couldn't believe what he was hearing. "That's horrible. What happened to him, Mother?"

"No one knows."

"Didn't anyone suspect her of being involved?" Tara knew Lady Aron could be cruel, but betraying her own brother to the Banshees? That she couldn't even begin to fathom.

"Some did suspect, but naturally, Lady Aron denied having anything to do with it. She was barely your age when it happened, Teren. And I don't think anyone wanted to admit that such a horrendous deed could be perpetrated by so young a girl—especially on her older brother."

"What makes you so sure she did it?" Tara asked.

"Your father overheard Firenza bragging about it to one of her friends—who, coincidentally, mysteriously disappeared in much the same way, a few days later."

Teren was visibly shaken. "If she would do that to her own brother, no telling what she would do to you, Mother—or Kandide, or one of us. Why didn't Father tell someone?"

"He did," Tiyana replied, "but Firenza's parents were extremely protective of their 'little girl,' and things were in such turmoil back then with the clan wars, that nothing ever came of it."

Tara rubbed her temples. All this was giving her a headache. "And Lady Aron is still getting away with murder—so to speak."

"Yeah, well, I still don't understand." Teren shot a confused look at his mother. "Why does all that make Lady Aron next in line for the throne?"

"Over the years, she grew more and more powerful in her own clan. I'm sure it was because most of the other clan leaders were afraid of her."

"Like most of the Council members are now." Tara scanned the empty Council seats.

"Some of them, anyway," Tiyana agreed. "In order to create a semblance of harmony—and to get the Fire Clan to sign the treaty—your father compromised by agreeing that if he died without an heir, Lady Aron would inherit the Gift and become the ruling queen."

"That's scary." Teren shuddered at the thought of Lady Aron ever becoming queen.

"I'm sure Toeyad felt the same way. But faced with more clan fighting, it probably seemed like the lesser of two evils. You must remember, Lady Aron has always commanded a certain following."

"Certain following or not, there's no way I'll ever let her become queen!" Teren stretched out his hands and two balls of flames appeared. "She'll find out what playing with fire is really like." He raised his arms, and the fireballs collided in midair, creating a blinding flash.

Tiyana covered her eyes. She could feel the intense heat from the flames. "Even with all your talent, Teren, you must remember, Firenza is incredibly powerful. Neither she nor her magic are to be underestimated."

"What worries me is that she said we won't be seeing Kandi again." A sudden chill ran up Tara's spine. "Mother, you don't think . . . ?"

"I admit, Lady Aron's comment is a concern. However, I don't see how she can possibly know about the V—" Tiyana's voice trailed off. She gazed at the dying embers that glowed in the chamber's hearth.

"Know about what, Mother? Please, you must tell us," Tara pleaded. "If Lady Aron is up to something, and she finds Kandi first, who knows what she'll do?"

"Firenza may be ruthless, but even she knows that the Gift must be deployed by Kandide, and that if it were to be transferred to someone else, your sister must give it up willingly. For that reason alone, I cannot believe that she will do anything to harm her."

"You don't know that, Mother," Teren insisted. "We need to find Kandide—and soon. Who knows what Lady Aron would do to convince her to 'willingly' transfer the Gift?"

Tiyana fell silent. *I hoped it would not come to this*, she thought, *but I fear there may not be a choice.* "I suppose you are right, at least about finding Kandide. There's more I must tell you. It happened when you were both quite young ..."

The two siblings listened intently as Tiyana revealed the story of Selena, and Toeyad's creation of the Veil. When she finished, Tara looked at her brother. "It seems the Royal Family isn't so different from one of your spell books, loaded with secrets waiting to be discovered."

"Yeah," Teren agreed, "and a lot of those secrets are just as dangerous."

Tara looked back at her mother. "I can't believe you never told me about Aunt Selena. I thought she transferred her healing talents to me because she was going to die and they would be lost forever. If I'd have known, maybe I could have gone to the Veil and continued trying to heal her wing."

"Maybe, Tara, but you were so young when it happened. And it's been a very long time since I've even seen my sister."

"When was the last time you went back to the Veil?" Teren asked.

"Your father and I quit going not long after we got Selena settled. We were worried that someone would discover what he had created. And now that you both know, no one else must ever learn of it," Tiyana warned. "It could destroy everything we worked so hard to achieve."

Tara reached for her mother's hand. "We promise we'll never reveal your secret, don't we, Teren?"

"Of course we won't. But I'm going there to find her."

"Teren ..."

"I'll be fine, Mother. I'm a mage. I'll be fine."

Tiyana's green skin paled as she began pacing the chamber.

"You have no idea of what you could be facing."

"It's the only way, Mother," Tara insisted. "We won't let you die."

Teren walked over to Tiyana. He was nearly as tall as she was. "There's no other choice. You have to transport me to the Veil so I can find Kandide. And, Tara, you need to call the High Council back into session, so you can tell them that you've decided to send me to search for her."

"I'm not sure what they'll say, but it'll give me great pleasure to tell them. Get ready to go, little brother. You're going to find Kandide!"

"Feet he may not have, but feelings,
I wouldn't be so sure."
Selena opened the door to Kandide's room.

SEVENTEEN

"It's all so very hard to imagine," Kandide told her aunt as they walked through elaborately carved double doors that opened into the château's long gathering hall. The two-story-high room was filled with Fée from many different clans, all of them busy. Some were weaving, some were sewing, still others were working on carvings or paintings.

"What's so hard to imagine?" Selena asked.

"What you're telling me—that all of this, everything here, was created by Imperf—um . . . I mean, the Fée who live here."

"Is it?" Selena stopped for a minute to examine a particularly beautiful vase. Its deep blue glaze sparkled with silver flecks. "This is the work of a master artisan, who also just happens to be unable to hear." Selena handed the vase to Kandide, and then signed to the Fée who had made it, "It's extraordinary."

"It is beautiful," Kandide replied, examining the delicate design. "It really is." She handed the vase back to its owner, who signed, "Thank you."

"What did he say?"

"He said 'thank you.'" Selena motioned for them to continue the tour. "Shall we?"

"I would have never thought—" Kandide frowned as she shook her head.

"You have much to learn, my child—so very much. Did I tell you that we also quarried and carved all of the stone that built this château? And we make all our own dishes and furniture, and weave and dye our own cloth."

"It's remarkable." Kandide still found it hard to believe that the Imperfects whom she'd always found so repulsive could create such extraordinary beauty. As they continued the tour, she noticed a very attractive young Fée with long dark brown braids that fell past her waist. Her skin was the color of milk chocolate, and she was dressed in delicate shades of blue, teal, and pink, with sparkling silver-jeweled spirals in her hair. Her wings were large and flowing, and shimmered in the perfect reflection of the colors in her dress. Kandide stared at her, searching for some defect, yet finding none.

"What's wrong with her?" she finally asked. "She seems to be perf—" Kandide stopped, realizing how judgmental she must sound. "I mean," she tried again, "what's her name?"

"She's called Leanne. Come. Let me introduce you to her." Kandide followed her aunt over to the pretty Fée. "Leanne, I'd like you to meet my niece, Her Majesty Queen Kandide."

"Your Majesty?" Leanne curtsied. "I didn't realize you—"

"It's all right, Leanne. There's no reason why you should have. Her visit was totally unexpected." Turning to Kandide, Selena continued, "Leanne is a healer. Her Talent is the most remarkable I have ever seen. Given time, she has been able to help—and in some cases completely heal—almost every type of ailment."

"It's my pleasure to meet someone with so much of the Talent." Kandide extended her hand.

Leanne, however, did not reach out to take it, instead replying, "Thank you, Your Majesty. I shall know your voice now."

"And we shall see you tonight at dinner, Leanne," Selena told her. "I want to finish Kandide's tour before it gets much later."

"Of course." Leanne graciously curtsied to Kandide, adding, "I look forward to it, Your Majesty."

"As do I." *There's something odd about her,* Kandide thought as she and Tiyana turned to leave. *She looks perfect, but . . .* After they had walked a few meters away, Kandide whispered to Selena, "What did Leanne mean when she said that she'll know my voice?"

"Oh, Leanne is without sight. Although some say she sees far better than anyone here."

"Blind? She's blind?" Kandide had never met anyone who was blind. "Then how can she heal others?"

"Goodness, child, it is her gift, that's how. Her Talent is truly amazing—perhaps even stronger than Tara's."

"Can she heal broken wings?" Kandide was almost afraid to hear the answer. *Maybe she can heal my wing. Maybe that's why Mother sent me here.*

"She can heal them to a degree. Leanne thinks that one day she might be able to make my wings completely straight. I can actually fly short distances now. I won't let her work on me as often as she'd like, though."

"Why not? Especially if she can make you perfect again."

"Perfection takes many forms, my child. Not all of them are in the shape of a wing or an arm or a foot. Besides, healing an old injury takes far too much of Leanne's strength. There are so many others here who truly need her help. She has, however, had excellent results with wings that are only recently damaged."

"How recently?" Kandide tried not to sound overly curious.

"Well, naturally, the sooner the better. Even after a few days, she can sometimes make a huge difference. Of course, it depends upon the severity of the damage."

As they were talking, Selena spotted Jake coming into the hall. In spite of her niece's wishes, she decided to call him over. "Jake! Jake, why don't you show Kandide what you have been doing with your prototypal wings?"

He acknowledged Kandide with a quick glance, and then replied, "I'm sure Her Majesty is far too busy to worry about things like artificial wings."

"Oh, but I'm not too busy," Kandide said with a smile. She had resolved not to talk to Jake ever again. *But maybe I'll give him one more chance*, she thought. *In case Leanne can't heal my wing, I really should find out about Jake's prototypals. Perhaps Teren could create something similar with a spell.* "I'm interested in what everyone here is doing."

"That's very gracious of you, Your Majesty." Jake half-heartedly bowed. "In that case, it would be my pleasure to show you our inventions."

"Please, call me Kandide." She returned his bow by nodding

her head ever so slightly.

"As you wish . . . Kandide." His words carried a tinge of mockery.

"And so I do . . . Jake." Her tone mirrored his.

"Oh dear, I didn't realize it was getting so late." Selena looked at the giant grandfather clock in the corner of the room. "It's nearly five," she said, more to defuse their silent tension than because of the time. "Perhaps seeing Jake's prototypal wings can wait until tomorrow. You must be very tired, Kandide. May I show you to your room? I'm sure you want to relax a bit before supper. Tomorrow we shall have a gala feast in your honor."

"That sounds lovely. I would certainly like to freshen up." Kandide was still looking at Jake. She couldn't help herself. *What is it about him?* she wondered. *It's certainly not his manners.*

"Good," Selena replied, "then I shall have a hot bath drawn for you immediately. I'm afraid your room is not quite what you're used to, but it is well-appointed and warm. Shall we?"

"Oh . . . yes." Kandide turned her attention to her aunt. "And I'm sure that my room will do quite nicely." Looking back at Jake, she said, "You will be joining us for dinner, won't you, Jake?"

"I have to eat." With a shrug and another mockingly low bow that included an elaborate flourish, he added, "Kandide."

Not to be outdone, she made a sweeping gesture for him to rise. "Then, please, stand up before you injure your back." A coquettish grin transformed her face into a flirtatious schoolgirl's, before she quickly regained her composure. "I really am feeling quite tired just now, and that hot bath sounds wonderful."

"I can well imagine. We'll see you at dinner, Jake." Selena

showed her niece up the stairs to her room, remarking, "It would appear that Jake is quite enamored with you."

"Me? Jake? Enamored with me?" To Kandide, the thought of her aunt actually considering such a thing was preposterous. "Why, he doesn't have any fee—uh . . . I mean feelings for me. That is well apparent!"

"Feet he may not have, but feelings, I wouldn't be so sure." Selena opened the door to Kandide's room.

With the reality of the situation staring
Kandide in the face, every ounce of adrenuline
that she had mustered to appear regal
and in control drained away.

EIGHTEEN

elena was right, Kandide thought as she followed her aunt into the sleeping chamber. Although bright and cheery, the room was not at all what she was accustomed to. *It doesn't even have an antechamber. But then, it was designed by Imperfects.* She glanced around at the neatly appointed furnishings. Two side chairs and a small settee were upholstered in delicate pinks and soft mint greens—her favorite color combination.

"I hope it meets with your approval." Selena pulled back a set of pink velvet drapes. Sunlight streamed in through a large bay window that overlooked the gardens below.

"Yes, it's quite lovely." Kandide walked over to a large vase of freshly cut pink and green ginger blossoms that was sitting on the dressing table. She inhaled their spicy fragrance. It reminded her of freshly baked cinnamon ginger cookies—and how hungry she was. "The flowers are beautiful." *And at least the bed looks comfortable,* she thought noticing the big fluffy pillows and perfectly turned-down pink satin sheets.

The bed was, indeed, an inviting sight. Only that morning, she hadn't been sure if she would ever enjoy a hot bath and a comfortable night's sleep again. Suddenly feeling extremely tired, Kandide yawned. "Oh dear, please excuse me, Aunt Selena, it's been a long day."

"Not at all, my dear. You must be exhausted. May I hang up your cloak?" Selena reached for the garment. "I am afraid we have no ladies-in-waiting here."

"No, thank you, I . . ." But Kandide spoke too late. Selena had already removed the cape from her shoulders. "I told you no!" She shrieked, jerking the cape away from her aunt. "How could you?" Kandide closed her eyes as though it would make her crumpled wing disappear.

"My apologies, Kandide. But please know it's all right," Selena gently responded. "I had a feeling this is why you came to us."

Kandide's eyes shot open. She was suddenly uncontrollably furious. "That's not true! I'm . . . I'm . . . I'm not an Imperfect! I am queen! You don't understand, Selena. I'm not like them." She pointed toward the window at two Fée who were walking in the garden. "I'm not! I'm just not!"

But even Kandide could not deny the reflection of her dull, twisted wing in the mirror that hung above the dressing table. With the reality of the situation staring her in the face, every ounce of adrenaline that she had mustered to appear regal and in control drained away. Everything that had happened over the past few days—the accident, the pain, the shame, her own mother sending her away—all of it collided at once.

Her purple-blue eyes filled with tears. "They called me a crumplewing, Selena—Kandide the Crumplewing! Can you imagine? I'm their queen!" She collapsed into a nearby chair. "Oh, Selena, what am I going to do?" Stabbing pains shot through her back and shoulder. Her wing was throbbing worse than ever. "What am I going to do?"

Putting her arm around her niece, Selena tried to comfort her. "Hush now, it's all right. Everything is going to be fine, Kandide. Of course you're a queen, and a very beautiful one."

Pulling away from her aunt, Kandide abruptly sat up. "No, Selena, it's not all right. It was Mother who sent me here! She's ashamed of me now. It's not enough that I'm so beautiful. Perfection is what really matters. You know that. My own subjects laughed at me when they saw my wing. They almost killed me. Everyone abhors me now—especially Mother!" Tears streamed down her cheeks. "Mother is ashamed of me— she hates me!"

"Tiyana doesn't hate you, Kandide. And no one here cares whether your wing is perfect or not. Outside, the world can be very cruel. Here, in the Veil, it's what's inside that counts. Come now, dry those beautiful eyes." She handed her niece a white lace-edged handkerchief from the dresser. "You'll stay here with us."

"With Imperfects? I can't! I couldn't stand— No. I must go away. Right now!" Kandide stood up, nervously straightening her dress. "You won't tell anyone, will you?" She clutched her aunt's arm, half pleading, half commanding her not to reveal her secret. "Please, Selena, don't tell Jake. I'll be gone as soon as I can fix my face. Just . . . just say I had to return home."

"As you wish, my child." Selena took the handkerchief and gently wiped a smudge of dirt away. "But only if you promise me that you will not leave until tomorrow."

"I can't go down to dinner. Not now!"

"I'll make your excuses and have your dinner sent up. Perhaps you will consider letting Leanne take a look at your wi—"

"No! No one else must know."

"Leanne is very discreet. She would never reveal your secret. We can merely say that you're tired and have come down with a headache from all of your travels."

The expression on Kandide's face changed from apprehension to hope. "Do you really think she might be able to heal me?"

"I think it's worth a try. Shall I ask her to come up?"

"You mustn't say why." Realizing that her plea sounded more like an order than a request, Kandide quickly caught herself and softened her tone. "I mean, you will swear her to secrecy?"

"I will inform her of your wishes. Now rest a bit. I'll be back in a few minutes." Selena left to find Leanne.

Alone in her room, Kandide tried to straighten her wing, but it was simply too badly damaged. The pain was unbearable each time she tried. As she stood there staring at herself in the mirror, more of her father's words came back to her: "It is your destiny to be a great queen, Kandide."

Sitting down in the pink and yellow upholstered side chair, she began reminiscing about when she was a young girl and her father taught her lessons in self-reliance. She thought about the day he first challenged her to partake in the battle games with the Royal Guard. Even though she returned covered with bumps and bruises, she did it. *I learned to fight—and really well!*

Kandide looked at herself in the dresser mirror. *And I'll win this fight too.*

Her spirits picked up a bit as images of that day saturated her thinking. It seemed so very long ago when King Toeyad sat her on his knee and said with a fatherly smile, "You are learning well, my daughter. You have shown the strength and the courage that you will need as queen."

"That's it!" Jumping up, Kandide was almost ecstatic for the first time since the accident. "Father's words—Leanne will heal my wing and I will fulfill my destiny. Father has said so!"

Again, she glanced in the mirror at her wing. This time her reaction was very different. "I will be perfect again," she vowed. "I will! Then I'll show them. I'll show them all. Even Mother will love me again."

Leave me!" Kandide was all but screaming. "Both of you, leave me!"

NINETEEN

"So, Her Majesty isn't coming to dinner?" Jake wasn't at all surprised when Selena told him that Kandide had decided to have her meal sent up to her room. They were standing in the hall just outside the main dining room. "I'll just bet she has a headache. Too good for us, is she? Well, it's her loss. I can't stand her kind, anyway."

"Now, Jake," Selena scolded, "remember, we don't judge here, even if the handicap is ignorance or prejudice."

"Or both! Besides, she's the one who judges—just because she's so perfect. She's not all that great looking anyway."

Selena summoned her last reserves of patience, not sure who was being more difficult—Jake or her niece. "You could be a little more forgiving, yourself," she told him. "After all, Kandide was raised to be queen."

"Yeah, and let's all give thanks that she's not our queen!"

Knowing that winning any argument with him was nearly impossible, especially one where so many conflicting emotions were involved, Selena returned to her original question. "In any case, have you seen Leanne? She might be able to help with Kandide's headache."

"I'm not sure where she is, but when you find her, see if she can also do something about Her Majesty's attitude!" Jake turned to go into the dining hall.

Shaking her head, Selena softly replied, "We can only hope . . ."

"Oh, Leanne, there you are," Selena spotted her walking into the dining hall with two other Fée. "May I speak with you alone for a minute, Leanne?

"Certainly. Is there a problem?"

"I'll explain as we walk." Selena apologized for pulling her away, and they headed up the main staircase.

Just as her aunt had promised, it wasn't long before Kandide heard a knock at her door. With her cape back around her shoulders, she cautiously opened it. Selena and Leanne entered.

"Your Majesty," Leanne curtsied. "Selena tells me you require my assistance."

"Yes. I command you . . . I mean . . . I understand that you may be able to help me."

"I've had some luck with wings and, though I cannot promise a full healing, I am honored to try."

"You already told her?" Kandide glared at her aunt.

"How else can she heal you?"

Kandide's annoyance transformed into panic. "How many others know? I must leave at once."

"If that is what you truly wish, my child. But I do think you should give Leanne a chance."

"Please let me at least try, Your Majesty."

"But you're blind." As Kandide spoke the words, she saw her aunt's expression change from concern to displeasure. *Well, she is,* she thought, in an attempt to rationalize her statement. Turning back to Leanne, Kandide tried to explain. "I'm sure you're very good at what you do, but I'm used to being attended by the palace physicians and none of them are, well, you know . . ."

"I understand how you feel." Leanne's words were soft and kind. "And just so you know, I heal with my hands, not my eyes."

"What if it doesn't work?" Kandide struggled with the idea of an Imperfect actually being able to help her. Everything she had come to understand about their value to society was being turned upside down.

"What if it does work?" Selena started to lose patience with her niece. "For your own sake, child, let her try. What other options do you have?"

"Well, I . . ." Kandide stammered, almost afraid to hope. "Do you really think you can do it?"

"I've had positive results with others who have injured wings." Leanne's words carried an underlying sense of confidence. "Would you like me to try, Your Majesty?"

"I . . . I . . . Yes, please." *Maybe it will work,* she thought, suddenly becoming excited at the possibility of actually being healed, even if it was by an Imperfect.

Leanne placed both hands on Kandide's wing, then quickly drew back.

"What is it?" Kandide tensed up. "What's wrong?"

"Nothing unexpected." Leanne calmed her fears. "It's just

that I felt what you've suffered—the horrible burning when the lightning struck. The way your wing curled in on itself. The stabbing pains you've been feeling ever since the accident. It's been dreadful, hasn't it?"

"Yes." Kandide didn't trust herself to say more. *Maybe it won't work*, she thought. *No, it has to. It just has to.* Her body was still tense. "Can you do it or not, Leanne?"

"Your wing is badly injured—one of the worst I've ever felt. But I do think I can help." Once again, she placed her hands on Kandide's wing.

Kandide could feel Leanne's immense power starting to flow through her shoulder and back. Mildly painful, it seemed to pulse and tingle at the same time. Her eyes were glued to the refection in the mirror. She couldn't believe what she was seeing. Within seconds, her crumpled wing started to uncurl. Its iridescent color came back, and it began to glow with a silvery sheen.

Kandide stared at the mirror. "You've done it, Leanne. I'm perfect again! I'm . . ." But her words were not to be.

When Leanne stepped back, breaking the flow of healing, Kandide watched in horror as her wing began to crumple, twisting back to its unsightly form. "Do it again!" she ordered, still excited about the success of the first attempt. "I know you can do it!"

"Perhaps if I can cause the healing light to flow from two directions," Leanne told her, "it will be stronger." She refocused her energies, placing one hand on the injured wing and the other on Kandide's upper back. As soon as the silvery strands of energy began to flow from her fingertips, Kandide's wing, once again, uncurled. It took a little longer, but nonetheless, it was full and beautiful.

"You're doing it!" Kandide began to flap her wing. But, once more, the minute Leanne lost contact with her, it deformed.

"Try again." Kandide felt a wave of fear. "I order you to do it again."

Growing ever paler, Leanne kept trying, but each time her channeling stopped, Kandide's wing returned to its crumpled state. Exhausted, she started to summon her magic for one last attempt.

"That's enough for now." Selena reached her hand out to prevent Leanne from continuing.

"Why are you stopping her?" Kandide pushed Selena's arm away. "I insist you let her try again!"

Having had enough of her niece's demands, Selena answered in just as firm of a voice. "Leanne is exhausted. She can try again later, when her strength returns."

"No! I want her to heal me now!" Half in tears and half-screaming, Kandide felt as though her entire world was about to implode.

"It may take several treatments, Your Majesty," Leanne tried to explain. "But I do think it will eventually work."

"Either you can heal me or you can't." Kandide turned away. "I don't want excuses. I should have known she couldn't do it!"

"Kandide!" Selena sharply scolded. "That is enough!"

But her niece was in no mood to listen. She turned on Leanne with a white-hot fury. "How dare you come in here with your promises? How dare you get my hopes up?"

"Begging your pardon, Your Majesty, I'm very sorry."

Still soft-spoken, Leanne attempted to calm her down. "You were so badly injured that it may well take more strength than I have at one time. We can, however, continue treatments a little each day. I'm sure I'll eventually be able to heal your wing. I can feel it."

"I don't believe you! You're . . . you're nothing but an Imperfect! And now, so am I!" Kandide collapsed onto the bed. All of the pain and humiliation that she had felt poured out of her. "There is no hope." She looked up at her aunt. "You lied to me. Father lied to me. I have no destiny. Leave me!" She was all but screaming. "Both of you, leave me!"

"Your Majesty, please, just give me some time to help you."

Ignoring Leanne's gentle words, Kandide sat up and glared straight at her aunt, shouting, "Take her out of here! I command it. I want to be left alone!"

"And so you shall be." Selena finally had enough of her niece's reprehensible behavior. "We'll discuss this in the morning, Kandide. Perhaps by then you will have returned to your senses." Taking Leanne's arm, she escorted her out of the room.

Anguish creased Selena's face. "Forgive me, Leanne. I should have never subjected you to that."

"No, Selena. It is I who am sorry to have failed you and her." Leanne lowered her head as the two of them walked away.

"The only failure, my child, is deep within Kandide. Her vanity, along with her fear and insecurities, have consumed all reason. With time, I'm sure she'll see things in their proper perspective."

"I know how difficult it is for her. I remember when I first lost my sight. I, too, was angry."

"Yes, but then you, Leanne, have always had an extraordinary spirit. I fear Kandide is not so blessed."

"I only wish that I—"

"There will be other days."

"I'm sure I can eventually help her, Selena."

"I'm not so sure. Kandide's wing is not her most serious problem."

The two of them continued down the winding stairs and into the dining room with Leanne still insisting that she could ultimately heal Kandide. "Perhaps we can find others to help channel even more power. I have two young students with the Talent who are showing a great deal of promise."

"Maybe, but right now, you've done all you can for her. Let's join the others for dinner. I'll have a meal sent up to Kandide a little later."

Jake spotted the two of them coming into the dining hall. "So, Her Majesty's headache isn't cured? Our queen won't be gracing us for dinner after all? She just can't stand being around us, can she?"

"Jake, please." Selena wasn't sure how much more she could deal with at that moment. "You don't understand."

"No, Selena, you don't understand. We live in our world. Kandide is one of them. She belongs in their world."

"Perhaps," Selena quietly responded. "Perhaps."

"That is very unkind, even for you, my dear,"
Lord Aron whispered.

TWENTY

"You seem unusually chipper, my dear." Lord Aron was standing with his wife on the balcony outside their suite of rooms in the castle, enjoying the warm December weather. Even with the sun beginning to set over the small lake near the edge of the courtyard grounds, the air lacked any of the crispness the season normally brought forth.

Looking out across the horizon and then back at his wife, the handsome brown-haired Fée couldn't help but admire how beautiful she looked. "The red and amber reflections in the water complement your loveliness, Firenza. Even the jewels on your gown seem to capture the fiery tones in this evening's sky."

"That they do," Lady Aron replied, watching the sun's fiery rays glisten on the mirror-like lake as it transformed into a glowing sliver. She turned back to look at him. "And you've always loved these colors on me."

"I don't believe I have ever seen you in anything else," he teased, taking her hand and softly kissing it. Lord Aron had fallen in love with his wife the instant he saw her at a Council meeting some three decades ago.

A flirtatious smile crossed her lips. "Well, lavender is hardly my color."

"No, I suppose not." Lord Aron brushed a wisp of fiery red hair away from her face. "What's making you so very happy tonight?" he asked. Throughout their marriage, he had never been able to predict her mood. She could be warm and caring one minute, and cold and icy the next.

"Why wouldn't I be happy, my darling?" Her playful smile turned to glee. "We no longer have to put up with that wretched creature."

"Am I to assume that you are referring to Kandide?" Looking into her amber eyes, he put his arms around her waist. A gentle breeze fanned the air. From the courtyard below, a harpist began to play, filling the moment with the lilting strains of an enchanted melody.

Lady Aron rested her head on her husband's chest. "And who else could I possibly be referring to?"

"That is very unkind, even for you, my dear," he whispered.

"Is it?" She looked up at him, and then slowly turned her face back toward the last glow of the sunset. "Even you must admit that Kandide's behavior is arrogant and self-centered beyond all reason."

"She has her rivals." Lord Aron grinned knowingly at his wife, hoping to counter a little of her obsession with the Royal Family, and Kandide in particular.

"She may have, but I certainly do not." Lady Aron's posture stiffened as she turned back to face him. "My concern now, however, is for the Gift. And as glad as I am that our former crown princess is gone, I am very worried about the Frost."

"As we all are, my dear. I don't think Tiyana thought about the Gift when she sent Kandide away. I'm quite sure she was more interested in just trying to save her daughter's life."

"You bring up a very good point. Fool that Tiyana is, it just doesn't make sense that she—"

"That she what?"

"That she would just blindly send her own daughter away like that."

Lord Aron eyed his wife suspiciously. "What are you getting at, Firenza?"

Putting her arms around his neck, Lady Aron attempted a cajoling smile. "You know me so well, my darling. But time is truly running out. I don't even want to think of the consequences if the Gift is not deployed—and soon. We must do something to find Kandide. She must be convinced to transfer the Gift."

"Kandide will never transfer the Gift."

"Perhaps she will have no choice."

"What do you mean?" His brow furled. Lord Aron had seen that look on his wife's face many times and it always preceded some sort of devastation.

"There are ways of persuading her." A chilling undertone crept into her voice.

Lord Aron removed her arms from around his neck. "Persuade how?" He had always known that she was in love with King Toeyad. And when Kandide was born, her disdain for the crown princess was instant. It was only after Teren was born that she agreed to marry Lord Aron. He had hoped that with the birth of their own son, she would be less spiteful toward Tiyana and the three royal siblings—and for a time she was. With Toeyad's passing, however, Lady Aron began reverting back to her old ways, openly displaying even more dislike for the Royal Family.

Aware of her husband's sudden annoyance, Lady Aron poured two glasses of sparkling peach wine and handed one to him. "Look, my darling, it is no secret that I don't like Kandide, but the Frost must take precedence. One spoiled, arrogant princess cannot be allowed to threaten all of nature. Even you know that."

"So what are you suggesting we do?" He accepted the fluted goblet with its golden rim.

"I have it on good authority that King Toeyad built a sanctuary for Imperfects somewhere." She lightly brushed her fingertips across the side of his face, and then traced the outline of his lips. "Tell me, my handsome husband, what do you know about a secret place that our dear king created somewhere in the Mists?"

Almost choking on the wine, Lord Aron backed away. "I love you, Firenza, but I will do nothing that would be disloyal to the crown or King Toeyad. Please don't ask me about this again."

"Well, I see we're finally getting to the truth." She held her goblet out over the balcony and poured out the wine. "Your loyalty to your wife seems to be emptier than this glass." With a snap of fingers, it flew up, out of her hand and shattered against the castle's stone wall. "But even if you don't care about me, I should think you would worry for our son." She motioned toward a portrait of a young Fée that hung on the inside wall across from the balcony. He looked neither like Lord nor Lady Aron, but instead a blend of the two with large blue eyes and honey-brown hair. "At the very least you could be concerned for Alin's future. Or is your allegiance to that . . . that Imperfect more important than to your own family?"

"You know that's not true, Firenza." He looked from his wife to broken pieces of glass that were scattered in the garden below. "In any case, you don't have to display your anger by destroying the five-hundred year old crystal my father crafted."

With another snap of her fingers, Lord Aron's wine glass flew out of his hand. It, too, smashed against the wall. The harpist stopped playing. Looking up at the two of them on the balcony above, he grabbed his harp and quickly moved to a more distant spot in the garden. Lady Aron was not someone he wanted anything to do with, let alone be in the middle one of the couple's many fights. A scathing glance from the fire Fée told him that he made the right decision.

Leaving the balcony to go inside their chamber, Lady Aron called back to her husband, "Perhaps I'm not the only one destroying things around here. Your so-called loyalty may well destroy our marriage and our son's future, not to mention Calabiyau."

Lord Aron followed her inside. Although rarely temperamental, he had to force back his anger. "My so-called loyalty may just be what saves Alin's future—and this beloved land." He took her hands in his. "Oh, Firenza, can't you see that preserving Calabiyau doesn't have to mean destroying Kandide—or her family—or even a bunch of Imperfects?"

"So," her amber eyes flashed with an intensity he'd rarely seen, "you admit you know about such a place?"

"I admit nothing of the sort—only that Kandide has taken the oath to deploy the Frost." Try as he would to remain calm, the blunt edge of anger finally crept into his voice. He waited a beat before continuing to speak: "Give her a little time; she will not allow this world to die."

"I'm afraid, my dear husband, her time has run out. You may want to leave Calabiyau's fate up to the whims of that self-centered brat, but I certainly will not. Now I must pick Alin up from his archery lesson. I'm taking him to Mother's, so don't expect either of us back this evening."

Before he could protest, Lady Aron vanished in a blinding flash of red light.

Kandide froze, staring, unable to believe her eyes.
There, just a few meters ahead,
inside a circle of twisted oaks, was one of the
rarest creatures in all the land.

TWENTY-ONE

The sun rose early the next morning, and with it, Kandide. *I can't remain here with all these Imperfects,* she told herself. *After all, I'm not anything like them.* Curiously, the pain in her shoulder had all but ceased. *Maybe Leanne did help my wing—a little.* She looked in the mirror at its still bent and twisted shape. *Well, not enough. Anyway, I must leave this place at once.*

Outside her window, the early morning sky was just beginning to show streaks of vivid pink and amber hues. It would be a good day for traveling, as there were no rain clouds and the air was warm. *I just hope the weather is as nice where I'm going—wherever that is,* Kandide thought, looking at the sun just starting to peek above the horizon. *In any case, I'd better be off.*

Remembering what Selena told her about where the château was located, and that she needed to be far enough inside the Mists—where the protection of the Veil ends—

in order to transport, Kandide began calculating the coordinates for her journey. Now that she had that information, she could transport to anywhere in Calabiyau.

Perhaps I should go to the Meadows—maybe by the waterfall. There's an old abandoned mill house there. It'll provide shelter until I decide what to do. Or, I could go to the edge of the woods near the lowlands. I wonder if Father's old cabin is still standing.

Her stomach rumbled as she considered her options. Before she went anywhere, she needed to find something to eat. Having stubbornly refused the meal that Selena sent up the night before, she was absolutely starving. With her cape pulled tightly around her shoulders, Kandide quietly tiptoed out of her bedroom and down the winding staircase. *There must be something left over in the kitchen,* she thought. Perhaps she could even pack a basket to take on her journey. Since she still hadn't decided where to go, or what she would find when she got there, a big basket would be nice.

Turning the corner to enter the kitchen, Kandide discovered that it was already bustling with activity. Had she not been so very hungry, she probably would have fled without stopping. But the mouthwatering smell of hot, freshly baked biscuits and honey was more than Kandide could resist. *Besides, what would a brief delay hurt?* she asked herself. *A good meal will give me strength. After all, I'll be on my own soon enough.*

"Why, good morning, Your Majesty," exclaimed a Fée who was missing both of her wings. Nevertheless, she was obviously in charge of the kitchen, darting from place-to-place, with a jump here and a leap there.

"Are you Margay?" Kandide politely asked. She had never

been very good at remembering the names of staff members, but Margay's shortbread had been unforgettable.

"I am," she said with a proper curtsey.

"Then thank you for the recipe. Selena had it slid under my door sometime last night while I was sleeping. A lovely surprise, and I assure you, my chefs will put it to good use. I was, uh, wondering if I might have a bite to eat."

"But of course." Margay, who reminded Kandide more of a short, rotund elf than a Fée, hastily ordered a place set for Kandide at a long serving table. "Would you not, however, prefer to eat in the dining hall?" Margay asked. "We're preparing a wonderful breakfast—fit for a queen." When she smiled, her entire face lit up.

"Thank you, but this will do just fine." Kandide took a biscuit from the tray Margay had placed on the table and nearly swallowed it whole. "They're quite delicious," she exclaimed, spreading fresh-made blueberry jam across a second one.

"Well, well, look who's up early." Jake suddenly appeared in the doorway. "Nice of you to come down for breakfast. You're welcome to eat in the dining hall, you know." Snatching a biscuit from the tray, he loaded it with fresh apple butter and took a bite. "Mmm. Margay, these are even better than usual."

"Now you stop that, Jake." She swatted at him. "In case you don't know who you are speaking to, this is Her Majesty Queen Kandide, and she's in a hurry."

"Well, then," Jake bowed to Kandide, waving his hand with an exaggerated flourish, "I beg your pardon—Your Majesty."

Kandide barely acknowledged his words or actions. Instead, she turned her attention to Margay. "It's quite all right, Margay.

I must be leaving now, anyway."

"Leaving?" Both Jake and Margay spoke at once.

"Yes. I have other duties that require my immediate attention. I would be most appreciative, however, if you would pack a basket for me to take on my journey. The biscuits are truly wonderful, and your jellies are some of the best I have ever tasted."

"Why, of course, Your Majesty. I shall notify Selena of your intended departure. I know she'll want to see you off."

"That won't be necessary. I, uh . . . have already informed her." Kandide motioned to the basket as Margay filled it with hot biscuits. "Perhaps a few more? And some fresh fruit would be nice."

"But, Your Majesty, I am sure Selena would wan -"

"Just the basket will do." Kandide was polite, but regally firm.

"As you wish." Margay filled the basket to overflowing, covered it with a bright blue gingham cloth, then curtsied and handed it to Kandide.

Nodding a courteous thank you, Kandide, with basket in hand, quickly departed.

As Jake watched her go, his expression revealed more than a touch of concern. "What I'd like to know, is how a Fée as kind and caring as King Toeyad could have raised such a daughter?"

"You knew her father?" Margay looked surprised.

"I served beside him in the after-wars. I was his first lieutenant. Queen Tiyana and I are from the same clan."

"Wow!" piped up one of the younger Fée who was counting out the plates to be used at breakfast. "You really knew King Toeyad?"

"Tell us about the clan wars, Jake," chimed in a red-haired Fée who snapped her fingers and a tray of biscuits floated into the open baking oven.

"Not again, Lindra," he pleaded. "I've told you those stories a hundred times."

"You haven't told me," said a green-skinned Fée with a long scar across his forehead.

A tiny member of the Air Clan hovered above his head. "Yeah, t-t-tell the re-re-rest of us," she added, trying her best not to stutter.

Jake smiled up at her. When he first found her huddled atop a dead tree in the Mists, she wouldn't speak at all. "Maybe later, Kaeta. I have a feeling I should tell Selena that her niece is leaving. I'm not so sure she is aware of it.

Kandide quickly left the protection of the gated wall that surrounded the château. She began carefully making her way into the Mists where the Veil would be thin enough for her to transport. Vines clawed at her from every direction, and the ground was as black and slimy as when she had arrived. It truly was a miserable place.

Selena said the edge of the Veil is about a hundred and fifty meters from the gate, she thought as she pushed a troublesome branch out of her way. *So, this should be far enough. Now, where should I go? To the old mill house by the lake. I can stay there until I decide what to do next.* But before Kandide could gesture to transport, she heard an agonizing shriek. Startled, she ducked behind the closest tree.

Was it a shriek or a whine? Kandide wasn't sure. Something,

however, sounded as though it was injured. *No, I don't have time to go and see. Besides, it might be dangerous,* she rationalized. *I must start thinking only of myself now.*

Once again, Kandide started to gesture to transport, and, once again, she heard the same pitiful sound. Something—she wasn't sure what—made her stop and look around for the source of the desperate cry. She scanned the area, peering through dead, gnarled trees and the thick black fog. *This is useless,* she decided. The fog was so thick she could barely see beyond the reach of her own arm. Then a movement caught her eye. She looked again. This time she saw something. "May the spirits help me," she said aloud. "It can't be."

Kandide froze, staring, unable to believe her eyes. There, just a few meters ahead, inside a circle of twisted oaks, was one of the rarest creatures in all the land. Its body was covered with gleaming white fur—all, except its head, neck, and shoulders. They were covered in white feathers.

Can it possibly be? She could not believe her eyes. *It is! A griffin. A real live griffin! But what is it doing in the Mists?*

"Okay, keep calm, Kandide. Keep calm. What would Father do?" she whispered under her breath.

TWENTY-TWO

K andide stood in the dense, misty forest, staring at a creature she never thought she would see. It had the head, wings, and talons of an eagle, the sleek body of a full-grown lion, and a tail that was forked like that of a mythical serpent. In spite of its powerful appearance, something was wrong—terribly wrong.

She cautiously made her way through the thick underbrush toward the frenzied animal. As she approached, she could see that it had gotten tangled in a snare and was desperately struggling to get free. But the more it tried, the tighter the thick brown ropes choked the creature's white-feathered neck. Its hind legs were restrained as well, and the harder the creature struggled, the deeper the ropes cut into its skin.

"I'll help you," she whispered, in an attempt to calm the frantic creature. But as she approached, the griffin began screeching at her, madly clawing the air. Kandide jumped back, just in time to miss a strike from one of its deadly talons.

"Okay, take it easy." She spoke in a soft, calm tone. "Who did this to you?" Griffins were known for their proud, fierce, and elusive nature, so how this one could have been captured, Kandide wasn't sure. "Don't worry, I'll get you free." She inched a little closer. Thankfully, it stopped clawing. Instead, it cocked its majestic head from side to side to look at her.

"You understand what I'm saying, don't you?" Kandide was almost close enough to reach out and touch it. She could see that the griffin's golden eyes were beginning to glaze over from being so tightly restrained. Its white neck feathers were stained bright red where the ropes had cut its flesh, yet it lifted its magnificent head to meet her gaze.

"I know how you feel—being helpless like this—but you must stay calm," she whispered, crouching down to seem less threatening.

The griffin looked at her, and this time Kandide was sure it understood. "I'll get you out of this, I promise. I just need to be a little closer so I can find out where the snare is fastened and how to release it."

As Kandide approached, she let out a gasp of astonishment. "May the earthly spirits help us, you're not just trapped, I think you're pregnant." The creature's bloated stomach looked as though its cub might be born at any minute. "I wonder if Selena knows?"

As she reached out to touch it, the griffin began screeching and clawing again, even more wildly than before. Kandide instantly drew back. "What is it?"

The griffin's neck was craned up. She had spotted something in the treetops. Kandide followed her gaze and felt the cold grasp of fear tighten around her chest. There in the branches above, a ghoulish beast had emerged. It dropped to the ground, landing only meters from where she stood.

With leathery, bat-like wings, and large white fangs that dripped a gelatinous green drool, it was the ugliest creature she had ever seen. Matted, patchy brown and black fur covered its long bony arms, and its hands ended in sharp clawing fingers. Its beady red eyes focused directly on Kandide.

"A garglan?" She dared not move. *At least, I think that's what you are.*

A cross between a goblin and a gargoyle, garglans, like griffins, were thought to be virtually extinct, *except maybe as guards to the Banshee caves—and that's only a rumor,* Kandide thought. This one, however, was certainly no rumor. *But how did it get here? The Banshee caves aren't even close to the Mists. It must have been hunting the griffin.* Now, however, the creature had found even more tantalizing prey.

When Kandide was in her tenth year, her tutor—over strenuous objections—had insisted that she memorize a bestiary, describing every sort of creature and monster known to the Fée. *Garglans,* as she recalled with a shiver, *consider the Fée a special delicacy. When devoured, our essence generates enough energy for it to live on for weeks—sometimes even longer.*

Unfortunately, the bestiary hadn't said anything about how to fight these creatures. *Okay, Kandide, keep your wits about you,* she told herself. Not sure what to do, she grabbed one of the biscuits from her basket and tossed it toward the beast. The creature caught it and, hissing with delight, greedily consumed the tasty treat.

"You like that, do you? Here, try this." She threw an apple off to the side, hoping to create a momentary distraction. Moving like a flash to catch it, the garglan instantly gobbled up the fruit. Drool dribbled down its chin. Its blood-red eyes darted back and forth between Kandide and the basket. "I have a lot more treats and I'll give them to you if you go away." She tossed it another biscuit.

In all her life, Kandide had never faced real danger. Battle games with the Royal Guard were one thing, but a creature such as this was quite a different matter. She didn't even have a bow, or a sword, or anything. "Okay, keep calm, Kandide. Keep calm. What would Father do?" she whispered under her breath.

As she stared at the dreadful beast, she suddenly froze. A second growling noise came from behind her. Her heart almost stopped. Another, larger and even more hideous-looking garglan leapt out from behind a dead tree trunk.

The griffin began screeching madly. Her large wings were flapping as she desperately tried to escape.

Before Kandide realized what was happening, the second garglan grabbed the basket from her hand. Hissing, it scurried up a gnarled tree with its prize. Howling in defiance, the first garglan darted up after it. The two began squabbling over the treats. Biscuits and fruit went flying everywhere.

Kandide had only moments to save herself. She started to gesture to transport, and then abruptly stopped. In her heart, she knew she could never leave the griffin. "If only I had a sword, I could cut you lose," she said in soft tone. It had stopped screeching, but she could hear the magnificent creature's breathing becoming more labored. "If I just could fly, I could release the snare. If ... if ... if! If only 'if' could help! Now stop that and think, Kandide," she told herself.

Her hand slid into the pocket of her cape. There it was—the feather King Toeyad had given her only days before. "Great! Why couldn't he have given me a knife?" she mumbled. *I certainly don't need to look beneath the surface to know what these guys are all about.*

There was, however, something strange about the way the feather felt. The silver spiral around its quill was hot, pulsing with energy. *Could Father have spelled it with some sort of magic?* she wondered, taking it out of her pocket.

A glint of silver in the mossy undergrowth caught her eye. *A fruit knife? It must have fallen from the basket when the garglans scurried up the tree with it,* Kandide thought as reached down to pick it up. "Look, girl. It's not much, but . . ." Incredibly, the power from the feather seemed to flow right through her body and into the knife. The blade began to glow white hot, as though it had been forged from molten steel that very moment.

Without pause, Kandide sliced through the first rope that constrained the exhausted animal. At least now, its neck was free. But just as the rope separated, the smaller garglan leapt from the tree. Its curiosity over the basket of treats obviously satisfied, it was now ready for a more substantial meal.

Kandide turned to face the hideous beast. She was determined not to let it near the mother-to-be. *Even if I don't survive,* she thought, *the griffin might still get away. Father, at least, would be proud.*

Clutching the feather even tighter, Kandide felt its power continuing to surge through her body and into the knife.

She slashed at the other restraint that was holding the griffin's feet. The ropes melted away like warm butter.

"Go!" she shouted, not daring to take her eyes off the garglan. "Hurry! You have to get back to the château!" Weighted down by the baby inside, and weak from her struggle to free herself, the griffin could barely move—let alone fly. "Just try," Kandide pleaded. "I'll keep the garglans distracted."

With all of her attention focused on the first garglan, Kandide didn't see the larger one leap out of the tree. Black fur smashed against her face and chest. The creature's enormous weight knocked both of them to the ground. A burning pain shot through her shoulder. She had landed on her injured wing.

With no time to react, Kandide was suddenly face-to-face with the garglan's razor-sharp fangs. Drool dribbled down its chin as its forked pink tongue made a hissing sound. She felt the creature's claws rip through her cape as they dug into her shoulders. Kandide's grip tightened around the knife. "I won't let you kill her," she screamed.

As if the knife were self-directed, the white-hot blade sliced across the garglan's right shoulder. Foul-smelling black ooze spurted onto her face and neck. She choked on the stench.

The stunned beast let out an agonizing howl, and it stopped fighting just long enough for the knife to strike again. This time, the blade slashed through its throat. Thick black slime sprayed everywhere. Kandide's face, neck, and shoulders were covered with the vile liquid.

The garglan stopped fighting. Its enormous dead body fell on top of Kandide. Her lungs felt like they would collapse from the sudden weight. But it was dead and that was all she cared about.

With all of her might, she shoved the creature aside.

Wiping the slime off her face, Kandide started to get up. *The knife,* she panicked. *I must have dropped it.* In just that instant, the smaller garglan spread its massive wings and leapt into the air. Hissing and snarling, its long, sharp claws were aimed directly at her throat.

"Go!" she shouted to the griffin, hoping that if the garglan was satisfied with her as its meal, the expectant mother might still get away.

From the opposite direction, a voice called out,
"Are you all right?"

TWENTY-THREE

The garglan let out a blood-curdling screech as its beady red eyes locked onto Kandide's. She dropped to the ground, blindly reaching for the knife. It was there, just inches from her fingertips.

Suddenly, all was silent. The garglan's claws never reached her throat. Less than a meter from where Kandide was kneeling, the creature slammed to the ground with a dull, heavy thud, its red eyes staring straight ahead.

Is it dead? Kandide was unable to make sense of what had just happened. *Or somehow faking, waiting for me to come closer? No, it flew toward me.* Her eyes traversed the body of the silent creature.

Then she saw it. "An arrow?" she murmured. "Through its heart? But who?" Looking around to find the projectile's source, Kandide caught a glimpse of a vivid red flash in an oak tree just a few meters away. *Could it be? Lady Aron, here?*

From the opposite direction, a voice called out, "Are you all right?" Startled, she whirled around to see Jake with a bow in his hand.

Despite being splattered with black slime, Kandide answered him in her most regal fashion, "I'm fine. Thank you, Jake."

"You're welcome—Your Majesty." He walked over and handed her his fresh white linen handkerchief. "Here you go."

She tried not to seem overly grateful, yet her expression revealed that she was extremely pleased to see him. She was also happy to wipe the foul-smelling stuff off her face and hands. "I was doing quite well, you know."

"I would say so," he answered, looking at the larger of the two dead garglans. "Just thought I'd lend a hand." A hint of a smile crossed his lips. His aim was perfect. The second garglan had died instantly without suffering.

"Good shot." She wiped more slime from her left cheek.

"Thanks." Spotting the small knife lying on the ground, Jake picked it up and handed it to her. "You killed the other garglan with this—a fruit knife?" Indeed, it was, once again, just a simple fruit knife.

"I did," she replied, with more than a tinge of self-satisfaction. "Did you see that bright red flash in the tree over there?" Kandide pointed in the direction where it occurred.

Before Jake could answer, the griffin let out a whimper. They both turned to see a tiny baby wiggle its way out from underneath its mother. "Jake, look!"

The griffin began licking her newborn cub to clean away the afterbirth. Kandide cautiously approached her. "Are you okay, girl? Are you okay?" The appreciative new mother responded with a soft purring sound. Her beautiful golden eyes glistened with gratitude.

"You just made a friend for life," Jake said softly. "Griffins may be fiercely independent creatures, but they're also intensely loyal when given cause."

Kandide gently stroked the soft white feathers on the mother's head. "Your little cub is beautiful," she whispered. The griffin nuzzled her hand in return, purring even louder.

Suddenly, Kandide froze. *My wing,* she thought, realizing that it was completely exposed. "I . . . I must be going now." She turned and quickly looked to see where her cape had fallen.

Picking it up off the ground, Jake handed it to her. "Please don't go." His green eyes shone with genuine concern.

"You . . . you don't understand. I must . . ."

"Why?"

"You can't possibly understand." She pulled the cape around her shoulders.

"I can't understand what?" Jake stood there looking at her. "That you aren't as perfect as you would have us believe? That, in fact, you're a crumplewing? There, I said it. You are a crumplewing—an Imperfect like me and Selena and Leanne, and all of the rest of us in the Veil."

"Thank you for helping me, Jake. I'll be leaving, now." Kandide's voice was filled with a queen's hauteur. "And you may return to your precious château."

"You didn't come to visit us, did you? You were sent away."

"I said you may leave now!" Kandide was practically screaming at him.

"No, I will not leave now." Jake's tone was almost too calm. "Might I remind you that this is my land, not yours."

"How dare you speak to me like that?"

"Why?" He responded with an air of flippancy. "You're not our queen. I doubt if you're even their queen."

"You repulse me, all of you!" *Why do I even talk to him?* she fumed.

"I don't think I repulse you, Kandide. I think *you* repulse you."

His words cut through her faster than the fruit knife had severed the garglan's throat, and just as deeply. She bit her lower lip. Then with calculated indifference, responded, "No one speaks to me like that." Kandide turned and started to walk away. *He thinks he's so smart. Well, he's not going to win, not this time.* She abruptly stopped, and turned back around, "Look at me, Jake. Go ahead, look at me." She lowered her cape, and turned to fully reveal her crumpled wing. "What is there for me? Everything I stand for is gone. My life is over."

"Really? Well, I saved it, so you owe me."

"That's highly debatable!"

"Not by my book." Jake crossed his arms, and smiled at her, which only served to make her even angrier.

"I didn't ask for your help." She mimicked him by crossing her arms.

"It doesn't matter." He shrugged. "Until you can repay me, you're in my debt."

"How dare you!"

"No, how dare you, Kandide. You, of all Fée, are sworn to obey the honor of the Codes—which means you are in my debt for saving your life. As payment, I demand that you help me take the griffin and her cub back to the château so we can care for them until they are strong again."

"I should think that you could handle that task on your own. *Besides, there's no way I'm going to spend even five more minutes with him if he's going to behave like that.* She turned to speak to the griffin, who had been carefully watching the two of them. "Goodbye, girl, I hope I see you again some day."

"I give up." Jake threw up his hands. "Fine, Kandide. Then stay here or go wherever you like. I release you from your debt." He walked over to the griffin, muttering under his breath. "How could King Toeyad have raised such a daughter?" Carefully lifting the cub into his arms, Jake started to head off.

"Wait!" Kandide called after him.

"What is it?" Jake turned back to look at her.

"The . . . the mother griffin, she's not following you."

"Come on, girl," Jake called, but the griffin didn't move. "Come on, let's go home." But no matter how much Jake called, she wouldn't budge. She simply stood there in the circle of gnarled trees, looking back and forth between the two Fée.

"You can't just leave us . . . I mean her out here all alone." She crossed over to griffin and began petting her. "Her neck is still bleeding from the rope cuts, and . . . and more garglans might come." Whether from fright, or perhaps from being rejected, Kandide wasn't sure how she felt. She only knew that she had found a proud and loyal friend who seemed as concerned about her, as she was about the new mother. *Maybe I should go back with Jake,* she thought. *At least until I know the griffin is safe. She does seem to want me to come with her.* "We could be eaten out here, you know."

"I doubt it. Any garglan would probably take one bite and

decide it wants a Fée that's a little more tender." Gently stroking the newborn cub, he again called the griffin to follow. "Okay, girl, let's go." And again she stubbornly refused to leave.

"Admit it, Jake, you do need my help getting her home."

"I'll manage." He called to the griffin once more. "It really is time to go, girl. You don't want me to take your baby by itself, do you?" He watched as the griffin just sat there.

"She's not going to go with you, Jake. Are you, girl?" The griffin shook her head from side to side. "See, you really do need my help. But first, there's something I need to ask you."

"What is it?" He walked over to her.

"Well . . ." She paused, nervously adjusting her cape. "If . . . if I agree to return to the château with you, will the others . . . I mean, will they—"

"Accept you?" Jake flashed that incredible smile. "They'll probably give you a medal. You just fought two garglans and saved the life of the only pregnant griffin in over half a century. Why, you're . . . you're a hero!"

"A hero?" Kandide stood up a little straighter. "Why, yes, I guess I am. Do you really think they'll accept me like that?"

"I think it's more a question of will you accept us?"

"Well, I . . ."

"There's only one way to find out."

"Very well, I shall return with you." Her tone sounded as though she was doing Jake a favor. "If you promise not to reveal my secret," she quickly added, glancing back at her crumpled wing.

Jake gave her wicked grin. "I tell you what, I promise to let you reveal your 'secret' first—as long as you don't take too long."

"Then I shall remain here!" Kandide flicked her braid back over her shoulder. "Won't we, girl?" She looked at the griffin, who slowly turned and looked at Jake with an expression almost as defiant as Kandide's.

Groaning, Jake ran his hand through his dark hair. "Fantastic. Now I have two of you against me. Females!"

"That we are, aren't we, girl?"

The griffin nodded.

Knowing that Kandide's pride was all she really had left, Jake gestured toward a fallen log. "Look, sit down for a moment, Your Majesty. Please."

"Stop calling me that. You yourself said I'm not queen."

"Title or not, you're every inch a queen. That no one can ever take away from you. Won't you please sit down for a minute, Kandide? Let's talk."

The beginning of a smile tugged at the corners of her mouth. *I guess it won't hurt for a few minutes*, she thought, joining him on the fallen tree. For all of her poise, it could well have been a throne.

The mother griffin walked over as well. Settling next to Kandide, she nuzzled her hand. Jake carefully placed the tiny cub by its mother and it began to nurse.

"In the after-wars, when I rode alongside your father," Jake explained, "I was a Perfect, too. Then the accident with the burning timber happened. Your father carried me back to camp in his arms."

"I didn't realize that you knew my father."

"Very well. My parents introduced him to your mother. My mother is from the same village as Tiyana. King Toeyad told me of a vision he had—that one day he would have a powerful daughter who would rule Calabiyau, and all Fée would live in harmony."

Kandide's eyes shifted toward the ground. "It's my sister, Tara, who must fulfill that destiny. She now rules Calabiyau, not I."

"But she doesn't rule all Fée. Some of us are still not allowed to live in harmony with the rest."

"But Imper—" Kandide stopped, realizing that she was no longer sure how she felt—about herself, Imperfects, or Jake. She looked into his green eyes. In spite of his impertinence, he had to be the most mesmerizing Fée she'd ever met. Trying to seem indifferent, she asked, "So then what happened?"

"Well, when the healers told King Toeyad that my feet couldn't be fixed, he assured me that I could go back to the castle and would be cared for. But I was far too proud, and ashamed—kind of like you."

"I—"

"And like you, I wouldn't let anyone see me. Not even my own father and mother."

"So, did Father send you away?"

"No, of course not. King Toeyad was true to his word. But I just couldn't imagine the humiliation of spending my life crawling around on my knees. As soon as my strength returned, I snuck out of camp—fortunately I could still fly. I went to an underground cave that I knew about and hid in it. Your father sent search parties out to find me. They almost did, so I moved deeper into the woods. I just couldn't face having anyone see me like that, nor did I want to disgrace my parents that way."

"Where did you go? How did you end up in here? What did you live on?"

"Hey, one question at a time," Jake responded with a slight laugh. "What I did, mostly, was feel sorry for myself. Kind of like you."

"I cert—" Kandide started to protest, but Jake kept talking.

"I survived by flying for as long and as often as possible. I couldn't stay airborne forever, though. So I learned to walk on my knees. It's a lot harder than you would think."

"I can imagine." The thought of Jake walking around on his knees made her smile. *I bet that knocked his ego down a bit,* she thought.

"Avoiding the occasional garglan was even more of a challenge."

"What did you do?"

"I made a short-bow and some arrows, and began practicing, since a sword isn't the easiest thing to use while kneeling."

"I guess not." Kandide chuckled. "So, how did you get here?" She glanced around at the dark, misty woods.

"One day, my father almost found me. So, I set transport coordinates—but I must have mixed up some numbers. The next thing I knew, I was here. At least I knew no one would find me. I built a small shelter in a rock cave, half beneath the ground."

"You actually lived out here." She cringed at the thought. "One night was more than enough for me."

"You get used to it—sort of." He, too, looked around, shuddering as he remembered those awful years—the cold, the dampness, and mostly how very alone he felt. "One day, when I was sitting there, feeling particularly sorry for myself, I heard what sounded like a young child crying, so I started searching. That's when I found Leanne."

"Leanne?"

"Yeah, Leanne. When she was five years old, she was sent away because she lost her sight. When I found her she was so weak from hunger and exhaustion, she could barely walk. I can't believe a garglan didn't find her first. Anyway, I picked her up and carried her into the cave."

"That's incredible, Jake."

"I'll tell you what's even more incredible—Leanne. She's a fighter. Puts me to shame. She'd bump into things, tumble over, then just get right back up and keep walking. Her determination was amazing. Nothing seemed to bother her. And she was so optimistic—something I hadn't been in years. After a while, I began to notice that she also had the gift of Healing. Ironic, isn't it—that she can heal others, but not herself? One day, an injured wolf found us and she healed its broken leg. We named him Trust because it took a lot of it to let Leanne help him. From then on, he was her constant companion."

"A wolf?" Kandide thought of the wolf she had met when she first woke up in the cave. "What happened to him?"

"He gave his life protecting her from an attack by a couple of garglans when I was off gathering mushrooms—they're about the only thing that grows out here. Anyway, Trust killed the first garglan almost immediately. But the second one jumped on his back and ripped open his throat. Even so, he wouldn't stop fighting. He died with the garglan's neck crushed between his jaws. Leanne was devastated, but there was nothing she could have done. It's the only time I've ever seen her truly depressed."

"I'm so sorry."

"Trust's offspring still live in the woods. Every once in a while, when a new litter is born, they'll introduce the pups to us as if to say 'Protect these Fée, they're our friends.' There's been one watching us for quite some time now."

Kandide looked up. Giving a start, she saw a huge wolf lying not more than a few meters away.

"That's Ari. He leads the pack now—and a more loyal friend you'll never find." As Jake spoke, Ari walked over and nuzzled his hand. He cautiously sniffed at Kandide and the mother griffin, who was busy licking her cub. The wolf, Kandide realized, was nearly as tall as the griffin.

"It's okay, boy, they're friends." The magnificent silver-gray wolf wagged his flowing tail and barked a quick welcome, all of which the mother griffin totally ignored.

"I'm surprised that you didn't see him when you arrived," Jake continued. "He usually stands in the shadows and growls so new arrivals won't start heading in the wrong direction."

"That was Ari? He was at the cave I slept in before I found the Veil. I thought . . ." She reached over to pet him. "You were there to help me find my way, weren't you? Thank you, Ari."

"That he was. Although, if you didn't know, I can see how he could be a bit intimidating." Jake scratched Ari's ears.

"After that, what happened?"

"As Leanne grew older, her ability to heal became even stronger. So did her remarkable optimism. She just wouldn't let me feel sorry for myself. It was Leanne who suggested that I make a pair of feet so that I could walk. At first, it was frustrating. I carved them out of wood, but I couldn't figure out how to make them work right. They kept falling off, or I would trip over myself." Jake stood up and began imitating his clumsiness.

Kandide started to giggle. "I bet dancing was tough!"

"Oh, I don't know!" Reaching out, Jake pulled her up and began purposely tripping all over her feet, while singing a lively tune:

> *Step to the left, step to the right.*
> *The faeries are out and about tonight.*
> *Watch them dance, watch them whirl,*
> *Faster and faster the Fée can twirl.*
> *Step to the left, step to the right.*
> *The faeries are such a wondrous sight.*

"Where did you learn that song?" Kandide asked as they danced around the small clearing.

"From King Toeyad. I haven't thought of it for years."

"Father used to sing it to me when I was a little girl. It's a human song." She began to sing along with him.

"Well, come on then. Pick up the pace a little. "Step to the left, step to the right." He began dancing faster and faster.

"Hey, watch it!" she told him, her toe having been the target of a misplaced boot.

"Oh, sorry." Jake lifted her up off the ground and together, they danced and flew, faster and faster. Finally, dancing, singing, and laughing so much, the two of them tumbled over, landing on the wet ground.

"It's good to see you laugh, Kandide. You're even more beautiful when you do, you know." Jake extended a hand to help her stand up.

For a brief second their eyes met and she couldn't move. *How could anyone be so handsome?* she thought. His impish charm, combined with that strong sense of inner confidence, was irresistible. And that incredible smile—it made her feel as though he could ease the entire world of all its ills. A warm tingling sensation swept over her body and went straight to her heart. Realizing that she had totally lost her composure, Kandide snapped back into her queen-like mode. She stood up and brushed off her dress. "Then you met Selena?"

"Yep," he answered, taking her hand and leading back over to the log.

"I don't understand why Father never told me about the Veil." Kandide sat down next to Jake. "I guess he didn't trust me as much as I thought."

"I'm sure that's not the reason." Jake tried to reassure her. "King Toeyad just wanted a place that no one, including the High Council, could find or know about—a secret place where *all* Fée can be safe and live in harmony with one another." "He probably just didn't think that it was . . . well, necessary."

Knowing that he was being kind, Kandide felt a pang of remorse. And this, too, was a new experience for her. "It's okay, Jake, I understand." And she did. If nothing else, Kandide knew that before her own injury, she'd never given a thought to the lives or the rights of the Imperfects. At times, she even said cruel things about them. "Father was probably right. I might not have understood." *And I can't believe I just said that*, she thought. Her back stiffened a bit. "In any case, you were telling me about meeting Selena.

"Right. Selena invited Leanne and me to join her. There really wasn't all that much in the Veil back then, just a one-bedroom cottage. But sleeping on a real floor was a lot better than living in a damp cave—or battling garglans."

"So, what about your feet? They seem to work perfectly now—well, almost." Teasing him, she rubbed her foot where he had stepped on it.

"Sorry about that. Not long after we moved in, Trump came along. He's a Banshee."

"A Banshee?"

"Yeah, and a terrific jewelsmith. He lost an eye in a freak accident. So of course the Banshees—"

"Sent him away. Rumors say that the Banshees feed their Imperfects to garglans." Now that she had actually seen the hideous beasts, Kandide cringed at the thought.

"They do. For some reason, Trump was allowed to just leave. He never said why. We found him in the Mists clinging to an enormous bag of jewels. He was half-dead from his injuries. Said he'd been out there for days."

"So you brought him into the château?" Her face shone with surprise.

"Well, we could hardly leave him there. Leanne healed his injuries, although she couldn't fix his eye, so he wears a patch."

Kandide was dumbfounded at the thought of a Banshee living among the Fée. "Weren't you afraid he might kill someone? I mean, he is a Banshee. His kind have been conducting horrible, brutal raids on the villages near our border with them. Father said they're the most vicious attacks he'd ever seen, and that their King Nastae is behind them. He wouldn't even tell me some of the atrocities they've committed. Are you sure—"

"I know what you're saying, but we try to judge everyone based on who they are as individuals—not what they are. I'll admit it did take a while for him to be accepted. To his credit, Trump knew he would have to earn our trust and respect, and he worked twice as hard as anyone to get it."

"You're telling me you actually trust him?"

"I do. It was Trump who helped me fashion feet that work almost like real ones. He took some of his diamonds and cut and polished them until they were round enough to serve as joints for my ankles and toes. Then he carved the feet out of hardwood. See?" Jake pulled off his boots to show the sparkling diamond joints. "Selena made the straps that hold them on. And look! They're almost as good as new." Jake stood up and did a little jig in his bare wooden feet.

"That's—" Kandide caught herself. The repulsion she felt when she first saw Jake without feet seemed to have vanished. "I mean, truly wonderful."

"Like I told you, we're working on wings now." Jake pulled his boots back on.

"I can't wait to see them." Kandide kept her voice cool, not wanting to betray the surge of hope she felt.

"Except we just can't seem to get them right."

"Why not?"

"I'll show you when we get back, but we had better be going." Jake held out his hand to help her up. "A garglan can smell death for miles, and we don't need any more of them to find us."

"What about them?" She pointed to the two creatures lying

in pools of black slime.

"One of their buddies will find them soon enough. I hear they eat their own dead. Even vultures won't touch a dead garglan."

"I can't say as I blame them."

Jake gave Ari a pat on the head, telling him to be extra careful. He barked once in response, then trotted off into the woods.

Watching him leave, Kandide hesitated before taking a step. "Are you sure the Fée at the château will accept me, Jake?"

"Probably," he teased. "I mean, I have." Flashing a flirtatious smile, he lifted the baby griffin into his arms. "Come on, let's go find out who accepts whom."

With the mother griffin at Kandide's side, the four of them set off toward the château. *Of course, they'll accept me. I'm a hero,* she reassured herself. *Even Jake says so.* But as they approached the gate, Kandide pulled her cape tightly around her shoulders.

"Take it or not." Lady Aron leaned back in her chair. *"The decision is yours, Teren."*

TWENTY-FOUR

Tiyana and Teren could barely keep up with Tara as she hurried along the winding hallway to the Council chamber. Her head was as high as her newfound confidence. *Teren was right. I can stand up for what I believe at the Council meetings,* she told herself. *I'll bet Lady Aron turns as red as a berry beetle when she hears what we've decided to do. I'm not going to let her push Mother—or me—around ever again.*

"Now remember, Tara, you're Queen," Teren whispered as they reached the tall double doors that opened into the chamber.

"That I am, little brother." The gold crown she wore, with its twelve different jewels—one for each of the clans—sparkled under the flickering oil lamps that lit the room. It was in complete contrast to her plain brown britches, green cotton shirt, striped socks, and lace-up boots, but on this day, she wore it well.

Seating herself on the crystal throne, Tara spoke with a regal sense of control that, up until that moment, even she didn't know she had. "Lord Rössi, please call the session to order, I have made a decision regarding Kandide."

"As you wish, Your Majesty." He bowed his head.

Although Tara felt more like a queen than ever before, those two words still made her flinch. *I'll never get used to being called Your Majesty,* she thought, watching Lord Rössi rap his gavel on the crescent-shaped table.

"The one hundred seventy-ninth session of the year 26,906 BT is now in order." He rapped his gavel again. "Queen Tara wishes to address the Council."

The "Tomboy Queen," as her subjects had started calling her, stood and then began to speak. "I have decided to send Prince Teren in search of my sister. He is to find her and bring her back so she may deploy the Gift of the Frost and the seasons can change."

"What?" Lady Aron leaped to her feet. "You're sending your little brother to find her? I can't believe General Mintz will agree to this."

"General Mintz has no say in the matter. As your queen, I am making this decision, and Teren will be going alone."

"Impossible!" Lord Revên objected. He, too, stood up. "If what Tiyana told us is true, and she doesn't know where Kandide is, then General Mintz must send troops to escort the boy. This is far too critical a mission to leave to a child."

He glanced over at Teren, who grimaced. *I'm fourteen; that's hardly a child.*

"You may sit back down, Lord Revên—and you as well, Lady Aron." Tara motioned for them to do so, and then seated herself. "I've made my decision." Although her pulse quickened, she held her ground.

"At the very least, Prince Teren needs to take guards," Lord Standish insisted.

"How will he even know where to search?" a very concerned Lady Karena asked.

"Perhaps I can send the forest snakes to scout for him." As the guardian of reptiles, Lady Alicia frequently asked for their help to locate lost children who had stayed out past dark on foggy nights and weren't able to collect enough moonbeams to light their way home.

"Or the lake fish," Lady Corel added. "I can ask the lake fish to help. Perhaps they've seen her."

"I thank you all for your suggestions. But they won't be necessary." *Hold firm*, Tara told herself, *you can do this*. "Teren will leave at first light."

"I personally think it's a good idea to let Prince Teren go." Lord Aron glanced up at his wife, trying to hide the sense of relief he felt. *If Tara is sending Teren alone, that must mean that Kandide was sent to the Veil*, he reasoned. *At least Firenza won't find her first*.

"In re-thinking the matter, I agree with you, my dear." Lady Aron sat back down in her chair next to her husband. "Teren should go alone." It was the first time since their argument that she had even acknowledged him, let alone agreed with him about a matter of State. "Let him have until the Winter Solstice to find her."

"But that's in three days!" Tara's voice shot up a notch.

"Yes, Your Majesty." Lady Aron leaned forward and rested

her arms on the table. "Solstice is in exactly three days."

"That's not nearly enough time," Teren protested. His mind flashed back to what Tiyana had told him, that getting to the Veil and back—if he could even find Kandide—would be difficult at best.

"Take it or not." Lady Aron leaned back in her chair. "The decision is yours, Teren. It is the only way we will agree to let you go on your own." She looked at the other Council members for any sign of dissent, but none spoke up. "The Frost simply must be deployed by the Winter Solstice. It's already becoming most perilous. The consequences after that date could well be irreversible."

Tara glared at the fire Fée. She took a deep breath before speaking. *Stay calm,* she told herself. *You know what she's like. Don't let her get to you.* "We all understand the consequences, Lady Aron. Some of us are simply trying to find a more realistic solution."

"Yes, some of us are, aren't we? And, as I see it, we now have two 'realistic' solutions: Teren returns in three days with Kandide—or, if he's not back, your mother uses the small portion of the Gift that Toeyad gave her to deploy the Frost. Will you agree to that, Tiyana?"

"As you have stated, Lady Aron, it may be the only other choice." Tiyana spoke without emotion.

"Well, it's not a choice Mother's going to have to make." Teren headed for the door. "I will be back in three days—with Kandide." *And right now, we need to get out of here before the other Council members start arguing about it.* "Mother, Tara, can you help me get ready? We don't have any time to waste."

"Good idea." Tara nodded. "The Council is therefore adjourned. As you have requested, Lady Aron, Teren will be back with my sister by the Solstice."

"So we all hope," Lady Aron mumbled under her breath. "And with that reassuring news, I, too, must be leaving." *This just gets more delicious by the minute,* she thought, vanishing in a flash of bright red sparks.

Moments later, the fire Fée reappeared outside the Royal Guards' quarters. She was just in time to spot Asgart who was getting off duty. Studying his new uniform, Lady Aron nodded approvingly. "Stripes suit you, Captain—I believe that is your title now."

"Yes, My Lady," he nervously answered. "Uh . . . could we go somewhere else to talk?" Asgart motioned for her to follow him, dreading what she might want. He had done as she asked, and the memory of it still repulsed him. *This,* he told himself, *had better be her last request.*

The two Fée walked to a seldom-used side garden. It was bursting with bright red poinsettias and golden chrysanthemums. "So, are you happy with your new rank?" she asked.

"Yes, thank you. It was strange, though, Captain Erley becoming sick like that—and so suddenly. I hope he recovers soon. He taught me a great deal when I served under him."

"Oh, I'm sure he'll recover—eventually. Now, were you able to appropriate the garglans? I'm in a bit of a hurry."

Making sure they were standing where they couldn't be seen, Asgart kept his voice to a whisper. "Begging your pardon, My Lady, garglans don't just grow on willow trees, you know. It was hard enough getting the first two for you. What happened

213

to them, anyway? I didn't see them at your villa, and why do you want so many more?"

"Questions. Questions. Questions. My dear Captain, when are you going to learn that I do the asking? Let's just say that I will sleep better knowing there are more garglans on the job— so to speak. Now, did you get them or not?"

"Yes." His voice revealed a hint of self-satisfaction. It was, after all, an almost impossible task. "There are fifteen more chained outside your summer villa. You have no idea what I went through to even find out where to get that many."

"Did the sleeping potion I gave you do its job? A few drops should have knocked the creatures and their guards out cold. You did take the anti-potion I gave you?"

"Yes and yes. Both potions worked just as you said they would. But if the Banshees ever find out who took their garglans—"

"Let's just make sure they don't. You've done very well, Captain. Once again, I shall see to it that you are handsomely rewarded."

"No! I mean, there's no need. You've already done quite enough for me. Really. Just consider us even now and I'll be on my way." He started to leave, but she caught him by the arm.

"Why, Captain Asgart, you risked your life to get me those garglans. And, by your own admission, you could still be in danger. As you said, if the Banshees ever learned who stole them—well, I don't even want to think what they might do. Besides, I couldn't possibly let such a brave deed go by without doing some little thing to thank you. And I think I have the perfect idea."

Asgart paled. Her ideas always meant trouble.

"I understand that Lady Socrat is in need of a lady-in-waiting. Perhaps your wife might be interested?"

"My wife?" He went white. *I won't let her drag Palara into this,* he thought. "Oh, my wife is doing fine. Truly, Lady Aron, Palara is more than content in her job."

"Are you sure? My sources tell me that just the other day she was complaining about how little money she makes working in the kitchen. You could use more money, now couldn't you?"

"We have enough, especially now that I'm a Captain."

"But you can always use a little more—everyone can. Besides, don't you think your wife also deserves the opportunity for a better position—Captain?"

His stomach began to churn. "Well, I—"

"I know, you think it's a lot to ask of me. But don't worry; I'm sure you'll figure out a way to return the favor at some point."

Asgart bit back his anger. *Why did I have to step on Kandide's cape? Just because she humiliated me when she was a child. I should know revenge always claims its owner.* He spoke in firm voice. "I will not have Palara—"

"Oh, don't be so controlling, Captain. Why, any decent husband would be proud to have his wife promoted to a position such as that." Lady Aron patted his check. Without another word, she vanished.

*Clutching her cloak tightly around her shoulders,
Kandide abruptly turned and rushed out of the room.*

TWENTY-FIVE

Of course *they'll accept me,* Kandide repeated to herself as she and Jake walked up the stairs that led into the château. The mother griffin was by her side. Her newborn cub was fast asleep in Jake's arms. Kandide clutched the white feather in her pocket with one hand and the top of her cape with the other. *This time, it won't come off my shoulders,* she told herself. *Besides, maybe Leanne can heal my wing—then there's no reason to tell anyone about it.*

Noticing how tightly Kandide held her cape closed, Jake whispered, "Remember, you're not only a queen, you're a genuine hero."

"Thank you." She relaxed her grip, but ever so slightly. "Right now, however, I feel more like a genuine mess." She glanced down at her muddy, slime-splattered skirt.

Seeing them enter the Great Hall, Selena rushed over. "Thank the earthly spirits that you're both safe." She looked at the mother griffin and the bright red blood stains around its white neck feathers. "Oh dear, what happened out there?"

"Kandide saved the griffin and her newborn cub from an attack by a couple of garglans." Jake carefully handed the tiny baby to Selena, who opened its eyes and yawned. Watching her cub, the mother griffin made a soft growling noise, nuzzling Kandide's arm. "They never would have survived if Kandide hadn't found them."

"May the spirits rejoice." Selena cuddled the snow-white baby. "Thank you, Kandide. He's the first griffin cub to be born in over half a century. You must tell me every detail about what happened. Oh dear, you both do look a fright. Are you sure you're not hurt?"

"Other than being a bit dirty, we're fine," Kandide replied, petting the mother griffin. "Her neck, however, could use a little attending to by Leanne. It doesn't look too serious."

"Of course, right away." Selena called to one of the serving Fée to fetch Leanne. "So, what happened? Where were you when you found her?" Kandide's aunt was, as usual, full of questions.

"I was in the Mists—about to leave—when I heard this cry. There was the griffin, caught in a snare, and—"

"And before Kandide could free her," Jake added, "a garglan leapt out from a tree." As he spoke, the room began filling with more Fée. They pulled up chairs and gathered around to listen. "Kandide killed the first garglan with just a fruit knife," Jake explained.

The assemblage broke out in applause and began chanting: "Queen Kandide! Queen Kandide! Queen Kandide!"

"Perhaps you'd better say a few words," Selena urged her niece.

Kandide raised her hand to silence the crowd. "Thank you. All of you." Although splattered in mud and slime, she couldn't have sounded more regal. "I did kill the first garglan with just a fruit knife, but it was Jake's arrow that killed the second one." Her hand slid back inside her cape pocket. She felt the silver spiral on the feather grow warm. Instantly, a burst of self-confidence flowed through her. "There's something else you must know. I . . . I'm not Calabiyau's queen—at least not right now."

A confused hush fell over the assembled Fée, who by now completely filled the large hall. Kandide looked at Jake for reassurance. His smile told her to continue. She took a breath. "I am, uh . . . I was sent a—" Visions of that day on the balcony suddenly flashed through her mind. The awful taunts of her subjects screamed inside her head.

No, she thought, *I'm their hero. I can't tell them about my wing. Not right now.* Clutching her cloak tightly around her shoulders, Kandide abruptly turned and rushed out of the room.

The mother griffin, who had moved out into the hallway to avoid the crowd, was nursing her cub. She sat up and unfurled her massive wings. "Oh, I didn't mean to startle you." Kandide held out her hand.

But the griffin just stared at her.

"You weren't startled," Kandide said slowly. "You're blocking my path, aren't you?"

The griffin nodded, stretching her wings even farther until they reached across the entire three meters of the hallway.

"Please let me by. You don't understand. I can't go back in there."

The new mother emitted a low growl and gently pushed her tiny baby forward. Smiling, Kandide picked him up. She sat down on a carved wooden side bench and began to cuddle the little cub. He rubbed his feathered white head against her arm.

"If this is your way of making me want to stay," Kandide looked at his mother, "it's certainly working." She gently scratched the cub's tummy. "Your baby is beautiful. He's so perfect." She looked at his tiny wings and perfectly shaped serpent tail. Although only a few hours old, his eyes were bright and sharp, as were his talons and yellow beak.

"Ouch!" She pulled her hand away. He had accidently scratched it "You're going to be a powerful little guy, aren't you?"

The mother griffin shook her head up and down; her yellow eyes sparkled. Then, hearing something, she quickly turned to look.

Jake was standing behind them. "All three of you are beautiful—and perfect."

"You know that's not true—at least not the perfect part." Kandide pushed a strand of hair away from her eyes.

"For me it is." He walked over and placed his hand on her shoulder. "Do you think any of us care if you have a crumpled wing?"

"I care." Standing up, she started to give the cub to its mother, but the griffin growled again, pushing Kandide back down on the bench.

"Looks like Gertie disagrees with you." Jake flashed the griffin a smile.

"Gertie? Is that her name?"

"Yep. Selena just told me."

"Gertie Griffin? That's silly."

Gertie glared at Kandide, and then let out another deep-throated growl.

"Oh, sorry. It's a lovely name. Really!" Kandide smiled sheepishly. "Look, I know you both mean well, but I'm just not—"

"Well, get over it, or Gertie and I will personally take you back out to the Mists and feed you to the garglans."

The mother griffin growled in agreement.

"How dare you speak to me that way—and you, too!" Kandide scowled at Jake, then at Gertie. She tried to sound angry, but the smile that crept through told otherwise. "You know, the little cub needs a name as well."

"How about Courage, in honor of his savior—and because that is what's needed right now?" Jake looked at Gertie, who nodded her approval.

"You want to name him Courage, in honor of me?" Kandide thought this was one of the nicest compliments she'd ever received. "I suppose I did save his life, but—"

"But?"

"But . . ." She paused before answering. *Maybe Jake's right. Maybe courage is what we both need right now.* The cub began to purr as Kandide gently stroked its silky white body fur. "Well, I guess if Gertie agrees, who am I to argue? 'Courage' it shall be." She hugged the tiny creature, who purred even more loudly.

"You know," Jake sat down beside her, "now that he's named Courage—in your honor—don't you have an obligation to be, well, courageous?"

Kandide rolled her eyes. "Only you, Jake, could turn naming

a baby griffin into a trap."

"It's not a trap—just a reminder of your true nature, Your Majesty." This time, there was no mockery when he called her by her title. "Now, I suggest you go back in there and act like the queen your father raised you to be—something about strength and courage."

Why does he have to have such an irresistible smile? Kandide thought. *And his eyes—they really are almost as gorgeous as mine.* "All right, Jake, let's just say that I tell everyone about my wing and they accept me. What can I do here if I stay? I have no healing gift. I can't carve or sew. I don't even know how to cook or weave."

"No, I don't suppose you do." Jake thought for a minute. "But you are a very brave queen, and that's pretty special. I suggest you go back in there and . . . well, why not be a queen?"

"You mean here, in the Veil?"

"Why not? We don't have one."

"Do you need one?" Kandide looked puzzled. "It seems to me that this place runs quite well on its own."

"That's true. And I don't think we need someone to rule, exactly. No one here is very good at being ordered around. But we could use a queen to . . . well, let's see, to represent us. Maybe someday, Kandide, you might even be able to convince the High Council that we're not worthless."

Maybe, she thought, slightly embarrassed by her earlier behavior. "Do you think, Jake, that this is my destiny—and that's what Father meant by serving *all* Fée?"

"I don't know," he answered. "But if anyone can do it, it's you, Kandide."

"If you really think so, perhaps then, I will be your queen." She set the baby griffin next to Gertie. With all the majesty she could muster, Kandide walked back to the Great Hall.

The moment the crowd saw her, they began clapping and shouting. "Kandide. Kandide. Kandide."

Standing just inside the doorway that led to Hall, she suddenly spotted Leanne, who was cheering the loudest. *My own kingdom hates me, but Leanne—she's even happy I'm back—after the way I . . .*

Jake took Kandide's arm and led her to the stairway in the front of the room. "Let's go up a few steps so everyone can hear you," he whispered. "And remember, strength and courage." He walked by her side as they reached the landing, midway up the stairs.

Kandide hesitated before speaking. The more she paused, the louder the cheering became. She wasn't sure what to say—only that whatever it was, it had to be the truth. "There's something I must tell you," she called out, quieting the cheers. "My sister, Tara, is Calabiyau's queen now. I was sent away. I'm an Imper—" She closed her eyes and swallowed hard. "An Im—" She couldn't quite say the word, but that didn't mean she couldn't show them. She let the cape slide off her shoulders and braced herself for the laugher to come. She could feel her body tensing.

But there was no laughter. No one jeered or hissed. She opened her eyes. All were sitting there attentively, waiting for her to continue. "I would like to stay here—and I think I can be of some help. It would be my pleasure to serve all of you."

Again, cheers broke out. Everyone stood up, applauding.

One young Fée called out, "Will you be our queen? We don't have one."

"Will you consider it, Your Majesty?" Leanne called out.

Kandide's eyes filled with tears. The sudden realization that everyone in that room had experienced exactly what she had gone through, swept through her thoughts. With true humility, perhaps for the first time in her life, she responded with a deep curtsy. "I would be honored—and promise to never order anyone to do anything—except maybe Jake." She winked at him, flashing a flirtatious smile.

The crowd went wild with laughter and applause. Selena joined Kandide and Jake on the landing, and finally quieted everyone down. "I suggest we prepare a feast to honor Her Majesty—the Veil's first queen." Again, cheers rang out.

Kandide felt a tug at the hem of her dress. She looked down to see Courage. The tiny cub pulled at her dress again. His golden eyes looked up at her like a child waiting to embark on a magical adventure. She reached down and picked him up. "Meet the newest member of the Veil," she told the crowd. "Well, the second newest, anyway. I guess I'm the newest. His name is Courage, because sometimes that's what we all need."

"Long live Queen Kandide. Long live Queen Kandide," the crowd began to chant.

Gertie let out an approving howl as she pushed her way through the assemblage and loped up the stairs to sit at Kandide's side. It was hard to tell who seemed more majestic— the mother griffin or Kandide. Crumpled wing or not, the Veil's new queen had never felt so beautiful or more perfect.

The glow from the Gift of the Frost radiated from inside her like an aura of shimmering platinum.

For the first time since the accident, Kandide felt a sense of deep inner peace. *Perhaps I have found a home,* she thought, slowly pulling her cape back up around her shoulders. *I shall serve all Fée, and someday Mother will see how much everyone here appreciates me for who I am—a hero. Then she'll be proud of me, as well.*

"May the earthly spirits protect you, my son."
Tiyana lifted her hand to gesture for him
to transport, then hesitated.

TWENTY-SIX

Tara sat on a swing woven from morning glories that hung from the exposed cedar beams in Tiyana's private antechamber. It was her favorite place to sit while chatting with her mother. She loved the bright purple flowers that blossomed on the dark green vines that entwined to support its soft upholstered seat.

This morning, however, she sat unusually quiet and still. Her stomach had an uneasy feeling. *Maybe I shouldn't let Teren go alone,* she thought, sitting there silently watching Tiyana adjust the straps on her brother's backpack. *Maybe Lord Revên is right. Teren is hardly more than a boy, even if he is almost as tall as I am.*

"Are you sure that you have everything?" Tiyana pulled the last strap on his backpack a bit tighter, then tied the loose end in a half-knot around the main strap.

"Yes, Mother," he replied for at least the tenth time. "You worry way too much."

"Or not enough." Tara slid out of the swing and walked

over to him. "Maybe we aren't worrying enough."

"Listen to your sister," Tiyana told him. "As far as I know, your father and I are the only ones who have ever returned from the Mists. Please believe me, Teren, when I say that the land surrounding Selena's cottage is very dangerous."

"I believe you, Mother. But you know I have to go. I won't let you risk your life deploying the Frost."

Tiyana fidgeted with his vest and collar. Just yesterday, it seemed, he was a little boy. "Maybe you should take guards."

"You know I can't." Teren threw up his hands. "You told us no one else can know about the Veil. Besides, Kandide might think she's being forced by the Council to return. Then she'll never come back. You know how she is. Anyway, I have my magic." He snapped his fingers and a pocketknife floated from a side table into his hand. With a flick of his wrist, it twirled around and then landed inside his right vest pocket.

With a loud sigh, Tiyana relented. "Very well then, but please, be extremely wary. There's a big difference between parlor tricks and using your Talent to be safe."

"Mother's right, Teren. Promise me you will transport right back here at the first sign of danger. Promise?"

"I promise." Frustration crept into his voice. *When are they going to stop thinking of me as a kid? I'm a prince and a mage.* He snapped his fingers again and the knife flew back into his hand. "I do know the difference, you know."

"Good, then take your father's sword and use this talisman if you are in any danger." Tiyana placed a small glowing orb, suspended from a golden chain, around his neck. "Should you need help, twist it three times clockwise, and I will be able to find you." She hugged her son.

He hugged her back, then strapped Toeyad's sword around his waist. "I'll be fine, Mother, don't worry. I love you."

"I love you, too. Remember, even though you are transporting, the journey will take several hours. The Mists are nearly a thousand hectares across, and the Veil sits at the extreme edge. May the earthly spirits protect you, my son." Tiyana lifted her hand to gesture for him to transport, then hesitated.

"It's getting late, Mother." Teren could barely contain his impatience. "The sun's already awake. Just send me there. I'll be all right. And from what you tell me, Selena will make sure of it."

Tara took her mother's hand. "Time is growing short, Mother. If Teren is going to go, you need to send him there now."

Tiyana knew she was right, and with a gesture, Teren vanished in a glimmer of yellow light.

"He'll be fine. I promise." Tara squeezed her mother's hand.

"Will he?" Tiyana's voice took on a bitter edge. "I hadn't realized that predicting the future was one of your Talents."

"It . . . it's not," Tara stammered. She'd never heard her mother speak that way. "I'm sorry. I just—"

Tiyana sat down on the arm of her favorite chair. "No, it is I who should apologize. Forgive me, Tara. The last thing you need right now is a mother who's lost control of her emotions. I'm just so afraid for Teren. I don't have any idea of what he may face in the Mists. And after losing your father and then Kandide . . ."

"I know." Tara walked over and put her arm around her

mother. All she could think of was how much Tiyana had been through these past few weeks. "But remember, Teren actually is a pretty powerful mage—even if he does use most of his magic for silly tricks. He's not really all that helpless."

Tara sounded as if she was trying to convince herself, as much as her mother. She looked out Tiyana's large beveled glass window at the pink and gold sky. The sun had pushed well past the horizon. "Teren's right about one thing, it is getting late. The Council will be in session soon and who knows what they'll be arguing about this time? I'd better go see."

With a gesture, Tara also vanished.

Jake's green eyes lit up with excitement. "You know, that just might work! What do you think, Egan?"

TWENTY-SEVEN

"So, what do you think, Kandide?" Jake held up a perfectly formed set of brown and gold wings that were shaped like those of a Monarch butterfly. They were standing in a large workroom off to the side of the château where Jake had been experimenting with different types of mechanical extremities, including arms, hands, and legs.

"I think they're quite preposterous." Kandide took the wings from him. "The color and shape are good, but they're way too heavy. How did you make them?"

"The spiders spin their silk in the shape we want. But that isn't durable enough by itself."

"So we tried dipping them in oak resin." Egan, the wingless young Fée for whom the wings were being created, spoke up. "That's what makes them so heavy."

"Next we tried a sugar solution," Jake continued.

"Sugar?" Kandide questioned.

"Yeah, and it was perfect, at least until it got wet. Poor Egan landed right in the lake." Jake started chuckling as he related how funny it was to see Egan's wings melt away, leaving him thrashing about in the water.

"That's terrible!" Kandide tried to stifle a giggle at the thought of wings melting.

"It wasn't funny!" the young Fée protested. With his slightly turned-up nose, big blue eyes, and honey-colored hair, he looked more huggable than indignant. "I could have drowned, you know!"

Born without wings, Egan had lived in the Mists since he was a baby. He was still quite young, no more than six in human years. He knew little more of his parents than which clans they belonged to, but that didn't stop him from taking pride in his heritage.

"Egan is of the Earth and Fire Clans," Jake explained, "and water is definitely not his favorite thing. He even avoids stepping across puddles. And since he can't fly, he's been known to walk for hours to avoid crossing the lake—even in a boat."

"My mother's clan doesn't swim," Egan insisted. "Fire and water don't go together."

"Well, in that case," Kandide looked down at him and smiled, "we really do need to solve this wing problem. I have an idea. There is a very old finish called shellac. It's light, can be thinned, dries hard, and won't melt when it gets wet."

"But it's made from little beetles!" Egan was aghast at the thought.

"That's right." Kandide nodded.

"My father's clan protects beetles. They eat the dead trees to make the soil better. I could never kill a beetle just so

I could fly!"

"We respect all life here," Jake explained, "no matter how small or seemingly insignificant."

"You're more like my father than you know, Jake. He, too, would never allow any creature to be sacrificed for his indulgence." Turning to Egan, Kandide reassured him, "Then we shall just have to find something else. Tell me, how do you make the prototypal wings flap?"

"Well, that's another problem we had to solve," Jake explained. "It's not perfect, but Egan moves his shoulder muscles back and forth, not unlike the way real wings work. Show her, Egan."

The young Fée demonstrated the motion with a wide back and forth motion of both shoulders.

"He can't fly as far as he would with normal wings, but at least he won't have to walk around puddles or the lake," Jake teased.

Kandide thought back for a moment, remembering her alchemy classes during her final-school training. She had never been particularly good at mixing solutions because she could never imagine that she would ever have to do as such. But now . . . "I have it! What would happen if you mixed sugar with a diluted solution of oak resin? The sugar will provide the stiffness, and the thinned sap might just be enough to seal it—so the wings won't melt."

Jake's green eyes lit up with excitement. "You know, that just might work! What do you think, Egan?"

"Maybe. Can you ask the spiders to spin a new pair so we can try it? Can you, Jake? Can you?"

"You bet." He walked over to a perfectly formed large web in the corner of the workroom. A blue spotted spider was putting the finishing touches on it. Jake clucked a few sounds, and several more spiders appeared. With few more clucking sounds, they immediately got to work spinning wings.

"And while they're doing that," Kandide looked straight at Egan, "I'm going to teach you how to swim."

"Oh, no you're not!" He started to back away. "I'm not going anywhere near that lake, ever again!"

Kandide reached for his hand to stop him from running off. "Grab his other hand, Jake. Egan is going to get a swimming lesson."

"Let me go! Let me go!" Egan protested, dangling between the two of them as they headed toward the lake.

Finding a quiet spot on a large rock near the edge of the water, Jake and Kandide finally released the squirming young Fée. Not, however, before Kandide evoked a promise from him not to leave.

"You won't throw me in?" he asked, eyeing both of them with extreme skepticism.

"No, Egan," she promised, "we won't." Kandide looked over at Jake, and then motioned toward the water. "Shall we?"

"Dressed like that?" He gestured to her overly formal clothes. "Allow me." With a flick of his wrist, both she and Jake were instantly wearing bathing attire. His was bright green, and hers was soft pink and sparkled like a thousand dewdrops. "That's better," he told her. "Just don't wear it in the ocean."

"Why not?"

"You'll make the mermaids jealous," he teased.

"And so they should be," she replied, striking a pose. "You don't look so bad, yourself." *Those shoulder muscles didn't come from sitting around playing chess,* she thought.

Watching the two of them, Egan scrunched up his face in disgust. "Are you going swimming, or do I have to sit here and listen to you all day? We have work to do on my wings, you know."

"You're right, Egan." Kandide agreed. "But first Jake has to tell me how he made our clothes change like that."

"Would you like a different color?" Jake flicked his wrist again and her bathing suit turned bright blue. "What do you think?"

Glancing down at it, she shook her head. "It's nice, but I think I prefer the other one."

"Me too." With yet another flick of his wrist, her suit turned back to pink.

"Thank you." Kandide really did like the pink suit better. The tiny dewdrops sparkled in the bright sunlight. They reminded her of early mornings in the Meadows when the dew had not yet evaporated from the flowers. "Now tell me how you did it—and promise me, Jake, that you'll never change my clothes again without my permission."

"It could be kind of interesting," he teased. "Just imagi—"

"You wouldn't dare!" Kandide looked horrified at the thought.

"Well, I mean . . . just imagine being at a ball and your gown changes color for every dance," he grinned.

"Jake!"

"Okay, I promise."

"So, how did you do it?" Egan spoke up.

"It's a little spell Trump taught me. Those Banshees are pretty clever."

"So, teach it to us," Kandide insisted.

"I will, but you have to catch me first." Jake dove into the water.

Kandide dove in after him. Coming up for air, she called out to Egan, "We won't be long."

The lake was cool and crystal clear, fed by mountain springs. Together, they swam to a tiny island not far from the shore, where Kandide immediately started a water fight.

"Follow me," Jake called, before diving underwater to avoid a carefully aimed splash. He led her through a spectacular underwater tunnel filled with freshwater coral, neon-colored fish, and graceful plants that grew in astonishing shades of turquoise, purple, and pink. They effortlessly swam through it to the opening on the other side. There, surrounded by steep, towering red rock cliffs, was a natural limestone pool with steaming hot water.

"What is this place?" Kandide asked, looking from jagged cliff to jagged cliff.

"It's a hot spring that's heated by underwater volcanic activity. Leanne says the water has healing powers."

"The warmth does feel good on my wing. It still aches sometimes."

"I'm sure it must, though I've never heard you complain."

"Well, you will if you don't bring me back here again—and soon! It's so beautiful."

"Almost as beautiful as you, Kandide." Jake's eyes reflected the sunlit ripples in the water. He reached out to touch her cheek, and her whole body tingled. But as he leaned closer to kiss her, she turned away.

"I've never been k . . . to a place like this before." Talking about where they were was far easier than talking about her feelings for him. "We shouldn't leave Egan alone for too long."

With a schoolgirl grin, she slapped her hand on the water, splashing Jake squarely in the face. He started to return the deed, but Kandide quickly dove beneath the surface. Coming up for air just in front of the underwater tunnel, she called, "I bet I can beat you back!"

"Think so? You're on!" The two of them began to race. Back through the tunnel and around the island they swam. While Jake could easily have beaten Kandide, chivalry dictated that he let her win—not, however, by very much.

"You didn't even try," she called out, arriving at the shore just a few strokes ahead.

"Oh, yes I did." He winked. "You just swam way too fast!" He took her hand and softly kissed it. "Why, Kandide, is that a blush I see?"

"Don't be silly!" She quickly turned her attention to Egan. "Come on in," she called, splashing him with water.

"I don't think so." Egan darted away to avoid getting wet.

"Oh, come on. You could be the first in either of your clans to learn to swim." Kandide spoke in her most encouraging tone.

"I could?"

"Absolutely." Jake nodded.

"Do you think I really can?" Egan was not at all sure about learning to swim, but the thought of being the first to do anything definitely appealed to him.

"Why not?" Jake replied. "Come on, we'll hold on to you." He flicked his wrist, and Egan found himself in bright orange swimming trunks. "You're already dressed for it."

"O-okay. I mean, maybe." Egan cautiously approached the edge of the lake. With a great deal more coaxing, he finally put one toe in the water, and then just as quickly pulled it out. "It's so . . . so . . . wet!" he objected.

"It certainly is." Kandide scooped up some water and let it pour from her hand. "That's why it's called water. Come on in. I won't let you drown."

Slowly, very slowly, Egan tiptoed into the lake, hesitating at every step.

"It's okay, I'll hold on to you." Jake reached out and took his hands. "Now lean forward and just relax. Keep your head up. See, you're already floating."

"I am!" With Jake's hand under his stomach, Egan was, indeed, floating.

"Okay, paddle your arms and kick your feet." Kandide moved his arms to show him how. "See, now you're swimming." For a moment, her thoughts flashed back to Teren. He was about Egan's age when she taught him to swim. "I think you're a natural, Egan. Even better than my brother, and he's part Water Clan."

Jake, with his hand still under Egan's stomach, turned him back toward the shore. "And I think that you've had a really good first lesson."

"So do I." Kandide helped the young Fée out of the water.

"Do you really think I'm better than Prince Teren was,

Kandide?"

"I do. Want to come back tomorrow for another lesson?"

"Really? Can we, Jake?"

"If Kandide says so."

"I may insist. But right now, let's go see about those wings." She smoothed Egan's dripping wet hair away from his face. "Here, better dry off." With a snap of her fingers, a fluffy white towel appeared, and she handed it to him. She snapped her fingers again, and two more towels appeared.

"Holding out on me, are you?" Jake whisked one of them from her and began drying his hair. "So, you teach me that spell and I'll teach you mine." With a flick of his wrist, Kandide was immediately dressed in the clothes she was originally wearing.

"It's a deal. Now, can you do something with my hair?" She shook her head, flinging lake water everywhere.

Jake ducked beneath the spray. "Sorry, I've never learned any styling spells."

"Then it should be next on your list." Kandide snapped her towel at him.

Dodging a direct hit, Jake grinned. "Of course, Your Majesty." As their eyes met, it was his turn to blush.

*Teren's arm flew back up—his fingers on one hand
were aimed toward the four garglans on his right,
and the fingers on his other hand
were aimed at the three on his left.*

TWENTY-EIGHT

Materializing in the middle of the dense, misty forest, Teren was not at all sure which way to turn. Gnarled and tangled vines covered almost every inch of open space. Although the sun was high in the sky, the dead tree branches were so thick that they shut out most of the light. *It's like a place of death around here,* Teren thought as he stood there not wanting to move. *Okay, now that's really getting carried away. Stay calm and remember what Mother said. The Veil is right around here somewhere.*

Teren's eyes scanned the forest as he tried to gather his courage. "She told me it could be dangerous, but she sure didn't say it was going to be this creepy," he whispered aloud. "I wonder which way I'm supposed to go." Taking a step forward, he slipped, landing flat on his bottom in the soggy under-marsh.

"I'm not sure either, but I think you'd better get up."

Teren whirled around. "Tara! What are you doing here?"

"You didn't think I was going to let you have all the fun, did you?"

"Does Mother know you followed me?"

"Not exactly." Tara held out her hand to help him up. "I was holding her wrist when she transported you, and I traced the coordinates."

"Where'd you learn to do that?" Teren brushed himself off.

"Maybe you should try actually reading some of those books in the Royal Library."

"Now wait a minu—"

"In any case, are you all right?" She looked him over.

"Yeah, but you won't be when we get back. Queen or not, Mom's going to kill you!"

"She may not have to." Tara grabbed Teren's arm and pulled him behind a tree. "Look!"

A hideous black form was standing not more that ten meters away. Its beady red eyes stared straight at her.

"Wha—what is it?" Teren stammered.

"A garglan, I think." The creature approached, creeping closer and closer. Its shrill hisses sent chills up and down Tara's spine. From working with the forest animals near her home, she knew when a creature was hungry, and this one looked as if it hadn't eaten in weeks. "I think we'd better go!"

"Where to?" Teren started to gesture.

"I'm not sure. This is exactly where Mother's coordinates sent you." Tara anxiously looked around. "The Veil must be here somewhere."

"We can't just transport to *somewhere*. Where do you want to go?"

"Let me think, okay?" Tara had no idea of where they should go.

"Well, while you figure it out, I think I can stop that thing." Teren mumbled a few magical words, then dramatically waved his hand in the air, pointing his finger directly at the beast. Instantly, the garglan froze. "There. Told you I could do it."

"I hope you can handle two of them!" Tara spotted a second garglan leap out from behind an old log. It was also madly hissing, and looked hungrier than the first.

"Sure I can. I think." Teren turned to point at the second garglan. But as he did, his finger left the first beast, and it shook free of the spell. Hissing even louder, its leathery bat-like wings flapped in the air.

"Uh. Teren, I think you—"

"Oops!"

"Oops?" Tara grabbed his hand and aimed it back at the first garglan. "What do you mean 'Oops'? Can you do this or not?"

"I've only tried it once on Kandide, and that was a game."

"Well, little brother, this is no game!"

She's right about that, he thought, standing with his arms spread and fingers pointing, one at each garglan. "I can do it, Tara." *At least I hope I can.*

"Then you'd better find some more fingers. Look over there!" She felt a rush of air, as another huge garglan flew onto a tree branch just a few meters away, hissing and snarling. Its pink tongue dangled out of one side of its mouth and slimy drool dripped down the other side.

"Got it!" Teren shouted. No sooner was that garglan frozen, than another garglan flew directly at Tara.

"Teren!" she screamed; then dropped to the ground.

The garglan's razor-sharp claws barely missed the side of her face. The creature howled in outrage, winging back around for a second chance at its prey. But Teren was faster. The beast, who had a wingspan of at least two meters, froze in mid-air, then plummeted to the ground.

"Thanks!" Tara quickly stood up. Her heart stopped as she heard a noise behind them. No more than a half dozen meters away, were three more of the hideous creatures. "How many more of these things are there?"

"I don't know, but that's seven. And after ten you're on your own." Moving his hands so that a finger pointed at each garglan, and muttering spells as fast as he could, Teren gasped for air.

"I need your sword." Tara dared not take her eyes off the beasts.

"Here." Teren started to lower his hand to give it to her.

"Stop!" she shouted. "Keep pointing! I'll get it."

Teren's arm flew back up—his fingers on one hand were aimed toward the four garglans on his right, and the fingers on his other hand were aimed at the three on his left. But it wasn't enough. The winged silhouettes of five more garglans appeared in the black fog. Their red eyes grew brighter and brighter as they crept closer.

"That's twelve," he whispered hoarsely. "And I don't have that many fingers." He quickly froze three of five. Stunned, the other two garglans sniffed at their frozen buddies.

"Over there!" Tara shouted. But before Teren could turn his head to see, a huge wolf leapt from the trees, landing directly in front of them.

"Ni— ni— nice boy," she stammered. Cautiously, Tara held out her hand for the animal to sniff. She had healed wolves before in the forests near her home. This place, however, was quite a different matter. She'd never seen a wolf so large.

Snarling and growling, the wolf lunged, not at her, but at the two garglans that weren't frozen. From deep within its throat came a loud ferocious howl. Three more wolves appeared. With fangs bared, they began to snap and snarl at the beasts in an attempt to keep them at bay.

"What do we do now?" Teren asked.

"Just keep your fingers pointed—and don't stop mumbling that spell. I think the wolves are our friends."

"I think we could use some right about now. My arms are getting awfully tired."

"Yeah, well, they're going to have a long time to rest if you don't keep pointing."

With sword in hand, and the wolves guarding her, Tara cautiously approached one of the frozen garglans. Normally, she couldn't bear to hurt any animal. *But these creatures,* she decided, *are a different matter.* Holding tightly with both hands to the hilt of the sword, she swung it in a smooth powerful arc. Her blade sliced cleanly through the garglan's neck.

"Oh, yuck!" Teren winced, as smelly black bile sprayed everywhere. "I think I'm going to be sick."

"Well, before you do . . ." Tara whirled around, just in time to see one of the garglans leap at the wolves. "Over there!"

"Got it!" He mumbled the spell again. "But remember, I'm back up to ten fingers."

"Just keep pointing."

"Just keep slashing."

Jake had just sat down to eat lunch on the outdoor terrace of the château's main dining hall. He nearly dropped the glass of cranberry juice he was holding, as a chilling, ferocious sound rang out. "That's Ari'!" He leapt to his feet. "Tori! Benji!" he called to the two Fée, who were seated a few tables away. "Come with me!"

They quickly followed Jake out of the hall, stopping only to grab their bows and arrows from the hall armory. Flying out of the château and over the gate, the three Fée headed toward the sound of the wolves.

At least Ari isn't alone, Jake thought as he heard other furious howls. He knew from their snarls, however, that the pack was in a desperate fight.

"Over there!" Benji shouted, pointing off to the left. He could barely see what was happening through the heavy mist. "It looks like a bunch of garglans have two Fée surrounded."

"Get closer, then release your arrows on my command," Jake ordered as they swooped through the fog. "And make them count. I don't know what is going on, but I've never seen so many garglans at once." He notched his arrow and took aim at the one crouched in a tree. "Ready, fire at will!" Jake watched his arrow blaze through the air. The huge beast drooped to the ground with an arrow penetrating its chest.

Tara and Teren looked toward the sky.

"Up there!" Tara pointed to the three Fée hovering overhead, then turned and slashed her blade through another frozen garglan's neck.

That's one brave girl, Jake thought as he watched her wield the sword. Notching another arrow, he easily killed another of the beasts.

"That's three for three," Benji called as the garglan he shot at dropped to the ground with an arrow through its heart.

"Make it four." Tori quickly released his arrow and it, too, streaked through the air, easily taking out another garglan. "Looks like the boy is using some kind of spell to freeze them."

"Yeah, well not that one." Jake spotted a garglan flying toward Ari. He unleashed his arrow. The garglan howled as it plummeted to the ground. Ari looked up. Seeing Jake, he barked a quick "thank you" before lunging at another of the hideous beasts. The creature's claws were dug into a female wolf's back.

Tara whirled around to see them and screamed. The garglan looked over at her and hissed. It was all the distraction Ari needed. He tore open the beast's throat. Oily black slime sprayed everywhere.

One by one, the garglans fell. Black ooze dripped from the last remaining creature as it screeched, and then ran off in a fit of madness. Jake's arrow had gone straight through its shoulder. Another well-placed shot put the beast out of its misery.

Benji, Tori, and Jake landed in the center of the curious menagerie. The stench burnt their nostrils, but the two strangers and all of the wolves were safe. Ari pranced over and licked Jake's hand.

"Thank you, boy!" Jake rubbed the wolf's head. "Good job!" He turned to the two Fée. "I'm Jake. This is Tori and Benji."

"And I'm very grateful." Tara replied, placing the sword back in Teren's sheath.

"Then, welcome, Very Grateful," Jake teased, then turned his attention to Teren. "And you are?"

"I'm her brother, Teren." His arms were still raised and his fingers extended, as if ready to cast more spells.

"Hello, Teren." Jake nodded to him. "I think it's safe to put your arms down."

"Oh! Right" He quickly lowered them and rubbed his wrists.

"Might I ask what you and 'Very Grateful' are doing out here in the Mists?" Jake looked from one to the other.

"My name is Tara," she answered, her tone polite but regal. Pulling a handkerchief out of her side pocket, she wiped black slime from her face and neck.

"Tara?" Jake looked at her more closely. "Her Majesty Queen Tara?" He and the other two Fée quickly bowed.

"Yes, and we've come to find our sister, Princess Kandide. Have you seen her? Do you know where she is?"

"Kandide?" Jake sounded hesitant. "What do you want with her?"

Teren eyes brightened. "You know her? Is she all right?"

"She's fine. But why are you looking for her, if I might ask?"

"My sister holds the Gift of the Frost," Tara explained. "And until she deploys it, the seasons can't change."

"I thought it was unusually warm." Jake rubbed his neck. "Kandide has the Gift? Of course, from your father."

"That's right. We're here to take her home with us." Teren picked up his backpack and slung it over his shoulder.

"Take her home?" Those weren't exactly the words Jake wanted to hear.

"If she doesn't return to the castle, our mother may die." Tara's lack of patience was beginning to show. "Please, if you know where she is, Jake, you must take us to her."

"As you wish, but first I need to do something." Jake walked over to the injured female wolf. Her back was bleeding from the where the garglan's claws had ripped through the flesh. "We'll need to take her back with us so Leanne can heal her."

"Perhaps I can help." Tara walked over and knelt down by the wolf. In a soft voice, she began speaking directly to the brave animal. "Hi, girl. Thank you for helping us." She held out her hand and the wolf licked her fingers.

"Your cuts look pretty bad," Tara told her. "Without treatment, I'm afraid they won't heal. May I help you?"

The beautiful silver-grey animal nodded her head.

"Good. It won't take but a few minutes." Tara held her hands just above the gashes on her back. Silver strands of light began flowing from her fingertips. The wolf's skin started to glow. As it did, the wounds slowly knitted back together until there was no trace at all of the injury.

"There, you're good as new!" Tara petted the she-wolf, who barked a thank you. "Is everyone else okay?" She looked at the other wolves. Ari also gazed around, and then barked once.

"That's good. Will they come with us, Jake?"

"No," he answered. "We've tried to get them to live inside the gates, but they prefer it out here."

With a low, guttural sound, Ari called to his pack. As quickly as they had appeared, the wolves bounded off into the black fog.

Tara turned to Jake. "Now, if you'll be so kind as to take us to my sister. We only have three days."

"And getting her to return," Teren added, "may not be all that easy."

"That is ridiculous, Kandi, and you know it!"
Tara scolded.

TWENTY-NINE

"This is amazing!" Teren exclaimed. He and Tara followed Jake into the neatly manicured courtyard just in front of the château. As Tori and Benji headed off toward the armory, Teren stood transfixed, staring up at what had to be the most spectacular palace he'd ever seen. Its matching gold towers blazed in the sunlight. The intricately designed stained glass windows shone like a kaleidoscope of jewel tones. And the gardens—he'd never seen so many types and colors of exotic flowers and botanicals. "This is nothing like what Mother described."

"It certainly isn't," Tara agreed as they approached the château's main entrance. "We thought it was going to be a little cottage." She looked up to see her mother's twin standing on the steps that led up to the elaborately carved front doors. "Aunt Selena?"

"Tara? Teren? May the spirits rejoice; can it really be you?" She rushed out to meet them. "I don't believe my eyes." Selena looked them up and down. The two siblings were splattered with black slime, but didn't seem to be injured in any way. "Goodness, are you all right?"

"We're fine, Aunt Selena." Tara gave her aunt a hug. "It's so wonderful to see you. Mother told us all about the Veil."

"Yeah, but she didn't say it would be anything like this." Teren looked around, still in awe of what he was seeing.

"I guess it has changed quite a bit from the days when Tiyana used to visit. Do come inside." Selena and Jake led the way into the Receiving Hall. "My, how grown up you both are," she continued. "And you, Teren, your smile is exactly like your father's. You must tell me what is going on in Calabiyau. First Kandide appears, and now the two of you."

"That's why we're here," Tara explained. "We need to talk to Kandide."

"I'll go fetch her," Jake offered, and then headed off.

"I think she and Egan are in your workshop," Selena called after him. "Please, do be seated." She motioned for Tara and Teren to sit on a pair of bright blue settees. "So tell me, I'm sure you both have missed your sister, but that's hardly a reason to brave the Mists. What's happened in Calabiyau since Tiyana sent Kandide to me?"

"It's the Gift." Tara told her aunt, explaining what was going on.

In Jake's workshop, Kandide and Egan were carefully applying the sugar and oak resin solution onto the young Fée's new wings. The two of them looked up as he walked in. Kandide couldn't quite make out the expression on his face. "Is everything all right out there?" she asked. "When I went down for lunch, Selena told me you had left in a big hurry. Ari's okay, isn't he?"

"He's fine. I have a surprise for you."

"A surprise? What is it? Not another baby griffin?"

"No. Your sister and brother are here."

"What?" Kandide's jaw dropped. "Tara and Teren are here?" She quickly pulled the protective apron off and set it on the counter.

"Yes. They want you to return home with them."

"They want me to go back to Calabiyau? That's wonderf—" She stopped short, glancing back at her crumpled wing. "No. I can't go back. At least not now." She looked at Egan, who nodded in agreement.

"Kandide, I think it's important."

"So is the work we do here, Jake."

"You must at least see them."

"Well, of course, I'm going to see them. I'm excited they're here. What I meant was, I'll not be leaving. How did they find me, anyway?"

"Tiyana sent them."

Why would Mother send them? Kandide thought, feeling a ripple of worry. "Is something wrong?"

"I'll let Tara explain."

"Egan, spray one more light coat of the oak resin on your wings," she told the young Fée. "Then let it dry. I'll be back later and we can try them."

Kandide and Jake hurried out of the workshop and down the hallway to meet her brother and sister. "Do I look all right, Jake?" She paused for a minute and straightened the collar of her tailored blue blouse before entering the Receiving Room.

"You look perfect. Would you like me to come in with you?"

"Yes, please." *Maybe he can tell them how important I am here,* she thought, *and why I can't leave.* Looking as radiant as ever, Kandide walked through the arched doorway.

"Kandi!" Tara jumped to her feet and rushed over to her sister. "Oh, Kandi, you're okay."

"Teren, Tara . . . I mean, Your Majesty, it's wonderful to see you." Kandide tried to contain the broad smile that crossed her face, but she just couldn't. She threw her arms around her sister. "I'm so glad to see you. And you, too, Teren." She gave her brother a hug, as well, and then stepped back, realizing that something dark and slimy had just stained her own brocade sleeve. Kandide glanced at it, then at his disheveled clothing. "Looks like you met some of our gatekeepers."

"Yeah, we took care of them, though," Teren replied a bit smugly.

"Especially after a wolf named Ari and his friends showed up," Tara added. "Oh, Kandi, we've missed you so." She hugged her sister again. "You should be queen, not me."

"No, the crown of Calabiyau is yours. The Veil is my home now. I'm its queen."

"What? Really?" Tara looked over at Jake. "You never said a word about that!"

Jake shrugged. "Well, I . . . I thought Kandide should tell you."

"And so I did. Please, let's sit down." Kandide walked over to a pair of yellow and white settees in front of the large picture window that looked out onto the front gardens. "Jake tells me that Mother sent you to find me?"

"She did." Teren sat next to his aunt. "And we need you to come back with us."

"You know I can't go back, Teren. And even if I could, I'm not sure I would. As Jake and Selena will attest, I'm loved and appreciated here for who I am, not just because I'm beautiful—or perfect."

"Oh, Kandi, I love you, too." Tara sat next to her sister on the sofa. "And so does Mother, and so does Teren. We all love you just the way you are."

"And we definitely appreciate you," Teren added. "But you have to come back. Mother may die if she tries to change the seasons."

"What? Mother can't change the seasons. I'm the only one who can do that."

"She thinks she can, at least this once," Tara explained. "The Council will force her to use the small amount of the Gift that Father gave her if you don't return—and that could take all her strength."

"The Council can't force Mother to do that. Besides, Father didn't give her nearly enough of the Gift to trigger the Frost. Even Lady Aron must know that." Kandide's answer held a curious indifference that surprised even Tara. "Do have some shortbread." She lifted up the bright blue plate that was sitting on the table in front of them and offered a piece to her brother.

Teren ignored the offer. "Don't you care?"

"Of course I care." Kandide set the plate back down a little too hard. "It's just that, well, it was Mother who sent me away. I know she blames me for hastening Father's passing. And that she's ashamed of me now because of my wing."

"That is ridiculous, Kandi, and you know it!" Tara scolded. "Mother sent you here to be safe. She knew Selena would take care of you. Isn't that right, Selena?"

"Of course that's why Tiyana sent you here, Kandide," Selena answered.

"It was the only thing she could do." Teren was as adamant as his aunt and sister.

"No it wasn't." Kandide's voice was cold. "Mother could have upheld my crowning. If Father were alive, he would never have let this happen. When Jake was injured, Father told him he could stay at the castle, didn't he, Jake?"

Standing off to the side, Jake chose his words carefully. He had a feeling that no matter how he answered, it might make things worse. "What you say is true, Kandide. King Toeyad did tell me I could stay, but I don't believe the Council would have ever let it happen."

"Think about it, Kandi." Tara placed her hand on top of her sister's. "Even with all of Father's support, he couldn't have persuaded the High Council to let you assume the throne—not as long as Lady Aron has a say. You know how hard it is to change the old ways, and you also know that the Council vote must be unanimous to amend the Articles."

Kandide slid her hand away and began twisting her braid around her finger. "Then why didn't Mother tell me about the Veil before she sent me—?"

"There wasn't any time!" Teren cut her off. "Mother was afraid for your life. You saw how fast that crowd turned against you. It was the only thing she knew to do at that moment."

"Please, Kandi, you have to return with us." Tara was practically begging.

"You'd do well to listen to your sister," Selena advised.

Ignoring her, Kandide picked up a piece of shortbread and took a small bite. "You both really should taste this. Margay's recipe is amazing." She offered the plate of biscuits first to Tara, then to her brother.

Hungry as he was, Teren wasn't sure if he should take a piece or throw the entire tray at his sister. "Mother could die," he said, emphasizing each word. "Don't you understand that, Kandide?"

"Now you're being silly, Teren. As I just said, the Council can't make her do it. When you get back, tell them that I absolutely will deploy the Gift—when I'm ready to do so. But for now, I am quite happy with the way things are." Kandide smiled at her brother, as if she'd just solved the problem, and then abruptly changed the subject. "Why don't I take you on a tour of the grounds?"

"We really don't have much time." Tara bit back her anger. "Teren had to promise Lady Aron that he'd be back in three days—by Solstice." *I can't believe we're even having this conversation*, she thought.

"Three days? Oh, well, then there's plenty of time." Kandide picked up the blue plate again. "Have some shortbread, and then I'll show you around."

"I don't think you understand." Tara stood up. Her checks were flushed with frustration. "While you're eating cookies, our subjects are worried that they may starve. If winter is delayed, then spring will be, too. If they can't plant crops, they won't have food."

Kandide reached out and took her sister's hands. "Now, Tara, you know I'd never let that happen. I've taken an oath to deploy the Frost, and so I shall—sooner or later." She also stood up. "So, would you like to see the gardens first or perhaps start with Jake's workroom? Wait until you see what we're doing."

She hasn't really changed one bit! Tara thought, at her wits end. *Somehow, we have to make her leave with us.* "All right, Kandi," she said at last. "We'll go on your tour. But only if you promise to return—and soon!"

"I promise I'll think about it. For now, however, I'm actually enjoying the warm weather. Aren't we, Jake?" She looked over at him.

He had been listening to the conversation with mixed emotions. He certainly didn't want her to leave, but could she really be as selfish as she seemed? Was this all meant to punish her mother? Jake was beginning to wonder if he knew her at all. It wasn't just Calabiyau Proper that would suffer. Without the Frost, all lands were in peril, including the Veil. "You really need to consider what Tara is saying," he told her.

Kandide reacted with more than a touch of indignation. "I said I would think about it, Jake, and I will." She turned back to her brother and sister. "Shall we go?"

"Can we at least wash this gunk off first?" Teren looked down at the spattered black slime all over his clothes.

"Oh, I can take care of that, can't I, Jake?" Kandide didn't wait for him to answer. "He taught me a wonderful new spell. I taught him one, too." She looked from her sister to her brother. "So, who's first?"

"What kind of spell?" Teren eyed her suspiciously.

"Let me show you." With a flick of Kandide's wrist, Teren was suddenly wearing an entirely different outfit. His green and gold vest changed into one that was dark burgundy with silver braid trim, and his stained brown trousers were now crisp and clean. Even his black boots looked new and shiny.

Teren looked at his clothes in amazement. "That's pretty good," he admitted. "Will you teach it to me, Jake?"

"Be happy too. But first, let's get Tara cleaned up."

Kandide flicked her wrist and Tara, as well, was instantly wearing fresh clean clothes. "I made you the same britches, shirt, and socks," Kandide told her sister. "Although it was tempting to put you in a dress."

"Don't press your luck, Kandi." Tara wasn't really in the mood for her sister's frivolity. "Nifty spells or not, I'm still pretty upset with you."

"Oh, Tara, relax. Let's go see the gardens. They're so beautiful right now. Are you coming, Selena?"

"You run along. I need to have rooms prepared for Tara and Teren."

"Okay." Kandide practically pulled her sister outside the château. With Teren and Jake following behind, they strolled through blue hydrangeas and stalks of lavender. Kandide veered off on a path that led to a smaller garden enclosed by a tall hedge. "This is one of the things I want to show you," she told Tara. "All of the plants and herbs here are for healing. I've never even heard of some of them." She spotted Leanne carrying a small basket full of green leaves from a lemon balm plant. "Leanne," Kandide called, walking over to her. "I want you to meet someone. Tara, Teren, come over here. This is my sister, Queen Tara."

"Queen Tara. It's an honor to meet you." Leanne curtsied.

"And you as well." Tara nodded to acknowledge her.

"And this is my brother, Teren," Kandide continued.

"It's a pleasure to meet you as well, Prince Teren. Your sister tells me that you are quite the mage."

"She did? Are you sure Kandide said that about me?"

"She did, indeed. And, Your Majesty, Selena tells me that your healing Talent is quite strong. Perhaps we can work together on Kandide's wing. It may take a number of sessions, but if we join our power, I'm sure we can help her."

"I would certainly love to try. First, however, perhaps you can help me convince my sister to return home to deploy the Frost."

"The Frost? So, that's why it's so warm this time of year," Leanne remarked. "It could also explain why the herbs are less potent this season—and flowers are appearing that shouldn't show up until spring. No wonder everything is confused. You must seriously consider returning, Kandide. It's quite late in the season already."

Ignoring her concerns, Kandide continued, "Leanne is blind, yet it doesn't stop her from doing exactly what she wants. Does it, Leanne?"

"I do my best. Nothing much stops your sister, either."

"You noticed," Teren muttered.

"Would you like to go to the lake with us, Leanne? Jake's coming, too."

"That's very kind of you to ask, Kandide, but I have several young Fée to attend to before supper. I was on my way to the clinic. There seems to be a terrible outbreak of scraped elbows today."

"Then we'll see you later." Grabbing Tara and Teren's hands, Kandide whisked the two of them away. "Come on, Jake. If we hurry, we can watch the sunset over the water."

Tara called back to Leanne, "Perhaps we can chat more over dinner?"

"That would be lovely, Your Majesty."

"Dinner, now that sounds like a great idea." Teren abruptly stopped. "I think we missed lunch. Come to think of it, we almost were lunch!"

"Don't remind me." Tara shivered at the thought.

"So, when's supper, Kandide? I'm starving!"

"Later, Teren. First the lake. Come on." Kandide grabbed his hand and they headed off.

Sitting on a large rock near the water, Tara gazed across the horizon. On one side of the lake were rolling hills with row after row of apple, pear, peach, apricot, cherry, and avocado trees that backed into the steepest mountains she'd ever seen. On the other side, vineyards and farmland stretched out as far as the eye could see. "It's really wonderful here," Tara told her sister. "I can see why you love it so much."

"And I've learned a great deal, as well." Kandide kicked off her shoes. Dangling her feet over the edge of the rock, she dipped them in the water. "You know the expression 'beauty is only skin deep'? Well, that's completely wrong. True beauty goes so much deeper."

If Tara hadn't been so frustrated, she would have been delighted that her sister seemed more accepting, at least in some regards. Now, however, she had to find a way to pull Kandide back to the subject that mattered—and the best way she knew to do that was to start with the subject she liked best—herself. "Look at your reflection in the water." Tara pointed at the mirror-like surface of the lake. "I've never seen you look more beautiful, Kandi."

"I know." She beamed, splashing water into the air with her toes.

Teren shook his head. *Kandide may have become more accepting*, he thought, *but she isn't any less vain.* "Did you know that Mother helped plant the original grapevines that grow here, Kandide?"

"She did?"

"With her own hands," he told her, surprised that Kandide admitted that he knew something she didn't. Was that progress?

"That she did, my child." Selena walked up to join them. "Your mother and I spent many a day getting those first cuttings started. Now just look at them."

"What worries, me, Aunt Selena," Tara looked out across the vineyard, "is that they still have their leaves. Those vines should be bare this time of the year."

"Tara is right, Kandide." Selena turned to speak to her eldest niece. "Not deploying the Frost affects everything."

"Is that why you came out here, to gang up on me?" Kandide crossed her arms. "Can't I just have a few minutes to enjoy the sunset?"

"Actually, I came out here to remind you that it's almost time for dinner. Are you hungry, Teren?"

"Starving!"

"Good. Shall we head back then?"

"Let's go!" Teren jumped to his feet.

As they all headed toward the château, Selena turned to Tara. "I think your father would have been so very proud of all we've accomplished. After the château was built, the lake was rechanneled to allow for watering the crops."

"Mother will be so happy to hear how very well you're doing. I know she misses you so much."

"I'm helping as well." Kandide caught up to them. "I'm making wings with Jake so Egan and Margay can fly."

"You're making wings?" Teren shook his head in disbelief. Kandide had never been known to make anything, unless it was another mirror to hang in the castle. He had to admit, however, that with just a wave of her hand, she could silver a piece of glass even better than the castle's finest mirrorsmiths.

"Come, I'll show you," Kandide lit up as she told her brother.

"But, Kandide." He stopped walking. "I'm hungry."

"Don't worry, little brother, Selena will hold dinner for us. Won't you, Selena?"

Her aunt looked at Teren, then at Tara and Jake and shrugged. "Some things will never change. Don't be too long."

"We won't." Kandide once again pulled her two siblings away. "We'll eat in a few minutes. And tomorrow we'll have a grand feast to celebrate your arrival. Then we'll discuss what to do about Mother and the Council, I promise. Right now, Jake and I are going to show you my idea."

"Kandide," Teren moaned.

"Did I tell you that we have a hot spring?"

"Can it boil a potato?"

Kandide regarded her aunt with suspicion.
"What do you mean?"

THIRTY

What a feast the morrow brought. Everyone drank from jewel-encrusted goblets that were filled with blueberry cider, rose lemonade, or sparkling white cherry juice. Teren stared at the tremendous silver platters that contained honey-dipped sweet potatoes, wild rice topped with acorn-stuffed mushrooms, fresh creamed rhubarb in a banana-lime sauce, and all types of other delicacies. He was determined to try everything.

Bright green avocados were tossed with cranberries, grapes, apples, mangoes, and pineapple to make a colorful salad. "This is the best I've ever tasted," Teren told Margay as he reached for a second helping.

"I'm pleased you're pleased, Prince Teren." Noticing an empty tray, Margay waved her large wooden cooking spoon, and another platter, this one piled high with whipped cream covered gooseberry crepes, magically floated in to replace it.

There were at least a dozen different fresh-baked breads,

cakes, and pies, plus nuts and berries the likes of which Teren and Tara had never seen. Baked pumpkin pudding topped with cinnamon, nutmeg, and cloves was served steaming hot. It smelled incredible and tasted even better. Twice, Tara returned to the great table lined with platters for more, and Teren had at least three helpings. Then he dove into the elaborately decorated marzipan candies and the dark chocolate swirls that were filled with almonds and purple cherries.

Neither sibling had ever been to a feast with so much incredible food, gaiety, and splendor. Tara's crowning party could not even begin to compare. Harpists and bards filled the great hall with music and wondrous stories—followed by dancing, juggling, acrobats, and magicians—then more delicious treats. Even Teren showed off a spell or two, much to the delight of the younger Fée. The feast lasted well into the wee hours of the morning.

Exhausted from so much dancing, Tara plopped down on the thickly upholstered green and purple chair next to her brother to catch her breath. "You know what's the most amazing thing about this place, Teren?" she whispered.

"The way my glass keeps magically refilling itself?" he answered, holding up his golden goblet. It was filled to the brim with a frothy blueberry cider.

"That is pretty amazing," she replied. "But I was just thinking—all of this splendor and happiness has been created by Fée who were discarded by their own, and sent away as though they were just so much rubbish."

"Yeah," he replied, "and if you look around, no one seems angry about it."

"I know." Tara scanned the crowded hall. "It doesn't matter if someone has two legs or none, is blind or missing an arm—they all just appreciate what they have."

"Well, I'd sure appreciate it if I could get the recipe for these chocolate-covered caramels." He popped a heart-shaped candy in his mouth. "Want the last one?"

"You can't be serious?" She held her stomach. "I don't think I'll ever eat again."

"Okay." He snapped his fingers, and the remaining piece flew off the tray and into his hand. "Good thing our chefs don't know how to make these. I'd be as big as Lady Batony!"

"Teren, that's not very nice. What happened to respecting everyone no matter what they look like?"

"I respect her. I do—crazy as she is sometimes." He helped himself to a candied ginger orange slice from a tray that floated past him. "These are really good, too."

"Everything's wonderful here. Why can't the rest of the world be like this?"

"I don't know." Teren sat his goblet down on the table next to them. "But maybe if Kandide can change—and she has, a little—there's hope for everyone else."

"Maybe. I just hope we'll be able to get her to return home tomorrow. I don't know what will happen if the Frost isn't deployed by the Winter Solstice, but it's not going to be good. You heard what Leanne said about the herbs. It's already affecting things I haven't even thought of." Tara watched her sister, who had been dancing all night—mostly with Jake.

Teren was also looking at Kandide. "I think she's in love with him."

"I think you're right. Maybe Jake can convince her to return with us."

"Maybe. It's not as if she can't come back here after deploying the Frost. Jake could even come along."

"That's a thought." Tara reached over and took a sip from Teren's goblet. "This cider is amazing."

"I know. My glass has refilled itself at least five times. Hey, maybe we could get Margay to come with us, too. She could teach our chefs some of her secrets."

"Not a bad idea." Tara took another sip of the cider. "Not that the castle chefs would ever listen to someone without wings."

"It's not fair, but I suppose you're right. Well, maybe Kandide could try deploying the Gift from here," Teren suggested. "It might work."

"You know it won't. The Frost can only be deployed from the castle."

"I wonder why?"

"I'm not exactly sure." Tara leaned forward and drew three intersecting lines on the table with her finger. "But I do know that's why the castle was built on that exact spot. It has to do with the convergence of the three lines of power that meet precisely at that point."

"Makes sense." Teren watched as his goblet, again, refilled itself. "So, I have another idea. If Kandide won't leave by tomorrow, I'll put a spell on her and we'll take her back that way."

"If all else fails, I certainly won't object. Do you think it could work?"

"It might." Teren stared at his open hand. A moment later, a tray of shortbread appeared on his palm. He tossed a piece into his mouth. "It's worth a try."

"Right now, I think we should both get some sleep." Tara yawned. "And you better stop eating or you'll pop! I have a feeling that tomorrow will be a long day."

The next morning, following a very late breakfast, Kandide and Tara joined Jake, Teren, and Selena around the large jeweled fireplace in the Great Hall. Tara was still pleading with her sister to return home. "We must go today, Kandi. You know time is running out."

"She's right, Kandide." As much as Jake didn't like the thought of her leaving, he had to agree with Tara. "If you don't return soon, Tiyana will certainly feel obligated to use what little of the Gift she has. It probably will take all of her strength."

"It could kill her!" Teren was desperate to persuade his sister to go back with them. "Mom's not all that young anymore, you know." Realizing that Selena and his mother were exactly the same age, he looked at his aunt rather sheepishly, adding, "I didn't mean it that way, Selena. She's not ancient, or anything."

Kandide ignored her brother. "The Council will just have to wait a little longer. I simply do not wish to go back right now."

"You're right, Kandide, you cannot go back," Selena calmly reassured her.

"What? Selena?" Tara was flabbergasted at her aunt's statement. "She must—"

Raising a hand to silence her young niece, Selena continued, "You can never go back, Kandide, even if your wing is completely healed. You can, however, go forward."

Kandide regarded her aunt with suspicion. "What do you mean?"

"The past is like . . . a library. It's perfect for learning, but not for living. What you must do now, my child, is to use what you've learned here in the Veil to teach others, so that they, too, can go forward."

Kandide had an awful feeling that her idyllic stay in the Veil was about to end. "How do you suggest I do that, Aunt Selena?"

"You have the power—and the opportunity now—to do what your father foresaw. You can create a better world for all Fée."

"And save Mother's life," Teren chimed in.

From behind a chair, Egan peeked out. His newly formed wings were firmly strapped to his back. Climbing onto Kandide's lap, he said, "Kandide, my mother sent me away, too. But if she could see me now, maybe she would change her mind." Egan's brand-new wings almost hit her in the face as he proudly fluttered them. "Even if she didn't, I wouldn't want her to die, just 'cause of me."

A deep frown creased Kandide's face. She placed her hands in the pockets of her cape. Suddenly, she felt a tingling sensation. The silver spiral around the feather her father gave her was, again, hot to the touch. A thought popped into her head. Kandide abruptly stood up, almost knocking the young Fée off her lap. "Oh, sorry, Egan, but you've given me a terrific idea."

"I did? I gave you an idea, Kandide?" Egan was beside himself at the thought.

Turning to Tara and her brother, Kandide announced, "We're leaving at once."

"Then you'll go?" Teren looked as though he wasn't sure he'd heard her correctly.

"You'll return with us, right now?" Tara was also staring at her sister in disbelief.

"Yes." Kandide nodded. "Jake and Selena must also accompany us."

"I'm afraid I can't do that," Selena replied. "I must remain here."

"Why?" Kandide's expression was puzzled. "Don't you want to see Tiyana again?"

"Much as I would love to see my sister, I fear that if I am seen in Calabiyau, it will raise far too many questions and the Veil might be discovered. Everything we've worked so hard to achieve could be jeopardized. You'll be in good hands with Jake."

"Then let's go!" Teren wasn't about to give Kandide a chance to change her mind. He gestured to transport, but nothing happened. He tried again, and still nothing happened. Neither he nor the others vanished. "Why isn't it working?"

"It's the Veil," Jake explained.

"In order to protect us," Kandide added, "Father created an enchantment on this area so that no one can transport directly in or out."

"Is that why we arrived outside, in the Mists?" Tara asked.

"It is," Selena replied. "It could be quite dangerous if just anyone could enter."

"It's pretty dangerous if they don't," Teren grimaced. "I could have done without that welcoming party we met."

"Normally, the garglans don't come so close to the château," Jake told him. "I've never seen so many of them. One or two, maybe, possibly even three, but never a dozen."

"Thirteen," Teren corrected him. "There were thirteen."

"Perhaps with the weather so warm, they're looking for fresh water," Selena suggested. "In any case, you must leave the grounds and go outside the protection of the Veil before transporting will work."

"Are you coming, Jake?" Kandide tried to make her words sound like a question, not a command. "I mean, will you come with us, Jake?"

"I guess I better." He opened a wooden chest in the hall and pulled out his quiver and bow.

"Thank you so much for everything, Aunt Selena." Tara hugged her aunt, and then walked toward the door, unable to keep the relief out of her voice. "We don't have any time to waste."

"Be very careful, my children," Selena called after them, as they headed out beyond the golden gate. She watched until they disappeared into the foggy Mists.

"This should be far enough," Jake told the other three, once he was sure they had cleared the protection of the Veil. "Keep an eye out for more garglans, and stay close so I can transport all four of us at once."

Looking around, Kandide spotted a sudden movement in the brush. "Over there!" she whispered.

"What is it?" Jake immediately pulled an arrow from his quiver.

"I'll get it!" Teren pointed his finger in the direction that

Kandide had seen the movement.

"Hold it!" Tara shouted. "It's not a garglan."

"It's me!" Egan popped out from behind a dead tree stump.

"What are you doing here?" Kandide scolded.

"I want to go, too." He flitted over to them. His new wings were working perfectly.

"Not this time, Egan." She knelt down to speak to him. "Maybe later. Now, let's get you back inside the gate."

"I don't think we can." Jake pointed to a nearby tree. "Look!" Two garglans were crouched in the branches above. "In fact, I think we all need to leave—right now!"

One of the garglans leapt from the tree. Instantly, Jake gestured and all five of the Fée vanished.

The garglans' only meal that day was a spray of faery dust.

It was difficult for Lady Aron to hide her glee. She could see herself finally wearing the crown.

THIRTY-ONE

Inside the chamber of the High Council, the anxious members were all assembled, as they had been the two days prior, since Teren and Tara left. Lady Aron got to her feet. Her fierce gaze swept the room, quieting the others. Ever since Kandide's injury, she had been determined to take control of the situation. While the rest of the Council had finally tired of arguing with her, Tiyana refused to bend to her will. But that was about to change.

"Really, Tiyana, how could you have let Tara go with him?" Lady Aron spoke in her most condescending tone. "How can we possibly view our queen's running off like that as anything but irresponsible?"

"I've already told you, I did not let her go." Tiyana was fed up with Lady Aron's nonstop badgering. "And, as you just said, Tara is our queen. I can hardly prohibit her from doing anything she wants to do."

"Well, you might have done more to discourage her," Lady

Corale said with a sniff.

"Indeed," Lord Revên agreed. "Surely, Tiyana, you still have some influence over *this* daughter."

"Tara is just trying to do what she thinks is best." Lady Karena defended the young queen's actions. "I'm sure she was concerned about Teren going alone."

Ignoring her, Lady Aron continued her badgering. "Well, Tiyana, have you at least heard from them?"

"No, I have not," she snapped. *And even if I had, I would not tell you*, she added silently.

"Well, since it appears as if you don't even know if any of your children are still alive, I really must insist that we proceed as though Kandide, and possibly even Queen Tara and Prince Teren, are not coming back." It was difficult for Lady Aron to hide her glee. She could see herself finally wearing the crown.

"It is Solstice, Tiyana," Lady Batony spoke up. "And as much as we all dislike the idea of your having to deploy the Gift, the little you have may well be our only hope of surviving."

"For once, Lady Batony, you are right," the Fire Fée told her. "Time has run out."

"Well, for fear of disappointing both of you, 'time' has just stopped." Kandide materialized in the doorway of the Council Chamber. Teren, Jake, Tara, and Egan all appeared with her.

A hush fell over the High Council. Everyone sat stunned and silent—all except Lady Aron, who let out a gasp.

"Kandide!" Tiyana rushed over to her daughter. "You're back."

"Yes, Mother, I am." She gave Tiyana a warm hug. "And as strong as ever."

Kandide glanced around at the assembly. "Good afternoon, everyone. I'd like you all to meet some very special friends of mine. This is . . . Egan?" Not seeing him, she realized that he was hiding behind her cape. "Well, the young lad behind me is Egan. And this is Jake."

"Jake? Can it be?" An astonished Lady Socrat leapt to her feet and rushed over to him. "It's really you!" Tears of joy streamed down her face.

"Yes, Mother, it's me." He gave her a tremendous hug, wiped away a tear, then hugged her again.

"What?" Kandide could only stare at the two of them.

"But how?" Lord Socrat, who had gone pale from shock, rushed over to Jake and his wife. "We searched everywhere for you, Jake, for years. What happened? Where have you been all this time?"

Kandide was as astounded as everyone else in the room. "Lady and Lord Socrat are your parents? You never told me."

With one arm around his mother and the other around his father, Jake's grinned. "It wasn't important until now."

No one, however, was more astonished than Lady Aron. "Kandide . . . Prince Teren . . . how did you . . . ? I mean—it's good to see that you're safe. You, as well, Tara." Quickly regaining her composure, she continued, "And you, Jake, it's been a while—a very long while. However, we have more important things to discuss right now than family reunions—as touching as they are. Kandide, you must relinquish the Gift of the Frost, and you must do it immediately!"

Kandide favored the Fire Fée with a dispassionate smile. "I have returned, and as you can see, the Gift is more radiant than ever." She gestured toward herself, turning for all to see her bright silver glow. "And I will, of course, be happy to deploy the Frost." *But I will never transfer it,* she silently vowed, *not now, not ever, not to anyone.*

Lady Aron glared at her. "Then at least do that much, immediately!"

"There is, however, a price." Kandide's words took the Council aback. They began murmuring among themselves.

"A price?" Lady Aron fired back. "How dare you? There will be no bargaining!"

"Fine, then I shall leave." Kandide turned to do so.

"Wait! I say, wait!" Lord Aron's attention had been momentarily diverted as he stared at Egan who was peeking out from behind Kandide's cape. He quickly turned back to the Council. "What is this price you seek, Kandide?"

Lady Aron started to protest, but he quickly silenced her. "Please, my dear, let us at least hear her out."

"What is your price, Kandide?" Lord Rössi asked.

Kandide stood tall, in perfect control. "For the Gift of the Frost, I respectfully demand a change in the Articles to allow Imperfects the full rights and privileges of the Fée."

"That is preposterous!" Lady Aron seethed with anger. Flames leapt from the tips of her fiery wings. "Never will we allow the superiority of our clans to be compromised by permitting Imperfects to live among us! They will have no rights, and they certainly will never be our equals."

"I ask only that they be treated equally," Kandide continued. "It's individual validity that I seek, so that *all* Fée have the same rights and privileges to determine their own destiny. I ask nothing more. No special treatment—just equality."

Teren listened in amazement. He couldn't believe his sister was actually facing down the Council this way. Kandide, he had to admit, had changed more than he ever would have guessed.

The members of the High Council, however, were not nearly as impressed. They began to talk over one another other, with each statement becoming more and more conflicted. Once again, it was Lady Aron who cut through the discord. "Your demand will never be met, not as long as I have a vote."

Kandide surveyed the group, stopping to focus directly upon the fiery Fée. "That's fine," she replied, almost too calmly. *Except I seem to be holding all the cards,* she thought. *Let's just see what happens next.* Turning to Jake and then to Tiyana, Kandide continued, "I'm sorry, Mother, but I have made my offer. Since it seems as though the Council will not even consider it, I see no reason to remain here any longer. I wish you all well. Shall we be off, Jake?"

*Kandide looked from Lord Rössi to Lady Aron.
"I shall give you one hour."*

THIRTY-TWO

"You can't leave, Kandi," Tara insisted. "As queen, I . . . well, I forbid it!"

"Bravo, Tara!" Teren was once again thrilled at seeing his sister taking control. "She's right, Kandide. You can't just walk out on us."

"With all due respect to you, Queen Tara, and you, Prince Teren, I can no longer remain here."

"And with all due respect to you, Kandi," Tara's words were as emotionless as her sister's, "I wasn't making a request. I am commanding you to stay."

Kandide took a step back, stunned by the resolve in her sister's voice. Never in her life had she heard her sister speak that way. "You're commanding me, Tara? May I remind you that I am no longer a subject of your crown? Mother banished me, remember?"

Tara met her sister's eyes. "Well, I'm un-banishing you." *There's no way I'm going to allow you to leave,* she thought, *even if*

Teren has to put a spell on you.

"Let her go, Tara." Tiyana's voice was weary. She placed her hand on her youngest daughter's shoulder. "Kandide is right to want to leave Calabiyau. Since the uniting of the clans, we have advanced in many ways, yet we are still so very barbaric in others. Many of you on the Council have lost loved ones because of these vile laws against Imperfects, and yet you continue to uphold them. Will we never gain a social conscience?"

"We have a social conscience, Tiyana." Lord Standish hurriedly spoke up. "And that is exactly why Imperfects are not allowed to live among us."

"We're not trying to be cruel," Lord Salitar added. "We just want what's best for everyone."

"Besides," Lady Batony added, "it's only been a hundred years since the different clans have lived in harmony. Imagine the discord of allowing Imperfects among us."

"She's right," Lady Alicia agreed. "I fear they would be mercilessly chastised, or even worse."

"Do you really want your young friend to have to deal with being treated that way?" Lord Revên motioned toward Egan's prototypal wings. "It's for their own good."

Kandide studied him. It was an excuse she had heard many times. "I hardly think being sent to the Mists is for anyone's 'own good.' And I won't argue that living here might be hard, at least at first. But shouldn't that be my 'young friend's' choice?"

"Some choices are better left to those who know best." Lady Corel insisted.

"And who might that be, Lady Corel?" Kandide walked over to the Council table and spoke directly to her. "You? Or perhaps

Lady Aron?"

The guardian of the seas shrank down in her chair as Kandide continued to speak. "My friends and I may not be perfect, but we are perfectly capable of making our own decisions. We're also perfectly capable of accepting Fée for who they are, not for what someone else thinks they should be."

"That's all very nice, Kandide." Lady Aron spoke as though she was addressing a child. "But you really are missing the point. The members of the High Council—as we have always done— simply have to consider what is best for everyone. Isn't it time you did the same?"

Kandide stood silent for a few seconds before answering. "As much as I hate to admit it, Lady Aron, you're right. It is time I start thinking of everyone's good. And since you've all made it perfectly clear that, as an Imperfect, I am not good enough to live here, I assume that means my request for equality is also rejected. Therefore, I have no reason to stay."

"Please, Kandide." Lord Rössi stood up, his brow deeply creased with concern. "Some of us don't feel that way at all. I had a sister who was sent away when she was fifteen. I would give anything to find her. Now you've given me hope."

"And Jake has survived all this time," Lady Karena hastily pointed out. "His injuries seem to have fully healed. Perhaps there are curative spells that we don't know about."

"I would say that I've overcome my injuries, Lady Karena, but not that they've been cured." Jake flew up into the air, leaving his boots on the floor.

"He has no feet!" Lady Batony gasped. She turned her head away and quickly covered her eyes. "Must you expose us to this?"

Lady Corel also covered her eyes. "How could you embarrass your father and mother like that?"

"We're not embarrassed," Lord Socrat said quietly.

"Well, you certainly should be." Lady Aron, having nearly fainted from the shock, fanned herself. "This is outrageous! I will have none of this mockery!"

"Nor shall I, Lady Aron." Kandide, with Egan in tow, turned and walked toward the door. "Shall we be off, Jake?"

"Stop! All of you." Every eye turned toward Tara. "As your queen, I command the Council discuss my sister's offer rationally. And you, Kandi, please—just give me this day so that I may make your case before the High Council. You're right; I cannot force you to stay. But I am asking."

Lord Rössi quickly banged his gavel on the table. "The Council accepts your order, Your Majesty. Will you give us this day, Kandide, so that Tara and I can try to make some sense out of all this with the Council?"

Kandide looked from him to Lady Aron. "I shall give you one hour."

"That is hardly enough time," the Fire Fée retorted, her amber eyes blazing.

"Take it or not," came Kandide's response.

"We'll take it." Lord Rössi stopped any more discussion. "It might, however, be better, Kandide, if you, Jake, Teren, and your young friend wait in the antechamber. Is that acceptable?"

"As you wish." Kandide graciously nodded. "We'll wait for one hour."

*"With all due respect, Queen Tara,
you know that isn't true."*

THIRTY-THREE

"Mother! Mother!" a young faery boy called out as he flew into the Council's antechamber where Kandide, Egan, Teren, and Jake were waiting. "Oh!" He landed rather abruptly in the center of the room. "Are you Princess Kandide?"

She looked at him quizzically. "Yes. And who might you be?"

"I'm Alin, son of Lord and Lady Aron," he answered with a sweeping bow.

Kandide thought back. She knew they had a son—she had attended the ritual Giving of Gifts when he was born—but she hadn't seen him since he was a baby. "You're Lord and Lady Aron's son?"

"I am. I transported here from Grandmum's house to visit my Mom and Dad. They don't know I'm here."

Egan, who was still hiding behind Kandide, peeked out from one side of her cape. To his surprise, he saw a young Fée who looked exactly like him, except for the boy's golden wings and flame-red clothes. Quickly, Egan leaned to the other side, so he wouldn't be seen.

Noticing the curious young Fée behind Kandide, Alin did the same, mimicking his actions from side to side, trying to get a better glimpse. Finally, he broke their game of back and forth. "How come you look like me?" he asked with an inquisitive frown.

"How come you look like me?" Egan mirrored his frown.

"I don't know." Alin shrugged.

Egan sized him up and down. "Are we twins?"

"Maybe. Why are your wings funny?" Alin pointed to them.

"Because they're prototypals," Egan proclaimed, standing up tall and turning to show them off.

"Oh." Alin was not all sure what Egan meant by prototypals. "Can you fly with them?"

"Sure I can. I'll show you." Egan opened his wings and gave a hopeful little hop. He dropped back down to the ground with a thud. There was no wind in the antechamber to help him lift off, so he couldn't quite get airborne.

Noticing that he was having trouble, Teren murmured a spell to create an air current, and Egan sailed right up, gleefully flying around the room. "See, I told you so!"

"Bet I can catch you." Alin flew up to him. Giggling, the two of them played a quick game of tag as they flitted back and forth.

Egan flew down and landed rather unsteadily. It was the part of flying he was still getting used to. "I can do something else, too," he told Alin. "I can swim!"

"No you can't." Alin shook his head. "You have to be from

the Water Clan to swim."

"No you don't." Egan shook his head. "Do you, Kandide?"

"Anyone can learn to swim," Kandide assured him. "Egan's a wonderful swimmer. He's my best student."

Alin studied him curiously. "Do you think you could teach me how to swim? My mother won't go near the water. She's from the Fire Clan and my father's from the Earth Clan, so he won't even try."

"Sure," Egan replied. "Can I, Kandide?"

"I don't see why not." The two of them started to run off. "Not right now, however," she called after them. "Stay here, where I can see you."

Kandide's words fell on deaf ears. Alin and Egan were already racing around a large chair on the side of the chamber, lost in discussions about leaning to swim. "They do look exactly alike," she commented to Jake and Teren.

"Yeah and both of them are from the Fire and Earth Clans," Jake replied.

"And the same age," Teren added. "It's an awfully big coincidence."

"Or is it?" Kandide watched the two youngsters. Egan was busily showing Alin how to move his arms and turn his head from side to side so he could breathe while swimming.

Inside the Council Chamber, the discussion was boiling over.

"Respectfully, Your Majesty, I must insist that you tell the Council where you found Kandide." Lady Aron was almost shouting as she attempted to force Tara into disclosing the secret of the Mists for all to hear. *If I can get our dear queen to reveal the existence of the Veil and an entire kingdom full of Imperfects,* she thought, *it will most decidedly cast doubt on her loyalty to preserving the sanctity of Calabiyau Proper. Not to mention the fact that she will be exposed as having lied to the Council about it.*

Tara took her time responding. "I've already told you, Teren and I simply ran into Jake in the woods. I have nothing more to say."

"With all due respect, Queen Tara, you know that isn't true. Do you not understand that by protecting Imperfects, the purity of all our clans is at risk?"

"I disagree, Lady Aron." Lord Socrat told her.

"So do I." Lady Karena chimed in.

"As do I." Lady Batony surprised everyone by agreeing. "I don't really want Imperfects running all over the place, however, when I was a young girl, my best friend—"

Lady Aron was beside herself. "When you were a young girl, Lady Batony, the individual clans controlled such matters. Perhaps it should be that way again!"

"Ladies, please!" Lord Rössi glared at the two of them. "We're running out of time. Can you at least try to stay on track—just this once?"

"For some of us, that seems to be quite difficult." Lady Aron leaned back in her chair and crossed her arms.

"And for others, downright impossible." Lady Batony responded by crossing her arms as well. "I do, however, think you should at least try, Firenza."

"I have an idea," Lord Rössi told them. "Why don't you both try?" He looked from one to the other. Neither said anything. "Good. Then as the Council Chair, it is my right to call an end to the discussion. As protocol dictates, each member is allowed to cast a single vote, using only one of the acorns placed in front of him or her. White is for yes; black is for no; green is to abstain. Only a unanimous vote may amend the Articles, and all abstentions will go to the majority side.

"The matter on the floor," he continued, "is to amend the Articles to allow Imperfects the full rights and privileges of the Fée. As Chair, I must place the first vote. While I do not believe that all Fée are ready to accept Imperfects, I do believe that history and my own experience have shown the alternatives to be far worse. Therefore, the acorn I place in the center is white.

"Lord Socrat, how do you vote?" he continued.

"Those Articles cost me a son. Now I may have him back. I vote Yea to amending them." Lord Socrat pushed his white acorn forward.

"Lady Socrat, how do ye vote?"

"I, too, vote Yea. May no other parent ever be forced to suffer such a loss." She pushed her white acorn forward.

"My fair Lady Corale?"

She, too, shoved her white acorn toward the center. "I follow their lead. Not because I think it best, but because I fear Kandide leaves us little choice."

"Lady Karena?"

"My clan has wanted to accept Imperfects almost from the time the Treaty was signed. I vote Yea." With her blue eyes sparking, Lady Karena eagerly moved her white acorn forward.

"Lord Salitar, how do you vote?"

"As Lady Corale has stated, there is no other choice. Kandide's terms are most persuasive. My vote is Yea." The tall, olive-skinned leader of the Healing Arts Clan pushed his white acorn to the center as well.

"Lord Standish?"

"I feel that my decision will not be well received by many members of my clan," Lord Standish began. His shoulder-length snow-white hair glistened as he slowly shook his head from side to side. "For as many centuries as I have been alive, they have held this prejudice. I am, however, designated to do what I deem best. Certainly, the argument for the Frost must prevail. Therefore, I accept the amendment." He placed his white acorn in the center with the rest.

"Lord Revên?"

Stroking his brownish-red beard, the keeper of the Sacred Arts gazed around the room before stating: "Prejudices are hard to change, even for those who seek truths. I may well be removed from the Council by my own clan's High Court for my decision. However, as Lord Standish just stated, the Frost must be given precedence. If the price for deploying the Gift is equality, then perhaps it is time for this change. My acorn is, therefore, white."

"Lady Alicia?"

"Perhaps, Lord Standish, all Fée will ultimately learn to accept Imperfects, and in doing so, we will all grow stronger." The dark-haired guardian of reptiles waved her hand, and like the snakes under her protection, the white acorn in front of her slithered to the center.

"Lady Batony?"

"As most of you know, it is rare that I ever side with the majority—although not rare that I disagree with Lady Aron.

In this case, I must agree that Kandide has left us no other choice. I am, however, compelled to say that it is a very disagreeable action on her behalf, and can only hope we aren't setting a precedent. Who knows what she may demand next year. Why, when I was young girl, my mother told me—"

Lord Rössi loudly cleared his throat. "Your vote, Lady Batony?"

She shot him an indignant glance. "As I was saying, the Gift, and therefore the Frost, must take precedence. White it is." Lady Batony snapped her fingers and her white acorn jumped to the pile.

"Lord Aron, how do you vote?"

He hesitated briefly, meeting his wife's eyes, then quickly placed his white acorn in the center of the table. "The time for acceptance is long overdue."

"Lady Aron, how do you vote?"

Scowling at her husband, Lady Aron picked up her black acorn and started to push it forward. But before she could, Lord Aron grabbed her wrist to stop her.

"Hear me, first," he said, and then turned to the Council. "Not so many years ago, Lady Aron and I bore two sons. Twins they were, identical in every way but one."

Lady Aron jerked her arm away. "How dare you tell the Council such a thing?" "It's time the truth is told, Firenza."

"You'd slander your own wife and lie to the Council—for what? A bunch of Imperfects?" Her entire body was red hot. "I won't have you saying these things!"

"And I won't have any more of your deceit." Lord Aron continued speaking to the other Council members. "My dear wife could not bear the shame of a son who was born without wings."

"You're lying!" she screamed. "Lord Rössi, I insist that you stop this blasphemy and you do it now!"

"And I insist, Lady Aron, that you obey the rules of this chamber. Stop your shouting and allow your husband to speak. When he is finished, you may have the floor. Lord Aron, you may continue."

"Firenza insisted that we send our newly born child away. Instead, I brought him to King Toeyad in hopes that he could help. It was the last I saw of our second son until today."

"You did what?" Lady Aron shrieked. Her wings flared with fire.

"What do you mean, today?" Tara asked.

Lord Aron sighed heavily. "May the earthly spirits help us, but I am fairly certain that the lad with Kandide is our other son."

"That is a lie! How dare you tell this despicable tale? Our second son died at birth, and he . . . he was perfect!" She was gripping the black acorn so tightly that it combusted in her hand. As she slowly opened her fingers, her eyes stared at nothing but ash.

Realizing what had just happened, Lord Rössi seized the moment. "How do you vote, Lady Aron?"

Looking at what was, just seconds before, a black acorn, Lady Aron realized that she could no longer vote Nay. "This is unfair." She pounded the table with her fist. "I demand another black acorn!"

"You know the rules." Lord Rössi held firm. "Each member

must vote using only the acorns given. How do you vote, Lady Aron?"

Having no choice, she angrily shoved the green acorn forward. Glaring at her husband, she cried, "You'll regret this day!" Turning toward the other Council members, her voice carried a chilling threat, "Mark my words, you will all regret what is done here!"

Ignoring her warning, Lord Rössi calmly proclaimed, "Since Lady Aron abstains, her vote goes with the majority. The Articles shall be amended. Let it be known that from this day forward, Imperfects have full rights and privileges."

Tara gasped. Could what she was hearing really be true? And yet, there were the white acorns piled in the center of the table—the lone green one off to the side. "It is a great victory for *all* Fée—and for that I thank you," she proclaimed, humbly bowing her head to the Council.

Standing near her daughter, Tiyana was speechless. *Perhaps Toeyad was right,* she thought. *He always said Kandide would find her way. Maybe even Selena can now return.*

Amid sighs of relief—for now the Council members knew the Frost would finally be deployed—Lady Aron put forth one final warning, "Your victory may seem glorious today, Tara, but I assure you, to the victor goes a price." Completely uncharacteristic of the Fire Fée, she left the chamber by walking through the arched double doors.

"Are you so sure they are lies?" Jake's question caused Lady Aron to stop and turn back around.

THIRTY-FOUR

Alin jumped out of his chair and ran over to greet Lady Aron as she entered the antechamber. "Mother, look, I'm here. And guess what? I have a twin!"

"Alin?" Grabbing her son's arm, the Fire Fée brushed past Kandide, Teren, and Jake and pulled him off to the side. "What are you doing here?"

"I wanted to see you and Father. And then I met Egan." His blue eyes shone with excitement. "Father said I had a brother who was lost when we were born. I think I've found him."

Egan stepped forward, even more excited than his twin. He had lived his entire life without his mother, and now, finally, she was there, standing before him. He gave a low sweeping bow, the sort he'd seen Jake give Kandide. When he straightened up, what he saw made him step back.

Lady Aron's face was full of disgust. She spoke only to Alin. "You have no brother. And if you did, he certainly would not be an Imperfect!"

"Excuse me, Lady Aron, but I won't have you speaking to Egan like that." Kandide met her face to face.

"And I won't have you filling my son with lies." Taking Alin's hand, she started to leave.

"Are you so sure they are lies?" Jake's question caused her to stop and turn back around.

"They have the same birthday, don't you, Alin?" Teren walked over to the young Fée.

"We do, Prince Teren. And Egan looks just like me, Mother. See." He pointed to his brother.

"It's merely a cruel trick of glamour. Your real brother died when he was born. Now, I'll hear no more of this outrage—from any of you."

"No. He's here! Really." Alin pulled his hand free and ran over to Egan. "Just talk to him, Mother—just for a minute. You'll see. Please?"

Lady Aron's amber eyes pierced right through Egan. His body was stiff with fear. "Your twin brother is dead!" She spoke as if wishing him to be so.

"But he's not . . ." Alin was practically in tears as his mother jerked him away.

"I should have known you would try to perpetrate something like this, Kandide. But even I never thought you would be so insidious as to involve my son." With a wave of her hand, Lady Aron and a sobbing Alin disappeared in a blinding red flash.

"Egan . . ." he called as his voice trailed off.

Egan clutched Kandide's hand. "Is she my mother?"

"Yes, she is. She's just not a very good one right now." Kandide knelt down and wrapped her arms around her young friend. "I'm so sorry, Egan, I should have never let you come with us."

"But I wanted to come. I thought maybe if—"

"You've done it, Kandi!" Tara raced into the antechamber. "Oh, Kandi! You've done it!"

But Kandide wasn't interested. "Not now, Tara," she said wearily. "Lady Aron said some terrible things to Egan, and I think it's time for us to be leaving."

"Kandide, you're not listening to your sister," Tiyana told her. "You won!"

"I what?" She stood up. "You mean?"

"Yes! The Articles are amended!" Tara grabbed her sister and whirled her around.

"Yes! Yes! Yes!" Teren hollered, jumping up and down and pumping his fist in the air. "You did it, Kandide!"

"I can't believe it." She stared at her sister in amazement. "That's why Lady Aron was so incensed. Oh, Egan, that's why your mother was so mean."

"Do you really think so?" A glimmer of hope erased his frown.

"Yes, I do." *And I think she is going to be even more angry,* Kandide thought, *when she learns that some of us may even live right here in the castle part of the time!* "I can't wait for us to go home and tell Selena."

"Maybe not, Kandide." Lord Rössi, along with the other Council members, had followed Tara out of the chamber. "The Council passed another resolution."

Kandide's smile faded. "Another resolution, Lord Rössi?"

"Yes. Now that Imperfects are to have full rights, at Tara's insistence, we voted to have you reinstated as queen."

"Oh, Kandi, please say yes." Tara took her hand. "Please."

"I . . . I . . ." Dumbfounded, Kandide had no idea what to say.

Lord Socrat continued to explain, "Tara has abdicated the throne to pursue her healing duties. That means that you, Kandide, may now assume your rightful place as Calabiyau's Queen."

She stood there silently trying to comprehend what he was saying. *But what about the Veil? I'm their queen now,* she thought, before answering. "No, Lord Socrat, I am afraid that I cannot be your queen."

"Kandi, you must!" Tara thrust her crown toward Kandide. "This thing doesn't even fit my head. And that throne chair is really uncomfortable."

"I will not be *your* queen. I will, however, be Queen of *all* Fée!" She winked at Jake.

"That's perfect!" Tara threw her arms around her sister. "I mean, as you wish, Your Majesty." She ceremoniously placed the crown on Kandide's head and then bowed, as did the rest of the High Council.

Kandide humbly bowed her head. *Is this impossible?* she thought, *and yet it's happening. Father was right, I will be a great leader—of all Fée.*

"We're really happy you are back." Lady Karena was smiling from ear to ear. "I knew in my heart that you would follow in your father's footsteps."

"Thank you, Lady Karena, for always believing in me."

"We're all thrilled," Lady Socrat added, extending Kandide a proper bow.

"Indeed we are, Your Majesty." Lord Socrat also bowed to his new queen.

Amid joyous congratulations from the rest of the Council members, Kandide spotted Egan sitting all alone in a corner. "Excuse me a minute," she told a very supportive Lord Rössi.

Egan quickly stood up as she approached. Attempting a smile, he bowed with a very well mannered, "Congratulations, Your Majesty."

Kandide extended her hand to him. "Would you hold my crown for me, Egan?"

"Sure." He reached out to take it. "It's really heavy."

"That it is," she replied. "And it comes with a great deal of responsibility. But right now, I want you to meet my mother, Selena's twin sister."

"Before you do," Lord Aron hurried over to them. "If may interrupt. I was wondering, Your Majesty, if you would do me the honor of introducing us?" He motioned toward Eagan. "I think it's about time we got to know each other."

Kandide could hardly contain her delight. *Now everything really is perfect,* she thought. "It would be my pleasure. Egan, this is Lord Aron—your father."

Egan's brow knitted with a wary frown. "You're my father?"

"Yes, I am. That is, if you will have me."

"But aren't you ashamed of me, too?" Egan glanced timidly back at his wings.

Lord Aron knelt in front of his son and held out his hands. "It is you who should be ashamed of me. Will you accept me as your father?"

Crown and all, Egan jumped into his arms, hugging him

so tightly that he almost knocked both of them over. "Kandide, I have a father!"

"And I have my other son back." Lord Aron stood up, with Egan still in his arms. "Thank you, Your Majesty."

"Thank you, Lord Aron. And now there's something else I must do." Walking over to the large beveled-glass window, Kandide opened it.

She closed her eyes, pushing all thoughts from her mind. When only the soft glow of a distant light remained, she began to speak, "Life's source, I summon, the Frost unbind. Your power I release, to the heavens on high."

No sooner were the words out of her mouth, than her feet began to feel like jelly. She grabbed for the window's edge, certain they would no longer support her. A flow of icy-cold sensations began moving upward from her toes—at first just a few prickles. But very quickly she started to feel as though an internal syringe was sucking every ounce of strength from her body. The feeling swept upward through her legs, stomach, and chest. Every vein felt drained of its life force, as though it would collapse.

Why does this always have to be so painful, she thought, forcing herself to remain focused. The silver glow radiating from Kandide's arms and hands became so bright that every Fée in the room had to close his or her eyes.

This surely would have killed Mother, Tara thought, watching her sister begin to tremor. But she dared not approach. The freezing cold emanating from her Kandide's body could be felt across the room. Water in a pitcher next to the window instantly froze solid.

Kandide ceased being able to think. A white void was all she knew. Her brain felt vacant—empty, like a hollow ball. Her body began to stiffen. Instinctively, she raised her arms, holding her hands, palms up, out the window. An intense beam of white light surged from her fingertips. Up, the cold fire climbed, higher and higher into the heavens.

All in the courtyard below stopped what they were doing and watched. Higher it streaked, until they could no longer see where it ended. There was a strange calm; not a squirrel chattered nor bird sang.

"It's not working," a young onlooker whispered to his mother.

"Maybe it's too late," she told him.

"Look!" another shouted, pointing upward.

Within seconds, a colossal streak of lightning, high in the atmosphere, lit up the entire sky. It silvery fingers expanded out like a blazing spider web. A split second later, Kandide was jolted out of her trance-like state by a booming clap of thunder. She could feel her brain begin to clear. "I've done it," she whispered, opening her eyes. "Winter will come. Life will be renewed."

The Fée outside the castle began cheering as they felt the temperature suddenly drop. Freezing air swept through the open window into the Council's antechamber. Inside, everyone began to cheer as well.

"Look, Father!" Egan cried. Jumping out of Lord Aron's arms, he pushed his way through the Council members to peer out the window. "The Frost, it's starting!"

All the land began to shimmer with a delicate blanket of ice crystals as the season's first Frost started to form. Leaves turned from green to red and golden brown. Flowers closed their blossoms. Songbirds ruffled their feathers to ward off the chill. It was, at last, time for Mother Nature to rest.

Pale and weak from having used virtually every ounce of her strength to deploy the Gift, Kandide managed to make it to the nearest chair. Her breathing was shallow and she felt completely drained. She looked down at her hands. The iridescent glow that normally surrounded her body was gone. Resting her head on the upholstered back of the stiff blue upright chair, Calabiyau's Imperfect Queen smiled. *The radiance of the Gift will build back up*, she thought, *and then I'll have another year of looking extraordinary. But now, I am Queen of all Fée, just as Father promised.*

Seeing Kandide alone, Jake left his parents' side and hurried over to her. He gently squeezed her hand and bowed. "Kandide, I'm so—"

"Shh . . ." She placed her finger on his lips. His sparkling green eyes told her all she needed to know. "Just stand there and smile. And for goodness sake, please stop bowing."

"As you wish, my Queen." Jake softly kissed her hand. *She doesn't need the radiance to be beautiful*, he thought. At that moment, he knew he was in love.

Still watching the goings-on outside, Egan spotted Alin and Lady Aron standing with a soldier in a far corner of the courtyard. He timidly waved to his brother, and then looked up at his father. "Do. . . do you think Mother will ever like me?"

With a heavy heart, Lord Aron watched his son, wife, and the Captain disappear behind an outbuilding. "Some Fée are just going to need more time. Come, I want to show you your new home—if you'll consider staying." He took Egan by the hand and they left the antechamber.

Teren made his way through the overflowing crowd to Tara. From serving staff to ladies and lords-in-waiting, it seemed as though everyone had come into the antechamber to congratulate Kandide. "Want to go out to the lake?" he asked his sister. "I'll bet it's icing over."

"I'd love to. I just need to see General Mintz first. His daughter came down with a case of the spots and I completely forgot about stopping by to help her. I can't tell you how glad I am to be finished with politics of any kind."

"Me, too!" With a snap of his fingers, two pairs of ice skates appeared in Teren's hands.

Tara took one set, and examined it carefully. "Next time," she said as they left the antechamber, "can you sharpen the blades?"

When the line of congratulatory Fée finally let up, Tiyana walked over to her eldest daughter. "Queen for only a few moments and look at what you have already accomplished."

"It was a stunning plan, wasn't it, Mother?"

"Yes, it was. I'm so very proud of you, Kandide."

"Thank you, Mother. Hearing you say that means more to me than you'll ever know."

Tiyana kissed her daughter on both cheeks. "How I wish your father could see you now."

"As do I, Mother." Kandide glanced over at Jake, who was standing with his parents.

"Why don't you ask him?" Tiyana whispered.

"Ask him what?"

"Why, to rule by your side, of course."

Surprised by her mother's comment, Kandide stammered, "I . . . Well, I—"

"He is crazy about you."

"Well, of course he is, but shouldn't he ask me?" Holding onto her mother's arm, Kandide forced herself to stand up. She still was feeling shaky.

"Protocol, my daughter. You must ask him. It is queen's etiquette."

"Is it now?" With Tiyana's assistance, Kandide made her way to the open window and gazed out. She inhaled the crisp air. It seemed to rejuvenate her body.

Snow was beginning to fall and everything sparkled with a crystalline glow. Winter was finally on its way, and the courtyard was full of younglings who were flittering about laughing and joking while throwing snowballs as fast as they could make them. Everyone seemed to be enjoying the change in the season. It may have been a late winter, but it certainly had all the makings of a great one. Perhaps, with the amending of the Articles, it was also the time for *all* life to begin anew.

Contemplating her mother's words, Kandide reached out the window and a perfectly formed snowflake landed in the palm of her hand. A pleased smile crossed her face. "A winter wedding. I do look wonderful in white!"

But her smile didn't last long. Her brother and sister came rushing back into the room.

"Kandide!" Teren exclaimed, racing up to her. "There's trouble."

She turned to see the panicked expression on his face. "What is it?"

"It's the Banshees," Tara replied. "General Mintz has just learned that their troops are amassing along our border."

"May the earthly spirits help us!" Tiyana exclaimed. "Your father feared that King Nastae might try something. That's one of the reasons why he wanted your crowning to take place so quickly, Kandide."

Unsure of what else to do, Kandide ordered, "Teren, tell Mintz to assemble all my generals. Tara, you inform the Council. We meet in the war room in an hour."

With a gesture, she was gone.

To be continued . . .

About the Characters

KANDIDE

Age:	19 (in human years)
Height:	5'5"
Eyes:	Purple-blue
Hair:	Gold and platinum
Hobbies:	Archery, aercaen, swimming, preening
Heroes:	King Toeyad and myself, of course.
Favorite Book:	Book One: *Kandide – The Secret of the Mists*
	Book Two: *Kandide – The Lady's Revenge*
	Book Three: *Kandide – The Flame is Fleeting*
Quote:	"Equality, like respect, my dear Lady Aron must be earned."

PRINCE TEREN

Age:	14 (in human years)
Height:	5'
Eyes:	Yellow-brown
Hair:	Sandy blond
Hobbies:	Spell-making, pranks, wizardry, aercaen
Heroes:	Merlin, Viviana, and most other wizards.
Favorite Book:	Book Three: *Kandide – The Flame is Fleeting*
	(Because I get to be a hero)
Quote:	"Gosh Kandide's vain!"

PRINCESS TARA

Age:	16 (in human years)
Height:	5'4"
Eyes:	Green
Hair:	Auburn
Hobbies:	Healing, saving forest animals, and keeping her brother and sister out of trouble.
Heroes:	Selena, Queen Tiyana.
Favorite Book:	Book Three: *Kandide – The Flame is Fleeting* (*I can't tell you, it would spoil the ending.*)
Quote:	"Why can't the rest of the world be like this?"

LADY ARON

Age:	*None of your business!*
Height:	5'6"
Eyes:	Amber and blue
Hair:	Flaming
Hobbies:	Archery, politics, and wizardry (Is there anything else)
Heroes:	Me. Who else?
Favorite Book:	Book Two: *Kandide – The Lady's Revenge* (*Isn't it obvious?*)
Quote:	"You will all regret what is done here!"

JAKE

Age: 27 (in human years)
Height: 5'11"
Eyes: Green
Hair: Black
Hobbies: Archery, swimming, reading, and dancing
Heroes: King Toeyad, Selena, Trump, Ari
Favorite Book: Book Two: *Kandide – The Lady's Revenge*
               (It's really an adventure)
Quote: "I don't think I repulse you. I think you repulse you!"

LEANNE

Age: 21 (in human years)
Height: 5'3"
Eyes: Brown
Hair: Dark Brown
Hobbies: Healing, dancing, singing
Heroes: Selena, Jake, Trust, Ari.
Favorite Book: Book Three: *Kandide – The Secret of the Mists*
               (Kandide comes into our lives)
Quote: "It's okay. I heal with my hands, not my eyes."

GARGLAN

Age:	37 (in human years)
Height:	5'
Eyes:	Red
Hair:	Brown and black patches
Hobbies:	Eating Fée
Heroes:	Me
Favorite Book:	Book Four: (Maybe we win in that one)
Quote:	"Grrrr . . . Hisssss!"

A Special Preview of Book Two

·K·A·N·D·I·D·E·

THE
LADY'S REVENGE

·K·A·N·D·I·D·E·
THE
LADY'S REVENGE
DIANA S. ZIMMERMAN
THE CALABIYAU CHRONICLES · BOOK TWO

The gale that fells the trees
oft starts as a simple breeze.
Be warned. Beware.
Enter this Council, only if you dare.

ONE

Morning arrived far too early. Kandide shed the cozy warmth of her blue satin comforter and forced herself to get out of bed. Calabiyau's young queen reluctantly stood up. Her purple-blue eyes blinked back the brightness as golden shafts of sunlight streaked through the tall, arched windows on the east side of her sleeping chamber.

Yawning, she struggled to overcome the lack of sleep from the night before. *I must have been awake half the night,* she thought, stretching her back and arms to loosen up her uncooperative muscles. *No wonder I'm so tired and stiff.* She twisted from side to side, and then rotated her shoulders and wings in an attempt to ward off the weariness. "That's better." She straightened her back. *I'm just glad I didn't tell Tara we'd go to the Meadows this morning.* There was nothing Kandide liked better on a warm summer day than slipping away from her royal duties and flying off to the Meadows with her younger sister.

But not today, she thought, looking out the window and

inhaling the rich spicy scent of the delicate white jasmine that surrounded each pane of glass like frilly lace curtains. The dainty, trumpet-shaped flowers were already basking in the morning sun.

Kandide watched as dozens of Fée flitted about in the courtyard, three stories below. They were doing their chores—going here and there with loafs of freshly baked bread and straw baskets brimming over with tomatoes, squash, lettuce, and fresh fruit of every kind. Other Fée tended to the castle's gardens. A young soldier led his horse out of the royal stable to begin morning rounds. The mane and tail of his white and black mare shimmered like silk from having just been groomed, and the silver-studded saddle sparkled with points of light.

Just beyond the ancient stone wall that surrounded the castle grounds, Kandide could see the pink, yellow, blue, green, and purple thatched roofs on the houses and shops that made up the sprawling village of Calabiyau Proper. It was teaming with activity as storeowners hung out "Open" signs or swept the walkways in front of their shops. On each side of the road, a chorus line of brooms danced magically, whisking from side to side at the direction of their owners.

It was a sight Kandide had seen each morning since she was old enough to sleep in her own room. Everything seemed normal enough, and yet she felt an eerie sense of foreboding deep down in the pit of her stomach. She opened the window and then stepped back with a jolt. Even the morning breeze felt odd, with a wet, prickly heat that brushed across her face. *That's strange,* she thought, wiping away tiny droplets of water. *It rarely rains in July.* Overhead, she noticed that dark clouds were beginning to gather.

Well, strange or not, there's no sense just standing here. I'd better get dressed. The High Council will surely have some ridiculous new proposal about something or another to suggest. She closed the beveled panes of glass to keep the hot air and moisture from coming in. Walking over to the largest of the five ornately framed silver mirrors that adorned her mostly blue bedchamber, Kandide brushed a wisp of golden-blond hair away from her exquisite face. *At least I don't look as tired as I feel. But then I never do,* she told herself.

Glancing at the gilded clock on her pearlescent white dresser, she realized that it was actually quite a bit later than her normal hour to rise. "Half past seven—why didn't Mylea wake me?" She pulled once on the deep blue velvet rope that hung next to the dresser. "Mylea," she called, "where are you?"

But only silence replied. Again, she called, "Mylea, are you there?" *What in the spirits' name is going on?* Wrapping a pink satin robe around her body, Kandide tied its belt, and walked out of her sleeping room and into the connected antechamber.

Instantly, the air turned icy cold. *It's the middle of summer,* she thought irritably. *Why is it suddenly freezing in here?* This was, indeed, a strange morning. Her body began to shiver from the sudden cold. With a snap of her fingers, a piece of dry wood from the tray next to her blue and-silver glass-tiled fireplace floated onto the iron grate. With another snap, she set the log ablaze. *That's better. The Fire Clan really does have some practical spells.*

Kandide held her hands over the growing flames and rubbed them together. The warmth from the fire felt good. As she stood there watching it crackle, a stream of horrific images flashed through her mind. Screams of terror reverberated in her head. She saw Banshee soldiers descending on a small village. Fée were running in every direction, trying to escape their attackers. Most did not.

With both hands, she clutched her forehead, hoping the awful images would go away. But they refused to leave. There was a familiarity about them, and yet she had no idea where she'd seen anything like this type of brutality before. Kandide had never actually witnessed a Banshee raid—*thank the spirits!*— and it had been nearly a year since the last attack was reported. Then she realized why they seemed so familiar. *My dream— the images, they were the same.* The gripping feeling in the pit of her stomach got worse. *No wonder I couldn't sleep.* Each time she had closed her eyes, she'd seen the same visions—Banshees attacking the Fée whom she was sworn to protect.

Why are these awful dreams coming to me? Kandide thought for a moment. Every Fée had slightly different talents. But being able to see into the future had never been one of her gifts— if this was the future. Her stomach twisted in knots. *What if the raids are starting up again and my dreams are a warning?* She had to speak with General Mintz at once—to let him know of her vision.

A sudden knock at her chamber door snapped Kandide's thoughts back to the present. "Come in," she called, hoping Mylea had finally decided to show up. For the almost twenty years (as humans measure time) that Kandide had been alive, Mylea had been her favorite lady-in-waiting. She was the only one, except her late father, the great King Toeyad, and her younger sister, Tara, who could put up with Kandide's vain and often self-centered ways for any length of time. "I said enter," she called again. "Don't you hear me?"

The door did not open. Walking over to it, she reached out to turn the handle. But it wouldn't budge. She tried it again. Still, the handle would not turn. "Mylea, are you out there? The handle is stuck." There was no answer.

"You needn't bother," a deep voice called out from behind her. "It won't open for you. I've spelled it."

Kandide whirled around. "What the . . . ?" The numerous mirrors in her antechamber reflected endless images of a tall stranger with a piercing stare. Her eyes darted from one reflection to another, finally spotting the intruder in a corner off to one side. "Who are you? How did you get into my room?" Her pulse quickened as he stepped out of the shadows.

"Who I am is not important." His voice carried an undertone of formality, as if he was a member of the court—*whose* court she could not imagine. She had certainly never seen him in her own kingdom of Calabiyau. "How I got in here *is*, Your Majesty," he said, adding, "For your own safety, you really should keep your room spelled. But be that as it may, I need to speak to you. It is most urgent."

"Urgent or not, how dare you break into my chamber?" Her shock was rapidly changing to displeasure. *I don't know who let you in*, she thought, *but you're not leaving the same way you came.* Kandide flicked her wrist and the heavy glass paperweight on her desk flew off the table, hurtling directly toward his head.

In a blur of speed, the stranger's hand reached up and caught the glass ball, just inches from his face. "Careful now."

He sounded amused. "You could break something."

A chill surged through her body. *He shouldn't be able to do that. No Fée is that fast.* She stood there watching as he pretended to examine the paperweight.

"Not to worry. It's fine." He held the frosted globe out to show her, then placed it on a nearby table. "I mean you no harm, Your Majesty, and I apologize for arriving unannounced. But now that I'm here, I respectfully request an audience with you. It is, as I said, most urgent."

"Then be quick about what you have to say." Kandide was not sure how else to answer. He obviously had powers beyond the norm—just how much beyond she did not know.

"And so I shall," he said with a peculiar smile, "be quick about it." Dressed almost entirely in red and burgundy, the brown-haired stranger wore a dark red cloak that fastened together at his throat with a star-shaped clasp made of five enormous rubies. "I've come to deliver this letter to you." He held out a scroll with a wax seal. It bore the name Cyndara—Cyndara, the Banshee crown princess.

Kandide's eyes squinted in disbelief as she focused on the bright yellow seal. "Princess Cyndara? Is this some sort of a threat?" Her mind flashed to her dreams. *Could this letter be related to them? We've never had any communication with Cyndara—only her father, King Nastae. And everyone knows that he is responsible for the raids.* She reached for the blue velvet chord near her silver writing desk. "One pull and an entire army of guards will break down my door to get in here—regardless of your spell. Now I suggest you tell me who you are, why you are really here, and how you got into my chamber."

"Your guards may well break down your door," the stranger replied. "But I assure you, they will not be able to enter. The spell I have cast is far too powerful. Even sound will not penetrate its veil. Once we have spoken, I shall release it—on that you have my word. And may I again say, Your Majesty, you really should shield your chamber from intruders. One never knows who might drop in." He held out the scroll for her to take.

Kandide made no move to accept the letter, instead eyeing it and the stranger with even more suspicion. "The entire castle is shielded," she replied. "Which means someone must have let you in." *And when I find out who . . .*

Again he looked amused. "You were not betrayed, Your Majesty. I assure you, I arrived entirely of my own accord. The shielding around your castle is not nearly as strong as you might think. Anyone with even a modicum of the Talent can counter it. I know of only one shield so invincible that it cannot be broken—the Veil that protects the château in the heart of the dead-land called the Mists." He paused before continuing. She felt he was searching her face for some sort of reaction. "I understand, Your Majesty, that you spent time in the Veil after your wing was injured. How is it that you managed to penetrate such a potent spell? Perhaps you know the source of its magic?"

"I was sent there," Kandide said brusquely, but her heart had nearly stopped at his words. "And it was through no magic of my own," she quickly added. *How could he know that I am that powerful? No, he couldn't possibly know that.* He couldn't know that the Gift of the Frost—her Gift, the one she had inherited from her father upon his passing, was what kept the Veil strong, protecting its château from intruders.

He would certainly know that since the beginning of time, Kandide's family had been the keeper of that most powerful of all spells—the Gift of the Frost. And that each year the Gift was used to bring about winter. For without the deploying of the Frost, summer's heat would last endlessly, spring could not set in, the crops could not grow, and all Fée would soon perish. It was this Gift that maintained the cycle of the seasons. But he couldn't possibly know that it was the spell's extraordinary power, which her father had linked to the creation of the Veil, that shielded the château and the Imperfects who lived there.

"What do you know about the Veil?" Kandide asked, trying to keep her voice casual.

The stranger shrugged. "What most know—that you are the one who made the once-secret château public knowledge when you convinced the High Council to welcome back Imperfects. Even Banshees know of your bold—perhaps foolish—act."

Kandide fought back a sudden flare of anger. How dare he speak to her that way? "There was nothing foolish about granting Imperfects the right to live in Calabiyau as equals. What does it matter if they have injuries or are not physically perfect? They never should have been exiled to the Mists in the first place. It's intolerance that is foolish. And," she added in a more controlled voice, "I believe that once they begin to return from the Veil, all Fée will learn to accept them."

"Perhaps," he said, sounding none too convinced. "But as I understand it, many Imperfects have no interest in returning to your kingdom. They prefer living with their own kind in the château and the surrounding villages that they've built."

"Where they live is their choice—as it should be. Just as it is yours or mine. Maybe one day, Banshees will even progress to that belief." Kandide was no longer interested in discussing politics with him. What she needed to know was how much he knew about maintaining the Veil. Did he realize that she was now the keeper of the spell, the one who held its extraordinary power? *No, he's just guessing,* she told herself. *Maybe that's why he's really here—to learn the secret of the Veil's strength. After all, why would Cyndara send a nobleman to deliver a message—especially one with his powers?*

Kandide chose her next words carefully. She was determined to find out everything she could about this mysterious stranger. "I'm pleased to know that someone who obviously has as much Talent as you appear to have cannot penetrate the Veil. So tell me, do you have a theory about the source of its strength?"

"No," he answered. "I do not."

"Then I guess the Veil's power shall remain a mystery—as it always has." Kandide knew he was lying, but decided not to challenge him. If she had learned anything from her father, it was to never underestimate her opponent. "Learn to look beneath the surface," King Toeyad would say. "Only then will you uncover the truth." *Especially with this one,* she thought. Well-groomed, he didn't look or act like the typical disheveled stringy-haired Banshee, and was clearly not a simple messenger. "You say you were sent by Cyndara, and yet you're not full-blooded Banshee—at least you don't appear to be."

"Her Highness' message has very little to do with my pedigree."

"Perhaps not, but your credibility does." Their eyes locked

again, this time in a duel for control. Having never met Cyndara, Kandide knew that by simply being a Banshee, the princess was undoubtedly cruel, ruthless, and certainly not to be trusted. He, more than likely, was the same. And yet, he made no attempt to harm her. His face held no threat.

"Once you read Cyndara's request, you'll understand," the stranger told her, then offered her the scroll again.

"So you say." She reached out to take the letter. "Perhaps you can also tell me what you've done with my lady-in-waiting, Mylea?"

"I'm afraid I don't know anything about your Mylea." His voice softened. "But I do wish to apologize again for appearing in your private chamber. Since time is of the essence, transporting directly here insured that I would speak to only you. And now that I have delivered Cyndara's message, I shall be on my way."

I'm not sure why, Kandide thought, *but for some reason I believe him—at least about Mylea.* She suddenly caught a glimpse of herself in one of the mirrors. Although she wasn't dressed to receive visitors, and her long silver-gold hair had not yet been released from its night braid, she still looked every bit a queen. Her high cheekbones, ivory skin, and confident carriage personified nobility. The bent tip of her right wing was the only imperfection in her otherwise perfect appearance. "You still haven't told me your name or why this letter is so urgent."

"My name doesn't matter. And if I may be so bold, there's no need to worry about how you look. You're quite beautiful, even though you aren't 'dressed to receive visitors' and your wing is still bent. Might I inquire as to why you don't allow your sister,

Tara, to finish healing it? She certainly is powerful enough."

How could he know my thoughts like that? Kandide wondered, suddenly feeling even more unnerved. "You ask a lot of questions for someone who is unwilling to reveal his own identity. Nevertheless, I shall answer you. The bent tip of my wing is my symbol—the symbol that all Fée are important, even those with physical imperfections."

"There it is again, that interesting concept," he said, "to embrace Imperfects as equals. One, I can assure you, that Banshees disagree with."

"And you, do you disagree with it?"

"I am but the messenger."

"You are far more than a messenger," Kandide told him, her patience wearing thin. "So please stop insulting me with your false humility."

"Very well, then I am a messenger with certain powers. And I must tell you that the seal on Cyndara's letter is also spelled. It can only be broken once I depart."

"Then how do I know it's even safe to open?" Kandide looked down at the scroll's yellow wax seal. "Perhaps it's some sort of a trick."

His brown eyes looked deeply into hers. "I don't deal in 'tricks,' Your Majesty." Kandide thought she caught a glimpse of indignation. "I only ask that you to consider her Royal Highness' message most carefully. And now, I fear I have overstayed my welcome." With a flourish of his right hand, the door handle clicked, as though a lock had been released. "I bid you a worthy day." In another gesture, the stranger vanished. The room instantly warmed up, and the burning fire flickered out.

Watching his shimmering essence fade from view, Kandide placed the scroll on her dressing table. For a moment she just stood there, staring at it. *I woke up to those awful dreams, and now this. It's just too much of a coincidence. I must see General Mintz right away*, she thought, trying to decide whether to open the letter or wait until she met with him. Looking back at her large mahogany day clock, which was just striking eight, she realized why her lady-in-waiting wasn't there. *Of course, it's Tuesday, Mylea's day off.*

Kandide opened the top drawer of her writing desk and placed the scroll inside. Tempted to break the seal and read it, she closed the drawer, deciding instead to wait. She picked up the portrait that sat on her desk. The face that looked back at her was a handsome dark-haired Fée named Jake. How Kandide missed him—even though she wouldn't admit it. To her, it seemed as though the entire world could be cured of its ills when he smiled.

For a brief moment, her thoughts left the strangeness of the morning and shifted to the short time she had lived in the Veil. It was there she and Jake first met. Kandide had been fascinated by all he had told her—how he'd become an Imperfect when he lost both feet fighting alongside her father in the Clan Wars. How he'd survived in the Mists. How, while living there, he met Kandide's aunt, Selena, and the two of them began rescuing other Fée who had been banished from their clans for being Imperfects. How they began building the château. How, over the years, Jake was able to develop artificial feet that were made of wood with diamond joints, and spelled with magic so that they worked almost perfectly. How he then began designing extremities for the other Imperfects—arms, legs, even wings . . .

"You really are clever," she said, smiling at Jake's portrait. "You should be here, instead of at the Veil. You'd know exactly what to do about Cyndara's letter and my dreams."

Although the Veil considered itself a community of equals, Jake and Selena were its leaders. He and Kandide did their best to spend time together, but it seemed as though each of them was always being pulled away to deal with their own complex responsibilities.

"In any case, you're not here." Kandide set his picture down a little too hard. "With or without you, I have a kingdom to run. And right now, I must get dressed and speak to General Mintz. Something is terribly wrong."

Looking in one of her many mirrors, she loosened her night braid. Soft, flowing waves of silver-gold hair fell around her face. "That half-breed Banshee is right about one thing," she said, brushing her curls, "I am beautiful, in spite of not getting any sleep."

Kandide suddenly grabbed her face. "Stop! Please." She pressed her fingers against her eyes. The visions, however, would not go away. This time they were very different . . .

About the Author

Like her novels, Diana's role in the performing arts as well as the business world transcends the ordinary. She has been a performer and businesswoman since the age of eight, when she invested all of her resources into a small magic trick. With a total capital outlay of forty-seven cents, Diana parlayed her investment into a spectacular twenty-five-year career as "America's Foremost Lady Magician." She has invented magic illusions for David Copperfield and Lance Burton, and is a highly respected lecturer, writer, and teacher in the world of magic. She also sponsors a young magicians' group—an organization she founded in 1974 with the help of Cary Grant at Hollywood's famous Magic Castle. Her transition to the corporate world saw the creation of CMS Communications, Intl., an international marketing communications agency whose clients include many of the Fortune 500. Diana is CMS' president and CEO. She is also an avid collector of faery art. With pieces dating back to the 1700s, her collection is one of the largest in the world. A painting by Australian artist Maxine Gadd, now in Diana's private collection, inspired the literary legacy of Kandide.

Coming Soon from Diana S. Zimmerman

KANDIDE – THE LADY'S REVENGE
Book Two of the Calabiyau Chronicles

KANDIDE – THE FLAME IS FLEETING
Book Three of the Calabiyau Chronicles

Continue the Magic:
Visit *www.kandide.com* - the Official Kandide Website.

- Play Video Games such as "The Attack of the Garglans."

- Read Secret Chapters from Book Two and Book Three

- Join Kandide's Fan Club

- Book Diana for School Appearances

- Send an Email to Diana

- Download Color Pictures of Kandide, Jake, Teren, Tara, Leanne, Lady Aron, and more

- Learn Cool Magic Tricks

- Read Stories from Student Authors – Get your story posted

- Check Diana's Tour Schedule

- Download the "Kandide Teacher's Guide" for Creative Writing

- Link to other Fantasy Sites such as FaerieWorlds™ and FaerieCon™

www.kandide.com

DATE DUE

APR 2 9 '10			
NOV 1 8 '11			